CULLEN

A PSYCHOLOGICAL THRILLER

SOLOMON PETCHERS

Images: Depositphotos and Canva

Cover Art: Ferry Susanto

Cullen

ISBN: 978-1-7374169-8-2

ISBN: 978-1-7374169-9-9 (ebook)

Contents

This story is dedicated to every person who's been chased, beat down, or endured physical and/or emotional bullying because of how you look, act, or identify.

It won't rain forever.

And for those of you who've never had to deal with such monstrosities, stand up for those who aren't quite ready to stand up for themselves.

Trigger Warning

Cullen is a story that deals with bullying and suicide ideation.

Bullying: If you or someone you love is experiencing bullying, there are many resources available to you and your loved ones. If you are dealing with bullying, please reach out to the people you trust: a friend, a teacher, and a relative. If you are the parent or friend of someone who is being bullied, please listen and look for the warning signs. Conversation starters and tips can be found at https://www.stopbullying.gov/
Suicide: According to the National Alliance on Mental Illness, suicide is the second-leading cause of death among people aged 15-24 in the U.S. Nearly 20% of high school students report serious thoughts of suicide and 9% have made an attempt. It is important to pay attention to our loved ones. If you have any questions, tips can be found at https://www.cdc.gov/suicide/prevention/index.html

CHAPTER 1

WILDERNESS CAMP - JUNE 2019

Branches pulled and scratched at Cullen Hickey's bare, chubby torso. In his panic, he was only remotely aware of where he was going. Going? It didn't matter. He just needed to get away from the half-dozen flashlights carving uneven beams of light. Their beams grew larger as they closed in, pushing him along. His chest burned, not only from the asthma that threatened his escape, but from whatever was poured on him. He recognized this feeling that usually started in his throat. Allergy enough to notice, but not enough to send him to the hospital or require an EpiPen. Not yet, anyway.

Ducking behind a fallen tree, he struggled to fill his lungs with air. Once again, he wiped away the muck that seeped through his hair and down his forehead. He needed to see, but what? The night usually scared him, but it wasn't the night he was running from. It was something far more nefarious. What made the night so scary was the unknown. Most of the time it was nothing more than irrational thoughts. This...this was different. This threat was real, but the terror he experienced was the same every time. How had he gotten here? One minute he was enjoying the campfire at Wilderness Camp with other eighth graders from his school and the next minute sticky syrup covered him, followed by some kind of powder. This night wasn't supposed to end like this. It was supposed to be the last hurrah of middle school before heading to high school. A time to celebrate with classmates and friends.

Friends. The only thing Cullen Hickey ever wanted was friends, but friends were scarce. It wasn't because he was some kind of jerk. Quite the opposite. If given the opportunity, people would see that he was a nice boy, as his mother often pointed out. He'd give you the shirt off his back if someone needed one, but that would mean exposing a back full of acne and love handles that dripped over his pants. The reason Cullen didn't have friends is that no one ever gave him a chance.

The awkward type and often dismissed for being different, Cullen was an easy target for those who got off on belittling others. He carried a target riddled with so many holes that only hints of color remained, its middle hollowed out by so many bull's-eyes—gaping wounds from verbal shotgun blasts and physical torment. The holes became permanent scars. Not carved into flesh and kissed away by a loved one but driven deep into the psyche. An emotional rollercoaster that only went down...down...down. No longer fun. No longer wondering if the ride will ever end because he knew it never would. And, as long as the target was there, new holes developed, merging with the scars.

Cullen's mother insisted that he attend the annual eighth grade field trip. He swallowed hard at the thought of two nights away from everything that was safe. It comforted him slightly when he overheard that Evan Stephens and Claire Matherson wouldn't be going. Something about getting caught. Getting caught. That was funny to Cullen. Evan and Claire got away with everything, especially with how they treated Cullen. Evan belted out the beatings and Claire doled out the tears, pretending to be the victim. They were both professional marksmen and liars. So, when Cullen heard the news, he was relieved. This would mean he might enjoy a weekend in peace.

Deep down, Cullen hoped things would be different in high school. He prayed the kids matured and grew up and took a stand against bullying. Yes, he hoped, but nothing *offered* him hope. Nothing had changed since fourth grade. A targeted cloak was thrown over his head like a Scarlet Letter. That year he discovered the cruelness of people. People his own age. People older and younger who stood around and laughed while he cried. It wouldn't matter that his hair was a matted mess of toilet water and urine. Teachers would intervene after each incident, dishing out an afternoon detention here and Saturday School there, but it was never enough. Over time, his predators just learned sneakier ways to abuse him.

Cullen rested briefly when he heard the voices call out a hurtful, childish play on his name. "Colon! C'mon out!"

The flashlights closed in and with them came cruelty. *Got to keep moving.* Sucking in a deep breath of air, he set off down the hill. Charging. Racing. Towards what? It didn't matter as long as it was anywhere but here. Wild thoughts flooded his mind. *Stand and fight! Don't be such a wuss!*

He'd tried that before. A couple of years ago. Something deep inside always smoldered, and after being pinned against the lockers enduring several punches to his pudgy side, a flame developed. Cullen turned around to face his assailants. Through curls weighed down by sweat, his eyes stared forward, tired and puffy from tears and pain. He glared at them. Not begging to stop. No, not that. His eyes asked for more. Daring them to do more. When Cullen righted his shoulders, he towered over most kids. Especially these kids. Younger than him. Looking to stake their claim. Pick on the easy target. But this time, even if it was only a moment, he faced his fears. His abusers muttered uncomfortably, not expecting this.

"D-Do it again," Cullen stuttered, out of character. The boys stared at each other, confused. The crowd that gathered to watch rather than intervene whispered uneasily. Suddenly, a punch landed on Cullen's neck. He didn't budge. Instead, he grabbed the boy by the shoulders and shook him. "Wh-Why do you do th-this to me? What did I ever do to you?!" The boy was a rag doll in his hands.

Then, a pop! A punch out of nowhere landed squarely on Cullen's cheek, dropping him in a heap. The boy he'd been shaking had an older brother. Evan Stephens. That was the last time Cullen stood up for himself. A brief, fleeting moment of bravery extinguished by a sucker punch. The sucker punch that did more than physically break Cullen. It crushed his spirit.

So, no. Cullen wouldn't stand up for himself. Not today. Probably never. *Wuss.* Tonight's mission? Make it through the night, no matter how long it would take. Run. Run as if his life depended on it. He was never really sure if it would ever come to that, but it wasn't outside the realm of his psyche. Even though those thoughts came to mind in situations like this, it was in those private moments that horrific feelings consumed his mind. It would put an end to all of this. An easy way out. A permanent solution. It wasn't the pain. He'd already endured as much pain as anyone could take. But he couldn't bear leaving his mother alone. He knew she would blame herself. Another person in her life who wouldn't stick around.

Instead, he ran. Whatever was poured over Cullen's head at the campfire continued to trickle down his face. His vision blurred in the darkness, so he never saw the smaller shrubs in his path. He stumbled, tried to catch his footing, but agility was never his friend and gravity hated him more. He tumbled. No matter how hard he tried, his momentum was a boulder rolling down a hill. He skidded. Like a plane landing without landing gear, his bare chest scraped across the dirt, roots, and sticks. For a moment, he assessed his injuries. A burning sensation tore across his front, from belly to neck and nipple to nipple. Part of his face felt as if it had peeled back, and he worried if only skeletal remains were left.

He cleared what he could of his vision in time to watch the flashlights close in on him. The beams of light brought a crescendo of maniacal laughter that didn't care whether Cullen had seriously hurt himself. Instead, they circled him, blinding him with their lights and recording his humiliation with their phones. They chanted, "It's raining. It's pouring. Colon's butt is flowing. Slipped on it and bumped his head. Ate it for breakfast in the morning!"

Panic etched into Cullen's eyes. This was beyond getting picked on in the hallways or at the lunch tables where there was always an adult to intervene. This was different. There was no one to break it up. A mob mentality. No logic. No mercy. Interested only in humiliation. Another hole in the target on Cullen's back. As his large frame struggled to stand and see faces, the lights blinded him, and only darkened shadows loomed behind them, laughing and chanting the awful nursery rhyme. He stuttered, "L-Leave me alone. I d-didn't do anything to you."

The hands moved closer. Slapping at him. This summer, he'd learned the term Purple Nurple and felt hands reach for his nipples, pinching and twisting them until they ached and changed color. The sweat and syrup that covered him made his body hot and cold at the same time and stung the scratches on his skin.

Now the flashlights circled him and chanted louder, "It's raining. It's pouring. Colon's butt is flowing. Slipped on it and bumped his head. Ate it for breakfast in the morning!" And then, the ultimate indignity...like a spider spinning a web around its prey, the horde wrapped him in rolls of toilet paper from all levels: his head, torso, and legs. "Every Colon needs toilet paper cause he stinks!" a teasing voice shouted.

"Cover up that turd!" another teased.

At first, Cullen tore off the first layers of toilet paper, but the supply never ended, and the battle became futile. And, as Cullen gave up all will to fight—like a spider's prey who knows his time is up—he dropped his hands to his side as the scratchy, single-ply toilet paper absorbed the syrupy substance, creating a thick layer as roll after roll spun around him. His body tipped over like a tree.

The flashlights weren't the only thing hunting Cullen. As his body laid on the ground, Cullen felt the dirt come alive. Tiny black worm-like fingers slithered from the soil, crawling over each other, probing for a way inside Cullen. They covered his face, tasting the syrup and sweat covering it. He felt the fingers infiltrate his ears, nose, and mouth, weighing him down. With his eyelids forced open, the fingers moved inside his head. Cullen felt himself pulled down...down into darkness. Not inside the soil beneath him, but into the dark recesses of his mind.

Suddenly, a whistle sounded in the distance. The last thing Cullen noticed was flashlights. The teasing students shouted something before they all scattered, running over Cullen's body in an effort to escape. Something switched off inside him. A light, perhaps. A light that dimmed slowly over his thirteen years; each incident, each direct hit, caused his light to fade, reducing it to nothing more than a flicker.

CHAPTER 2

"CULLEN. ARE YOU OKAY? Cullen?" one teacher asked, pulling at the toilet paper covering his face, exposing scratches and bruises.

Cullen's eyes blankly stared into nothing. The teacher looked helplessly at the other adults and shook his head.

Another teacher, Ms. Saunders, a teacher Cullen liked, knelt beside him. She was one of the few teachers that, unlike most others, didn't dismiss him. She brought her head down towards his ear. "Cullen, sweetie. It's Ms. Saunders. Can you hear me? Are you hurt?" she asked, knowing well the obvious answer. He'd recover from physical injuries. It was the other injuries that she was most concerned with. The kind that pushed a person to this state. Cullen turned his head ever so slightly towards Ms. Saunders' voice, but his eyes continued to stare off to somewhere else. She reached for his hands, freeing them from their mummified binds. Taking his right hand into both of hers, she tried again. "Cullen. It's me. Ms. Saunders. Can you hear me?" Cullen lightly squeezed her delicate hand. "You *can* hear me. We're here for you." Ms. Saunders looked up to the other adults and smiled concernedly.

Then Cullen's hand squeezed her hand again. Gently, at first. Then, gradually, his hand turned into a vice grip. He squeezed…and squeezed…and squeezed. Ms. Saunders looked down at the blank stare in Cullen's eyes as she winced. "Cullen, you're hurting me. Please let go." When his grip increased in force, she shouted to her colleagues, "He's crushing my hand!" Her groans quickly progressed to a scream as she tried to tear her hands from his grip. "Cullen! Let go! You're hurting me!" she shouted, but the vice tightened and tightened. Ms. Saunders looked to the others for help as the pain intensified. "Help me!" she pleaded. The three others struggled to free her hand. Cullen's eyes held no anger, no rage. They just stared absently.

Suddenly, one by one, the crunching sound of bones echoed from her hand. Ms. Saunders screamed as her free hand desperately punched Cullen's arm. One teacher mounted Cullen, but nothing he did offered relief. Ms. Saunders planted her feet into Cullen's chest and forced her way back, but she was a mouse in the grips of a python, and it squeezed until every single bone shattered. She shrieked, "Cullen Hickey! Let go of me!" Then, as quick as it started, it ended. He just let go. His eyes were still absent and distant.

That evening, an ambulance brought both of them to the hospital. Ms. Saunders ended up in a cast, given something for the pain, advised to visit an orthopedic doctor, and released after a few hours. After they cleaned Cullen up, he was admitted. His blank stare didn't change. *The trauma set his system into shock* is what the doctors said, but the truth was, they didn't really know the true trauma. Not just this incident, but the countless incidents before this. Layers upon layers.

Margaret Hickey spent days whispering support into her son's ear. Cullen, unresponsive except for the occasional flutter of his eyelids, stared off into...emptiness. After two weeks and a steady cocktail of meds, the doctors recommended that Cullen be transferred to Saint Mary's Psychiatric Hospital.

Feeling helpless, Margaret could do nothing but cry. Alone. Lost, with no one to turn to. The measured responses of the doctors and nurses assured her that Saint Mary's was the best possible place for Cullen. Then there was the visit by the social worker, but she offered little in the way of support. Just intrusive, rehearsed questions about Cullen.

Sandra Doyle, fresh out of college with a head full of ideas about how she would make a difference in peoples' lives, cautiously approached. "Hello, Mrs. Hickey. My name is Sandra Doyle. I'm with Child Services and have been assigned to your case."

"Margaret. Call me Margaret. What do you mean, assigned?"

Unsure of how to approach, she struggled. "This is all just standard procedure whenever a child in Cullen's condition comes in. We want to be certain we have the full picture."

"Condition," Margaret stated, not a question at all. This wasn't a condition. This was abuse.

Sandra forced a smile and handed Margaret a Kleenex. "Yes, Mrs.– I mean, Margaret. Do you mind if I ask you a few questions?" Margaret nodded her head. "I want to understand the situation before the hospital transfers him tomorrow. Walk me through it. Cullen was at a camp when this happened. Is that correct?"

Margaret shook her head. "It was supposed to be the big send off before high school."

Sandra scratched a note into her notebook. "Does he experience this at school? You know, being bullied?"

"Yes." A tear trickled from her eye as she looked over at Cullen. His eyes were still vacant. "It's happened from time to time. Cullen is a good boy, but people, especially those his own age, just don't connect with him."

"I understand." More notes. "And how are things at home? Does Cullen seem withdrawn?"

Margaret narrowed her eyes. "No, Cullen isn't withdrawn at home. He's a quiet boy. Not withdrawn," Margaret's voice ticked up a notch as Sandra turned the page in her notebook and penned more notes.

"How would you describe your relationship with Cullen? Are there issues at home?"

"Issues at home? This isn't something that happened at home. Why do I feel as if this is an interrogation?" Margaret seethed. "What is it you're writing about?"

"Again. I'm just trying to get the big picture," Sandra tried to reassure her and smiled sympathetically.

"Things are *fine* at home. Cullen is a sweet boy. He does his chores and gets his homework done. He's a normal kid in that respect."

"Okay," Sandra scratched more notes, each one a nail scratching across a chalkboard in Margaret's mind. "And you said he's experienced some bullying at school?"

"Yes. What is it you want to say?" Margaret huffed in frustration.

Sandra took a deep breath, clicked her pen, and placed it on the page she was writing in and closed the notebook across her lap. "If you knew about the potential for Cullen to experience bullying, then why send him to Wilderness Camp?"

A fire burned inside Margaret as she struggled to keep her control. To suggest this was a mother's doing was of the highest insult. "Ms. Doyle, was it? If you are suggesting this is my fault..." She felt her face grow hot and couldn't finish the sentence. "Do you have children?" Sandra shook her head. "Of course, you don't. How can you understand if you don't even have children yourself? I bet you are just a few years out of college, aren't you?" Sandra didn't respond. "I have a question for you. Is it so bad to want my child to have the same opportunities as other kids? Why can't I send my child to a camp that was supposed to celebrate children? Celebrate their achievements? Yes, Cullen isn't like other boys. He struggles with making friends. He has a noticeable stutter. However, if someone just gave him a damn chance, they'd see there's something special about him. You shouldn't be questioning me about whether it was a good idea to send him away. You should question the counselors and teachers that attended that trip. Why weren't they there to help my boy?" Margaret stamped out each word as if imprinting them into concrete.

Sandra pursed her lips, searching for the words to say, and settled on, "I understand this is hard and I'm sorry if I–"

"How can you possibly understand how hard this is? Cullen isn't your child. You have no connection to him. I believe we're done here. My son needs me," Margaret shouted.

Sandra pressed back against her chair. "Yes, Margaret, you're correct. It's true, I cannot possibly understand what you're going through. I apologize if you felt I've overstepped. I'm just trying to do my job. And despite what you may think, I really do care about what happens to Cullen." She waited for a response. When none came, she continued, "We can be done for now." Sandra paused. "Is it okay to contact you? I may have some more questions. But, mostly to check on Cullen?" She forced a smile.

Margaret looked into Sandra. Wondering what *check on* really meant. More uncomfortable questions? Yet she knew Sandra was just a kid. A kid doing a job. Following a script. Instead of answering, Mrs. Hickey simply turned her attention back to Cullen.

Somewhere hidden in the recesses of his mind, Cullen stood in the middle of a dimly lit room. Black walls, painted with a texture that looked poured on instead of spread with the smooth strokes of a paint roller, echoed with a dull hum. Embedded in the paint, silver flecks twinkled, not like the night sky, but like a dark forest dotted full with eyes of predators looming in the near distance. Alive. A breathing, knowing thing.

Goosebumps danced between the hairs on Cullen's arm. He embraced himself and investigated the room, searching for a way out. The walls, which made him uneasy, provided no answers. No doors. No windows. Just walls. And when he touched one of them, the blackness melted over his hands. At first, he found himself fascinated, but as the black advanced over his arm, fingers extended from the walls, grabbed hold of him, and dragged him slowly in like quicksand. Curiosity quickly turned into panic when he attempted to pull away. Cullen put his other hand upon the wall to give himself some leverage, but the wall absorbed his other hand, and small black, worm-like fingers crept up both arms. The laughter of children resonated within each finger as it slithered up his arms. Not playful laughter children used with each other, but sinister sneering of those who'd tormented him. Within the laughter, he heard someone or something whisper, "Why do you let them do that to you?" The wall let go, sending Cullen sprawling to the floor. And then, silence.

From somewhere else, voices echoed. Not the whispering wall. Not the children. Cullen stood up, closed his eyes, and allowed his ears to pinpoint its origin. His mother? A smile crept across his face. She sounded pained and tired, but at least it wasn't the voices inside the walls. However, the stress in his mother's voice concerned him. Who was she talking to?

"...all just standard procedure whenever a child in Cullen's condition comes in. We want to be certain we have the full picture," Cullen heard a woman say after introducing herself.

Condition? What condition? Where am I? Cullen thought.

"So, Cullen was at a camp when this happened. Is that correct?" The woman asked.

Camp. Yes, that's where I was. Why was I there? Wilderness Camp. It was supposed to be safe. That's why I agreed.

"Does he experience this at school? You know, being bullied?" Cullen heard the woman.

Yes, Cullen answered in his mind.

"It's happened from time to time. Cullen is a good boy and people, especially those his own age, don't understand him," his mother responded.

From time to time? I think you mean almost every day.

"And how are things at home? Does Cullen seem withdrawn at home?"

"No, Cullen isn't withdrawn at home. He's a quiet boy. Not withdrawn."

Yes, I am, Mom. I'm quiet because home is the only break I get. A break from running. A break from hiding. I'm exhausted.

"How would you describe your relationship with Cullen? Are there issues at home?"

"Issues at home?" his mother asked, frustration edging in her response.

Cullen felt a scream in his throat, but when he tried, his voice failed him. *Issues at home? She wants to know if there are issues? Not anymore. Not since Dad left.*

"We are just trying to get the big picture."

The big picture? Ha. Since when does anyone want to get the big picture? Let me paint it for you. I spend most of my days getting teased or sometimes worse. And no one wants to do anything about it. How would you like your face buried in the toilet? There's the big picture.

"I'm concerned that if you knew about the potential for Cullen to experience bullying, then why send him to that camp?" the unfamiliar voice asked.

Yes, why? Why did I agree to go? Why did I think it would be a good idea?

"Ms. Doyle, was it? If you are suggesting this is my fault..." His mother's voice echoed in the room of his mind, causing the dark walls to ripple in circles like dropping a pebble into still water. "Do you have children? Of course, you don't. How is it that you can be in the position you are in if you don't even have children yourself? I bet you are just a few years out of college, aren't you?"

Mom. Stop. It's not worth it.

She continued, "I have a question for you. Is it so bad to want my child to have the same opportunities as other kids? Why can't I send my child to a camp that was supposed to celebrate children? Celebrate their achievements? Yes, Cullen isn't like other boys."

I try to be.

"He struggles with making friends. If someone just gave him a damn chance, they'd see there's something special about him."

Special? There's nothing special about me. I'm nothing.

"You shouldn't be questioning me about whether it was a good idea to send him away. You should question the counselors and teachers that attended the trip. Why weren't they there to help my boy?" He heard the all too familiar emotional crack in his mother's voice when it came to matters concerning him.

Yes, where was everyone? Why weren't they there to protect me?

Cullen squeezed his hands together. For a moment, the tone of the walls changed from black to a deep red. The color of coagulated blood before a scab forms. As he clenched his fists, the sounds of breaking bones filled the room. It wasn't enough to make him stop. He squeezed his hands together even harder until a voice from somewhere else screamed, "Cullen Hickey! Let go of me!" He loosened his grip.

Who's there?! He spun around, panicked, searching the room for the voice.

Cullen moved to the middle of the room and sat, waiting in the dark room for something. He wasn't sure what, but he didn't like this place very much. He knew his mother needed him, but there was no way out.

CHAPTER 3

Saint Mary's Psychiatric Hospital - August 2019

For two months, Cullen remained a prisoner inside the room of his mind. Although he had no reference for how long he walked alone, he knew that his heart ached. For some reason, this place felt familiar like using breadcrumbs to leave a trail in an unfamiliar forest only to find out that something had eaten the trail.

Something extended outside these four walls, but he dared not investigate. They warned against such things. And then there were the voices that called to him from inside the walls and beyond. The ones within the walls taunted him, but others from outside were different. He learned to recognize some of them. His mother's, of course. Others, he assumed to be friendly, probed with questions from their distant place.

"Cullen, how are you today? It's me. Dr. Morris."

As good as I can be.

"Do you think you might try to get up today? Perhaps go for a walk?"

No. Stop asking. I'm fine where I am and mostly safe here.

"No? That's fine. Let me help you up and we can go for a ride around the grounds in the wheelchair. Your mother will join us today. Isn't that exciting?" Dr. Morris asked, forcing a chipper tone.

From inside his mindroom, the room tilted from side to side like a room in a funhouse–except there was no fun here. The movement sent him sprawling across the floor and into the sticky walls as Dr. Morris and someone else assisted his gigantic frame into a wheelchair. Although his physical body didn't offer resistance, he felt the sensation of moving from inside his mind. Cullen, only faintly aware of what was happening, learned early on that he didn't like the walks. The light from the outside played with the walls, exposing whatever menacing threat that lurked within it. On those days, he cowered. The room, devoid of hiding places, exposed him. Blending into the corners wasn't an option. That's where *they* hid. Faces of his tormentors lay in wait, taunting him on all sides, pressing themselves against the walls, hurling insults. He knew they wanted to take him; consume him.

Why do you let them do that to you? A voice called from inside the room, not from the walls. *Stand up for yourself.*

Cullen scrambled from side to side, helplessly moving away from the faces while trying to pinpoint where the other voices were coming from. Once he made it to one side, presumably safe from the faces, another would appear, pressing against the walls, threatening to break through at any moment. These daily walks, designed to be peaceful, added to the torment happening inside Cullen's mind.

On the outside, Cullen's body sat motionless, staring blankly, only acutely aware of the late-summer breeze. Dr. Morris turned to talk to a colleague in the gardens and didn't see Margaret Hickey approach.

"There he is," she said to Cullen, wondering if today was the day he would respond. She knelt on one knee and met his eyes, pushing his curls aside, which had grown long since his arrival at St. Mary's. "Oh my, every time I see you, you seem to look more and more like a man." She kissed him on the forehead and gazed into his face, searching for any sign of what used to be her boy. As he'd gotten older, he'd taken on his father's features. Margaret found her mind shifting back to her marriage with Cullen's father. A marriage that had started to fall apart within the first year.

Bruce Hickey had been looking for furniture for his new home. Margaret, a sales representative, had helped him. At first, he'd been just a sales mark; someone to help her sales rank within the company. With a steady dose of flirtation and flattery, she encouraged him to not only furnish the living room and kitchen but the bedroom as well. Margaret's plan had worked so well that Bruce came back the next day to ask her to dinner. She didn't make it a habit to do such things, but she didn't want to come across as rude. More importantly, she didn't want him to renegotiate the two thousand dollars he'd spent. It also didn't hurt that he was strikingly handsome and easy to flirt with. So, part of her wasn't faking it.

From there, things moved quickly. Within a month, she moved in and tested out the furniture she sold him. She remembered that when she was selling it to him; she picked all the things that she would have liked if she could afford all those furnishings, never realizing that one day she would use the furniture. Within three months, she was picking out an engagement ring. Everything changed when Margaret became pregnant at six months. Bruce promised to make an honest woman of her. They were off to the Hall of Justice the next day and were married.

They spent the better part of nine months preparing their three-bedroom home for the arrival of baby Cullen. On January 19, 2007, a ten-pound baby boy was born. Because of his size, Margaret was slow to recover. To help, Bruce took more time off of work. As days turned into weeks, Cullen never developed sleep habits that both parents so desperately needed. When he was awake, his disposition was pleasant. His eyes always seemed as if he were looking through you. As if he could see into your soul. Whenever he fed, his eyes never left his mother's until he dozed off. But naps were brief and sleep never lasted more than a few hours. As if he could sense whenever it was nap time, his pleasant disposition soured. For hours, he'd wail.

It was during these long nights; Margaret noticed a change in her husband. She'd catch a frustrated glance towards her or a heavy sigh when it was his turn to get Cullen, who'd only been asleep for a few hours.

"Parenting is hard," she'd remind him. To that, he'd force a smile that wasn't genuine. The polite kind of smile reserved for a stranger. She knew he knew it was going to be hard, but knowing and experiencing were two different things.

From behind, Dr. Morris' voice broke into her thoughts. "Hello, Mrs. Hickey. How are you today?"

Startled, Margaret jumped to her feet. "Oh, hello, Dr. Morris. I didn't hear you."

"My apologies. I didn't mean to scare you."

"Oh, it's no problem. For obvious reasons, I'm finding myself easily distracted these days."

Dr. Morris pursed his lips. "You do know it may benefit you to seek someone to talk to. A professional." Margaret tilted her head in disapproval. "It's nothing to be ashamed of. Cullen's condition is a lot for a parent to deal with." He smiled pleasantly.

"If there was only time. Besides, we have more pressing issues to worry about. Like Cullen. How's he doing? Any changes?" She searched Dr. Morris' eyes for any signs of encouragement.

"Well," he smacked his lips, "there haven't been any major changes, but I will say he's been sleeping better the last couple of days. Sleeping for a good six to eight hours."

"Without sedation?" A smile broke across her face.

"Yes, ma'am."

"I feel so terrible that I had to leave town. What mother leaves her child when he's in the hospital?"

"Don't beat yourself up. The wheel keeps turning. We're hoping that Cullen continues to push the needle in the right direction, and I think he will."

"Let's hope so. This is good news. So now what?"

"Well, unfortunately, it doesn't change much," Dr. Morris admitted. Margaret felt her stomach sink. "But this is good. This little development means that his brain is likely healing from the trauma. As you know, when he sleeps, we've been connecting him to an electroencephalograph which measures brainwave activity. What we've noticed is that during sleep, the brainwave activity has shifted to the frontal lobe." He pointed to the front of his head. "This is where the brain looks at things logically and makes sense of experiences."

Mrs. Hickey gently squeezed Cullen's shoulder. "So, what was the *electro-whatever-you-called-it* machine reading before?"

"That's the fascinating part. Because of the trauma our Cullen was going through, the readings were lighting up primarily in what is commonly called the Reptilian Brain. It dwells at the base of the brain where the spinal cord connects."

"The Reptilian Brain. Like that of a lizard?"

Dr. Morris gave out a hearty laugh. "Yes, I guess you can say that. It's more of a primitive part of the brain that we all have.

Think about a time you've been scared. How about earlier? When you didn't see me coming, and I startled you. Your brain went through a moment where it had to decide whether you wanted to run, punch me in the nose, or make sense of the situation. Thankfully for my nose, you didn't choose to punch me." Dr. Morris smiled.

"Oh Doctor, I would never," she laughed, embarrassed at the notion.

"Thank goodness. This shift is good even though Cullen still isn't responding to the world around him. We have also noticed that when he is awake, his eyes are moving around more frequently. It's almost as if he's dreaming."

"Dreaming? While he's awake? Like daydreaming?"

"Well, sort of. Have you ever heard of Rapid Eye Movement?"

"Yes. It's called R.E.M. or something, right?"

"Uh-huh. Have you ever observed someone when they are sleeping? You may notice that while their eyes are closed, the eyes move around under the lids. We've noticed that Cullen's eye movement has taken on the same patterns as someone who is sleeping. R.E.M. sleep not only suggests that someone is dreaming, but it is also a sign of brain restoration. Before Cullen's eyes just looked off in the distance, but now, they are moving around, as if they're searching."

Margaret knelt again and looked at Cullen's eyes. Sure enough, his eyes dashed back and forth. "Doctor, you're right. At least they look like they have some kind of life in them. Before, it was as if he was someplace else," she agreed, kissing Cullen's forehead as she stood up. "So, what does this mean?"

"To be honest, I don't know. But...I am cautiously optimistic. Any change, as long as there is no decrease in brain function, is a move in the right direction for Cullen." Then, he smiled as if something were on his mind.

Noticing his hesitation, Mrs. Hickey asked, "Dr. Morris. Why do I sense there's something more you want to tell me?"

Dr. Morris took off his glasses and held them to the light. After noticing a smudge, he retrieved a cloth from his jacket and rubbed both sides of the lens. As he settled them onto the bridge of his nose, he noted, "Mrs. Hickey, Cullen has been here for two months now, right? Although this recent development is promising, his progress has been painfully slow. Especially for someone who hasn't suffered brain trauma because of a contusion."

"But he has suffered something in his brain, right? He's not faking it."

"Oh dear, no. There's no faking this. Cullen has clearly suffered a traumatic experience."

"Then, what is it you want to say, Dr. Morris?" Margaret crossed her arms.

He smirked like a child who wanted to ask permission for something but was afraid the answer would be no. "Mrs. Hickey, given all Cullen has been through, I would like to try something a little less conventional."

"Doctor, if you are thinking about putting Cullen on some kind of medicinal cocktail, I'm against it. He may be the size of a man, but he's just a boy."

"It wouldn't be possible for me to agree any more. There are some alternative therapies that we can consider."

"I'm all for therapy, but Cullen isn't even conscious. How can he receive it?"

"I've been working with post-traumatic stress syndrome for several years now. PTSD can show itself in different ways. I think we could both agree that what's happening to Cullen is just that." He waited for a response. After Mrs. Hickey nodded, he continued, "I've been working on a therapy which combines two lesser-known therapies. One is Exposure Therapy, and the other is called Eye Movement Desensitization and Reprocessing therapy."

"Well, that's a mouthful, don't you think?"

Dr. Morris let out a quick chuckle. "It certainly is. In psychotherapy, we simply refer to it as EMDR."

"Well, isn't that a relief? So, tell me what these therapies are?"

"Well, let's start with EMDR. It's when I noticed the eye movement changes in Cullen that the idea came to me. EMDR is a lesser used therapy that uses bilateral movement in patients to help them deal with trauma. It could comprise of alternating hand taps, headphones with sound alternating between the ears, or following something back and forth in front of the eyes. Anything that crosses from one side of the brain to the other. When I noticed Cullen's eye movement, I tested to see if I could get him to track my fingers."

"And did he?" she asked excitedly.

"Not at first, but after a few rounds, he did. See for yourself."

Margaret and Dr. Morris shifted their attention to Cullen. Dr. Morris pointed his index and middle fingers in the air and slowly moved them in front of Cullen's eyes. Margaret watched intently, praying and hoping to see her boy respond. After a few passes, Cullen's green eyes, slowly at first, tracked Dr. Morris' fingers.

Margaret felt her heart jump. It was a small thing, the tracking, but it was at least something tangible to prove Cullen was still in there. "Doctor, you're right! Look at that!" Tears spilled from her eyes. "Okay, so tell me more about EMDR."

"Okay, I believe we can use EMDR to help Cullen deal with the traumatic experiences of being bullied. I've been working on a headset that would cover his eyes and ears. While Cullen is tracking a light with his eyes, we will send positive messages into his brain through the headset alternating into each ear. For a patient receiving EMDR with a therapist, he or she would focus on the stimulus while being asked to conjure feelings and emotions. This is where we would be at a disadvantage because obviously Cullen cannot currently communicate. So, this is where the Exposure Therapy would take place. This is where I'm concerned with attaining your consent."

"Well, it doesn't sound so bad so far."

Dr. Morris collected his thoughts. "With Exposure Therapy, we would expose Cullen to the things that essentially put him here in the first place."

"Wait. What are you saying?"

"While he is wearing the headset and following the light during EMDR therapy, we would alternate the light with images of people and places that have caused him discomfort. We would show him pictures that may be uncomfortable. Situations of bullying and teasing."

"Dr. Morris," Margaret challenged, shaking her head. This time, tears of terror overran her tears of joy. "Are you telling me you want to flood my boy's mind with images that have been a living horror movie for him? That can't possibly be beneficial. Absolutely not."

Dr. Morris tightened his lips. "I understand but listen for a moment about how Exposure Therapy works. The research is there. It works. Let's say someone has had a traumatic experience with a spider. Perhaps they've been bit or found themselves traumatized by an uncomfortable situation involving a spider. Because of this, the person may experience nightmares or irrational anxiety. The very thought of a spider sends shivers down their spines, causing them to sweat and shake. With Exposure Therapy, we would expose the subject to pictures of spiders. They would hear stories of spiders. Over time, they might even hold a fake spider. These situations would desensitize the person so that every time, the threat lessens. In the next phase, we put strategies into place to deal with spiders if they come in the presence of one. Finally, we would expose the subject to a real spider. The idea is the person would feel less stressed and the tendency to freeze up or overreact lessens the more we expose them to it."

"We're talking about the difference between a spider—a bug—and human beings. People who bullied Cullen don't give a damn what kind of therapy he's been through. They will keep coming. You know what the other difference is? At the end of the day, a person can squash a spider. Game over. Sorry, Doctor, but I won't subject him to that, especially in the state he is in." Margaret looked at her watch. "I have to go. You've taken all the time I have when I could have been spending it with Cullen." She shook her head and turned to walk away.

"Mrs. Hickey," he called after her. "There will always be more spiders."

Margaret spun around quickly. "What are you saying, Dr. Morris?"

"There will always be bullies, just like there will always be spiders. Don't you think it is time for Cullen to face his fears and give him strategies to help him stand up to adversity? I think by trying this therapy, there's a legitimate opportunity to bring Cullen back and give him a fighting chance."

A tear escaped Margaret's eye as the resistance that she held onto so firmly moments ago melted away. "A fighting chance?"

Even Dr. Morris couldn't escape the moment. Inside, emotion washed over him, and he fought hard to keep it in check. He rarely allowed himself to tiptoe away from objectivity. "Yes, Mrs. Hickey. A chance to not just be told how to handle his situation, but to possess tools to truly help him face it."

"Do you believe this will work? Will it help Cullen return to me?"

"I do."

"I hope you're right."

A smile broke across Dr. Morris' face. "Does this mean you will consent?"

Margaret's eyes flitted back and forth, glancing toward Cullen and back to Dr. Morris. Her mind swam and searched for reasons not to, but the prospect of Cullen getting better outweighed any thoughts that stood in the way. "Yes, Doctor. I trust that you have Cullen's best interests in mind. What is it you need from me?"

"I do, Mrs. Hickey. I want what's best for him, and I think this may be a way to bring him back to us. Once he does, I will personally see that his therapy continues until you feel comfortable. It's important you are there every step of the way. I know this may be a big ask, but is it possible to give me the names of Cullen's aggressors? Pictures too, if you can access them."

"Excuse me?"

"Yes. We will need this for the Exposure Therapy. I will have to program his therapy with images of those that caused him pain. I understand this may be difficult."

"Spiders?" she asked. Her heart pounded at the thought of exposing her son to the very monsters that had sent him here.

"Yes, spiders," Dr. Morris responded. "It's the only way this will work."

"I will get you this list tomorrow," she responded. Walking over to Cullen once more, she kissed him. She peered at his eyes that darted back and forth. As she passed Dr. Morris, she told him, "Tomorrow. Take care of my boy." She exited the courtyard like a woman with a place to go, determination etched into her mind.

28

CHAPTER 4

LATER THAT EVENING, DR. Joshua Morris read an email from Margaret Hickey, relieved she agreed to try the EMDR Exposure Therapy. As he waited for the images she sent to download to his computer, he gently picked up the small picture frame sitting on his desk and tilted it to cut down on the glare. A thin smile crept across his lips. A perfect beach day, which he remembered like it was yesterday. They'd spent the weekend in San Diego. Before heading back to the beach house, his wife and son lounged in their beach chairs, taking in the salty air, waves and the sun offering one of its magical departures of orange and pink cotton candy skies.

With the perfect moment begging to be captured, he switched his phone to camera mode and called out to them, "Johanna. Jakob." When they turned around, he captured the picturesque moment. His wife's perfect smile on her sun-kissed face. Her windswept hair framed her face, giving even the most exquisite supermodels a run for their money. And Jakob. Joshua's thumb caressed the glass over his son's face; his son's infectious smile and his newly applied braces on his teeth, on which he insisted on getting green and blue rubber bands.

An impromptu break down the coast for a few days. He remembered the look on Jakob's face when he and Johanna surprised him at school. Jakob loved the beach. That trip had brought so much joy to the Morris family. Unfortunately, it turned out to be the beginning of the last happy days.

Joshua placed the picture back on the glass table. Without breaking his gaze, he poured himself another drink. He took a gulp and directed his attention to the attachments on his computer. Images of students who'd harassed and tormented Cullen filled his screen. *It's funny*, he thought. *They always looked like normal kids*. Kids you'd never suspect of being capable of such cruelty. Dr. Morris knew all too well that anyone can pass off a pleasing smile and still be capable of bad things. He wished he could have deciphered the difference, but he couldn't. He was a psychiatrist, for goodness' sake. Trained to recognize sociopaths. Heck, he even assisted the police department in creating criminal profiles. But when it came to matters that were close to home, he missed all the signs.

All. The. Signs.

He knew deep down he had failed his son. His wife. Himself. He took another sip of his drink, now his third one, and stared at the pictures on the screen. So many faces. His son had several but really only one ringleader. The head of the snake. The one that made it okay for others to join in. He'd been too late to determine who it was in his own son's life.

But Cullen? Five pictures filled the screen and ten more names that needed images. With each picture, Mrs. Hickey wrote a detailed description and what they'd done to Cullen. How had there been so many? Joshua read the descriptions, trying to determine which one was the ringleader. When he got to the lengthy paragraph about one student, he knew he found him. Evan Stephens.

"There you are," Joshua commented, bringing the last of his drink to his lips. "You will be the catalyst for Cullen's recovery."

Dr. Morris worked late into the evening programming the EMDR Exposure Therapy into the headset. Uploading pictures. Recording phrases. Arranging the light therapy for the EMDR. In his heart, he knew this would help Cullen. It had to. After losing his own son, he'd made a promise to himself that he would make this his life's work.

CHAPTER 5

TWO DAYS LATER, AN orderly wheeled Cullen into a comfortable room, much like a traditional therapist's office, complete with a couch for sessions. Bach played just below the conscious level, enhancing the relaxed atmosphere. Dr. Morris, on the phone, looked up at the orderly, smiled, and pointed to the corner of the room. "Excuse me for one moment." He covered the receiver of the phone with his palm and ordered, "Thank you. Please put him beside the sofa. That will be all."

Before returning to the phone call, he glanced at Cullen and was pleased to see that his eyes still appeared as if they were searching for something. An optimistic smile broke across his face. "I'm sorry, Mrs. Hickey. Cullen is here now. Well, he looks the same, which is good. Okay, no, I won't begin without you. Ten minutes. Yes. I've authorized the front desk to just send you back. It's F104. Yes, I won't start. Please be careful. See you in a few."

Inside Cullen's mindroom, he sensed this as a different place. This wasn't his usual walk through the garden. The walls didn't change. Black. Sticky. Alive. Cullen found comfort in this because as long as the walls stayed this way, it meant the faces didn't haunt him. No voices either. He sat on the floor in the middle of his mindroom and awaited what would come next.

Soon he heard the familiar voice of who he now knew to be Dr. Morris. "Hello, Cullen. I hope you're well today. I'm so very excited." His voice echoed off the walls of the mindroom. "Today, we start the journey to get you healed. I hope...I know this therapy will work."

The therapy that you talked about in the garden? I'm scared. Cullen thought inside his mindroom.

Dr. Morris looked at his watch and then rubbed his hands together. "Cullen, today is the first step in getting your life back." He put his hand on Cullen's shoulder and gave a gentle squeeze. The Cullen sitting in the chair didn't react, but inside his mind, he felt the light pressure. Although this frightened Cullen a bit, he found comfort that he could sense something other than fear.

"I sense you haven't been in control of your life for quite some time. Chaos. Fear. Imagine finally having the coping skills to look at those monsters of your life and finally being able to do something," Dr. Morris spoke.

As he sat on the floor, listening to the echoing voice, tears filled Cullen's eyes. *But what if this is all I'm made for? Prey can't change who they are. Forever hunted. Maybe that's my purpose in life.* Wild thoughts swirled inside his mind as memories where he endured bullying flashed to a cacophony of maddening taunts.

Just then, a soft knock came to the door before opening. "Oh good. Cullen, look who's here."

"Pardon me for walking in. I don't know what came over me. I guess I'm just anxious," Margaret noted, fidgeting with her hands over the top of her purse.

"Oh please, it's nothing. I understand. Preparation for Cullen's therapy kept me awake most of the night. I stayed up coding the last bit of programming. Please come sit down."

Margaret swiftly glided to the couch next to Cullen and kissed him on his forehead. "His eyes are still moving," she noted.

Inside his mindroom, Cullen felt pressure on his forehead from his mother's kiss. Although it didn't feel quite like a kiss, he knew what it was. He touched the skin just behind the curls that fell over his eyes with satisfaction.

"Yes, I noticed. I was just giving Cullen a little pep talk before we begin."

Mrs. Hickey smiled apprehensively. She hadn't slept all night. Doubts crept in about this therapy, and she slipped down a rabbit hole, looking up EMDR and exposure therapy on the Internet. She unearthed articles of patients who swore that these therapies had changed their perspectives on life and given them the coping skills to deal with adversity. Yet, there were those who felt this type of science comprised of crackpot therapists looking to make a dollar and a name for themselves. Margaret glanced over to the wall where Dr. Morris proudly displayed his degrees from Duke University. *He couldn't be a crackpot, right?* she thought. *He went to Duke, for Pete's sake.* Her heart ached for Cullen. Deep down, she knew things had to change for him. He couldn't continue this way. She'd heard the horrific stories of children who just gave up instead of getting help. Parents who wondered if they could have done more. Suicide. Margaret didn't want to think of the word, but as hard as she tried to put it out of her mind, it barged its way through.

"Is something wrong, Mrs. Hickey?"

Snapping back from her thoughts, she curled the corners of her mouth. "I just want my Cullen back."

"Me too. We are going to do that, and he'll return better than ever."

"That's a tall order there, Doctor. It might be best to scale back on the expectations," she smiled at him.

"Fine. Let's just settle on bringing him back."

"Agreed. So, what do we do? Is this the headset?"

Like a child with a new toy eager to show it off, Dr. Morris lifted a virtual reality headset from the table. "Yes, this is it. A one of a kind of tool. There isn't another like it in the entire world."

"How do you know?"

"Because this, Mrs. Hickey, was created by yours truly."

"I've seen these advertised on television."

"Well yes. But what's on the inside is truly special. Specifically designed software for Cullen."

"Oh? Call me impressed."

"Thank you."

"So, how does this work?"

"Are you familiar with VR?"

"Virtual reality?"

"Yes! Well, I've essentially taken VR goggles and converted them with programming, including images, sounds, and sayings."

"Which is why you requested the pictures of those kids?" A bitterness bit at the last two words.

"Yes. I've rewired the goggles and added headphones, so now both the goggles and headphones work seamlessly together and can be used for both EMDR and exposure therapy."

"You know, Doctor Morris. I've been doing a little research on these therapies."

"As I hoped you would."

"These two therapies haven't been used together. Well, not in my exploration."

"This is true. Cullen will be the first."

"You know that this makes me anxious."

"As I would expect it to. You are a mother. *His* mother. I'd be concerned if you didn't have reservations." Dr. Morris took his glasses off, held them to the light, and retrieved a microfiber cloth from his pocket to rub the lenses. "Mrs. Hickey, I understand the apprehension. I was a parent, too."

"Was?"

"I mean, I guess you never really stop being a parent once you become one. My son passed away nearly three years ago."

Margaret gasped. "Oh, my goodness, Dr. Morris. I didn't know."

A faint smile broke across his lips and disappeared quickly. "How could you?"

Tears pooled at the corners of her eyes. "I couldn't imagine. I'm so sorry, Dr. Morris."

Like any parent, Margaret had mentioned that she couldn't imagine losing a child, but that was a lie. It was what she feared most in this world. She'd seen Cullen at his lowest and wondered helplessly if, one day, he would have had enough. This nightmare ended with coming home and discovering her little boy dead.

Dr. Morris interrupted her thoughts. "Mrs. Hickey. I only want to help, and I believe I can."

Margaret looked lovingly at Cullen. She watched the way his eyes flitted back and forth, wondering if they were actually searching for a way to come back to her or if he was lost for good.

"Okay, Dr. Morris. Let's do this. Explain to me the procedure." She shook her hands as if any doubt that she held onto could be flicked away.

"Sounds good," he began as a satisfied smile settled across his face. "Of course, I will put the headset on Cullen. In increments, lights will sync up with the movement of Cullen's eyes. The hope is that he notices them on a subconscious level and follows them. Once the lights are calibrated, images will display."

"*Those* images?" Margaret asked with hesitation.

"Yes, but other images, as well. The idea of Exposure Therapy is that we desensitize Cullen from those images and partner them with more appealing images. Smiling faces. Sunsets. Puppies. That sort of stuff. They would be a combination of intense photos and more pleasant ones until the association changes."

"Okay, and then what?"

"While the therapy presents images to Cullen, pre-recorded words and phrases will alternate in each ear. Words of encouragement. Words of affirmation. Phrases that I hope will rewire Cullen's mindset. If we can change the way he thinks about himself and how he perceives dangerous, stressful situations at a subconscious level, then he may have the tools to moderate his perception of such things in the real world."

"Theoretically," Margaret pointed out.

"The more we believe, the better his chances. Yes, theoretically, but great things have been done with EMDR and Exposure Therapy. I believe it on a scale higher than just theory."

"Yes, Dr. Morris." Margaret looked at Cullen and pushed some curls that hung in his eyes. "Okay. Let's get started."

"He's lucky to have you, Mrs. Hickey. I can tell you're his source of strength."

"Well, I think it's the other way around. I wish there was more I could do to help him." She kissed Cullen on his head again.

He picked up the headset and smiled. "Let this represent a start." Then, Dr. Morris faced Cullen and adjusted the headset onto his head. "Okay, Cullen, are you ready to take the first step?"

CHAPTER 6

FROM INSIDE HIS MINDROOM, Cullen listened to his mother and Dr. Morris talk through the process. The walls weren't pulsing as much as they had earlier, but that wasn't what relaxed him. When his mother spoke, the color of the walls changed from their sticky, lurking darkness, waiting to consume him if given the opportunity, to a lavender tone. In the trapped air of his mind, the familiar smell of her perfume and hand lotion filled the space.

Cullen stood up. This development was new to him and for the first time, he didn't feel trapped, even though nothing offered a means to escape. Walking over to the walls, he hesitated. Something pulled him to touch it. Extending a finger out, he wondered if the wall would grab him as it had done before. But something inside him told him that as long as he was able to hear his mother's voice, everything would be okay. The lavender color extended like a tentacle and met Cullen's finger halfway. The wall swirled playfully in and around his fingers. For the first time in what felt like ages, a smile crept across Cullen's face. The purple tentacle extended across his palm and up the wrist. It didn't feel as cold or sticky as it had.

Instead, it was welcoming and pleasant and even warm. Cullen reached out with his other hand, and the wall gently played with it the same way it had the other. Cullen cupped his hands, and the lavender spilled into his hands like scooping water from a magical lake. Then, a stream of purple rose from the small pool and looked Cullen in the eyes. Taken aback for a moment, Cullen felt a flutter of panic move over his body as a purple finger inched towards his face. His fears subsided once the tiny stream touched his nose playfully, like the way a parent would "boop" a child's nose. Cullen and the lavender finger stared at each other. He knew it was his mother and struggled to hear her voice come from the thing. Instead, her voice came from outside his mindroom. "I wish there was more I could do to help him."

You being here is enough, Mom. I'm trying to find my way back to you. I hope this works. With that, the thing pressed against his forehead. His eyes filled with affection.

Then, a hum grew from the walls. Fearfully, Cullen spun around, expecting the walls to come alive and take him. From the corners of his mindroom, the sticky black color crawled across the lavender, consuming it like a plague. A pungent odor slowly replaced the scent of perfume and lotion. When Cullen turned back towards the lavender pool in his hands, the black pulled at the color, extending little fingers and setting hooks into what remained of the soft color, dragging it back into its darkness.

The darkened walls hummed louder. Then, the already dark mindroom grew darker. Colder. A storm moved in. Cullen scrambled to the middle of the floor, fear etched in his eyes, searching the corners, anticipating an attack. Moments ago, he felt as if things were going to be okay, but now he wasn't sure.

The walls moved in waves. A light pulsed in the middle of the walls from left to right and right to left. Cullen grew more and more mesmerized with the light until finally he stood in one place and focused on it. Then, a voice sounded in his mindroom, "Hello, Cullen, don't be afraid. I'm here to help you."

Who is that? Who's there?

"Do your best to breathe. This will not be painful," an unfamiliar woman's voice tried to reassure him. "I am here to help you."

Is this the therapy?

"Rest assured that you are safe, even though some images you will see will be unpleasant, others will not. It is best that you continue to follow the light and breathe deeply. There is nothing else for you to do."

What do you mean, some will be unpleasant? How the heck am I supposed to just breathe deeply? Even as Cullen sought answers, he anxiously squatted to a seated position in the middle of his mindroom, his eyes pacing back and forth in sync with the light. Left to right. Right to left. Left to right.

Outside of his mindroom, Dr. Morris and Margaret watched the computer screen. Inside the headset, within the light, a camera tracked Cullen's eye movement. Dr. Morris cheerfully announced, "See, I was right. See his eyes? They are tracking the light! This is exciting news."

A smile broke across Margaret's face. "I don't know what this means, but it's good to see my boy responding to, well, anything. So, what now?"

Any excitement that was there a second ago tempered. "Now, we start therapy." Dr. Morris tapped the keyboard of his laptop and clicked enter.

Inside the mindroom, Cullen waited for whatever would come next. His eyes continued to follow the light, and he forced himself to breathe deeply. The light carved a wake through the walls like a boat cutting through calm waters. The voice returned, "Initiating sequence."

As Cullen's eyes paced the streaming light, images displayed. He felt his heart reverberating off the walls as one image came into focus. Claire Matherson. One bully that Cullen faced off against throughout his middle school years. Her image seemed to step out of the light and stand in the room with him. She said nothing, but inside Cullen's mind, insults from her sounded off. "Why are you so creepy, Loser?!" Her lips didn't move, but she stared at him. No. *Burned* into him. Although the image uploaded into the computer was of her pleasantly smiling in her yearbook picture with the perfect amount of makeup on, Cullen's memories showed her as he remembered her: mean and callous.

Claire was a pretty girl. Perhaps the prettiest girl Cullen had ever seen. The kind of pretty that was hard to look at because he knew he'd never be enough for her to even look his way. It would never be Cullen. That's how the bullying started with Claire. Cullen would catch himself staring at Claire's beauty. Not in a creepy way like the way a stranger would stare at someone, but in the way someone would admire a pretty face in an advertisement for a Revlon commercial or artwork in a museum. While he waited for the bell to ring outside of his classroom, Claire waited across the hallway. Mesmerized by her, he stared at her. When she locked eyes with him, he didn't know where to look. She walked across the hallway and popped a bubble in his face. "Do you like to stare?" Cullen dropped his head. "I know I'm pretty. Everyone stares at me." She twirled a dirty blonde curl around her index finger.

Just then, Evan Stephens approached. "Is Cullen bothering you?"

She smiled at Evan and then pouted her bottom lip. "Yes, he keeps staring at me."

"Is that so?"

Cullen tried to put his words together. "I-I'm sorry, Evan. I really wasn't st-st-staring. J-Just d-d-daydreaming."

"Oh, so I'm not pretty? You weren't staring at me?"

"No, I mean yes. You are pr-pretty, but I wasn't st-staring at you," Cullen's stutter heightened with the stress.

As a small crowd built, Evan slapped his hand against the wall behind Cullen. "So, what are you saying?"

"I'm saying. N-Nothing. I just w-want to be left alone," he stammered. It was then a teacher broke up the crowd. That was the day Claire Matherson teamed up with Evan Stephens and made Cullen their target.

Inside his mindroom, Cullen felt nervous being in the same place with Claire's glaring image. Then his eyes followed the light behind Claire's image as it shifted to the left side of the room, where another image showed up. Someone he didn't recognize. She was an edgy type of girl with hints of blue streaks in her short black hair. A small gap between her front two teeth exposed itself when she smiled at him. This girl was also pretty, yet edgier than Claire. She stepped forward into the room, blew a bubble with gum she was smacking on, and rested her hands on her hips. Then the light moved to the right and Claire appeared again. When the light moved more quickly from left to right, both images of the girls emerged from the walls and stood before him.

A voice bounded off either side of his mindroom and coordinated with the pulsing lights. "You matter," sounded in his left ear. "Know your worth," echoed in his right ear. Back and forth, the phrase repeated in succession. So now, the images of the girls stood prominently in his room as the light moved behind them and the voice repeated the phrases.

Cullen tried to control his breathing. His mind, confused at the images, sensed that one was threatening and the other wasn't. Then, before his eyes, the two girls blended together as one. Claire's menacing smile morphed with the other girl's gap-toothed smile, making Claire less scary. The light moved from left to right expressing the phrases, "You matter. Know your worth."

Who are you? Cullen asked in his mind.

The image of the girl with the blue streaks separated from Claire's. "I'm Val ." Her voice bounced off the walls.

Val?

"Yes, Val."

Are you here to help me?

"No. I'm not here to help you. I'm here to remind you."

Remind me? Remind me of what?

"That you matter," Val declared. Echoed voices repeated in the room.

Cullen mouthed the words as his eyes traced the light and images back and forth. Suddenly, the lights slowed down, and the images stepped back into the walls and disappeared. The lights stopped. Outside of the mindroom, it had only been a minute, but inside felt longer. Much longer.

Margaret looked up from the screen and at Cullen sitting in the chair. She hoped for some change, but Cullen remained still. A bead of sweat spilled down his face.

"So, what now?" she asked Dr. Morris.

A satisfied half-smile rested on his face. "Well, it's going to take some time, but I'd say this first run was a success. Although Cullen had several spikes in heart rate, his eyes tracked the images the entire time."

"What images did he see?"

"The girl. Claire."

"She's not his biggest problem, Dr. Morris. Why not start with the other one?"

"This therapy is new for Cullen, and I don't want to show the images that caused him the most pain right away. It's something we need to build on...for Cullen's sake."

"I see. That makes sense."

"We will proceed with this version for several days, maybe a week. Cullen won't always be this relaxed. In order for Exposure Therapy to work, we have to be consistent and then progressively intensify the therapy. Let's give him a minute or two and then proceed with another round."

From his mindroom, the room chilled suddenly. He hadn't expected to see Claire. She looked so real, as if she were really in the room with him. Over the past three years, he feared her as much as Evan Stephens. Her lies had become so convincing that Cullen caught himself wondering if perhaps her truth was the actual truth. That's how good she'd gotten. Cullen lost the will to defend himself verbally, especially with his stutter, and physically, even though the bruises had been evidence enough. No, she hadn't hit him. She'd never. But she'd convince teachers that Evan had to defend her because Cullen had done something to her. He hadn't, but she was dramatic enough to turn Cullen from victim to culprit.

You matter.

Cullen hadn't mattered to many around school. Just another kid taking up space. Nothing Cullen did at school mattered. People treated him as if he wasn't there. He felt worthless.

Know your worth.

The words inside his mindroom had told him this. *You matter* was something he could understand. But to know his worth, Cullen had to convince himself that he was worth something at all. That would take more, and even as he thought the words, he would need to persuade himself that he mattered to anyone outside of his home.

The sticky black walls hummed and came alive again. Cullen sat on the floor and waited. The light came from the wall and paced from the left side to the right again. He tracked the light as the same announcement filled the room. "Hello, Cullen. Don't be afraid. I'm here to help you. Do your best to breathe. This will not be painful. I am here to help you." This time, he didn't ask questions. He just waited and followed the lights and took deep breaths. "Initiating sequence," the voice announced.

The image of Claire came to the room much quicker this time. This time she stood over him with that look he'd grown used to. The one where she lied easily about something and had gotten away with it. A dark uneasiness grew inside Cullen. This time a memory displayed on the walls as tiny fingers came alive with light to show it. It was one in which Cullen knew well.

It was the beginning of the seventh-grade school year. Cullen and Claire had shared the same math class. He sat in front of her. To assure that all students participated, Mrs. Caldelion used popsicle sticks with all the students' names on them, so at any time, she could call on anyone. Cullen didn't mind this for math class because it was the one class that actually made sense. In other classes, like language arts, words and letters often played tricks on him. Something that should make sense became jumbled in his mind.

In math class on this day, Cullen's name had been called, but the answer he'd given was incorrect. He'd immediately realized his mistake and tried to correct himself, but Mrs. Caldelion had already pulled the next popsicle stick. Under her breath, so that only the surrounding kids could hear, Claire whispered, "He's got to be the dumbest person alive." Cullen felt his body stiffen. Dipping his head down and looking back at her, he glared. She whispered, "What? It's true. Now turn back around before I tell Mrs. Caldelion that you're threatening me." Cullen did what he was told. He always did as he was told.

They exchanged no words for the rest of the period. Near the end of class, as students lined up at the door awaiting the bell to dismiss them, Cullen glared at Claire. Not directly, but through his curls so as not to be noticed. When the bell rang, the kids filed out into the hallway. Cullen's nearly six-foot frame lumbered out last, where a crowd of students encircled the classroom doorway.

In the middle of the throng, Claire stood in her tight, ripped jeans and a form-fitting red top. She announced, "Hey everyone, I want to read you a letter I got today." The hallway grew silent. "Dear Claire, I don't know if you know this, but I've liked you for a really long time."

The crowd of kids called out, "Ohhhhh."

Claire continued, "I'm so glad we have a couple of classes together so we could get to know each other. Maybe you want to get to know me the same way. You are the prettiest girl I've ever seen. Maybe we could kick it sometime."

"Ohhhh," the crowd called out. One student whistled a catcall.

"Please let me know if you're down," Claire read from the folded piece of composition paper.

She waited as the crowd cheered again. Claire locked eyes with Cullen, who waited in the middle of the circle of kids. Sweat beaded on his upper lip and his hands trembled.

"Who's it from?" a kid in the crowd shouted out.

"I thought you'd never ask." She looked down at the letter. "Yours truly," she paused and purposely waited for the tension to build. "Cullen," she shouted and pointed at him.

The entire hallway exploded with laughter. As Cullen watched the memory play out on the walls of his mindroom, he knew the worst part wasn't over. The faces of the mocking crowd felt as if they encircled him inside the mindroom. Cullen mouthed the words he'd said in the hallway that day, "I-I didn't wr-write that."

"Excuse me? So, you don't think I'm pretty." The crowd of kids laughed. A few threw wads of paper at him.

"I-I do, but I d-didn't wr-write that letter," Cullen pleaded.

"Then you think I'm pretty. Well, duh." A few kids whistled again. "But don't you want to get to know me better this year?" She pouted her lips and made a sad face. The crowd in the hallway silenced.

"I-I mean, you aren't very n-nice to me. I b-b-bet there's a nice side t-to you." The kids fell over themselves with laughter.

"Well, Cullen, I'm not a nice girl. And, as far as your love letter to me is concerned..." She held the letter up to his face and slowly tore it. "... I'd never be caught dead getting to know a fatty like you. A loser. A worthless piece of meat that just takes up space in this school. If you left this school, no one would notice."

The crowd howled with laughter and then someone started the chant, "Loser! Loser! Loser!"

Cullen was momentarily stuck in place. Tears pooled in his eyes and spilled down his cheeks. "I - I didn't write that letter," he stuttered in his defense. Of course, it didn't matter that he didn't. Claire had proclaimed it and people believed it.

Words filled his mindroom as the memory faded into the darkness of the walls as the phrases, *You matter. Know your worth,* traded from ear to ear. Cullen tried to cover his ears, but something prevented his hands from moving. The light paced back and forth behind Claire's image in the room. Her eyes locked with his and with it came a sneering smirk.

Then Val's image appeared in the mindroom. She exhaled to form a bubble. As it popped, she gave a confident look at Cullen. Her blue streaks radiated in her hair. "You matter. Know your worth." The image of Claire retreated slowly from the room and just became an image on the black walls. Val watched the image of Claire disappear and looked down at Cullen and smiled. Not a teasing smile, but one encouraging confidence. The blue streaks from her hair fell just in front of her eyes. She mouthed, "You matter. Know your worth."

How do I find my worth? I've never known how. The teenage girl nodded at him one last time before fading back into the walls. *Please don't go, Val. Tell me what I have to do. How do I find my worth?*

The light returned and pulsed back and forth. Its pace slowed, and the light dimmed until it was gone. The humming of the walls stopped as well. Cullen remained in silence on the floor of his mindroom, panting.

In his office, Dr. Morris tapped a key on the keyboard to de-activate the therapy session. He lifted the headset from Cullen and placed it on the table. "Doctor, look," Margaret announced. From the corners of his eyes, tears spilled down the edge of Cullen's nose. "Is...Is he crying?"

Dr. Morris cocked his head to the side. "I can't tell, Mrs. Hickey. But, if he is, this is certainly something unexpected." He reached for a penlight from his shirt pocket and shined the light in Cullen's eyes. They continued to dart around the room. "Everything seems to be okay."

"I hope so," Mrs. Hickey worried. "The idea of Cullen being sad enough to cry without being able to release his emotions just tears me apart."

Dr. Morris sat back in his chair. He looked out of the window and drifted momentarily, lost in thought. Finally, he spoke, "Do you want to know what I'm thinking? With EMDR Exposure Therapy, we are exposing him to stressors in his life. Maybe in his mind, he's actually facing them. The exposure therapy part would suggest that it will take some time to desensitize him to this. I believe, Mrs. Hickey, that those were indeed tears."

"Do you think he's hurting, you know, inside?"

"With the amount of PTSD Cullen has experienced, I'd imagine there has to be some level of emotional distress he's experiencing."

"I'm not sure I'm comfortable with this. He needs to express himself, Doctor. He's never had to sort through this before."

"I understand, which may be the reason he's in the state he's in. With all the pressure he's felt over the years, regardless of how much he's expressed to you, something had to give. So, instead of exploding, Cullen imploded. But I want you to think about something. Any emotion is better than what we've seen these past few months. Wouldn't you agree?"

"Yes. When you put it that way, it makes perfect sense. I just worry about him."

"It's your mother's heart." Margaret smiled briefly at Dr. Morris, then looked at Cullen. She squeezed his hand gently. "So, that will be enough for Cullen today. We will continue the same therapy for some time. I will make a few tweaks to the program. Keep the same stressor. Start with the girl and then work our way to the others."

"How often will he receive the therapy?"

"Daily. A few times a session and build from there."

"I will do my best to be here." Just then, an orderly came in to retrieve Cullen and take him back to his room. "I'm going to walk back with Cullen, if you don't mind."

"Of course," he responded. Then to Cullen he affirmed, "You did a great job today, Cullen. It won't be long. You will be back with us soon."

He watched as the orderly and Margaret Hickey moved towards the door. Margaret turned and looked back before leaving. "Tomorrow?"

"Tomorrow," Dr. Morris reassured. "Have a good evening."

For the next two weeks, Dr. Morris brought Cullen deeper and deeper into confrontation with Claire Matherson. Inside his mindroom, he'd grown accustomed to the daily therapies, which brought on more and more painful memories in his dealings with her. With one memory, he'd been led to believe that someone was interested in him, only to be humiliated by a crowd of students and then a video was posted onto Instagram and SnapChat. Another time, Claire dared a guy friend to pour chocolate milk down the back of Cullen's pants, so it looked like he'd had an accident. And, of course, they convinced everyone at school he had. That was the day the school started calling him Colon instead of Cullen, a name that would be an easy target from then on.

Each time, Val continued to show up and offered support. *You matter. Know your worth.* As days passed, more affirmations came. *You are your power. The meek will prevail.*

Other voices from somewhere else asked, *Why do you let them do that to you? Protect yourself.* He wasn't sure where these voices came from, but they didn't seem to come from therapy. Regardless, Cullen found himself less and less afraid of the memories of Claire.

When he wasn't in therapy, he faced off against the walls. Each time, it was as if the walls dared him to get closer, pulsing deeply as he approached. Although he didn't utter the words, his mind spoke them for him. *I am my power. I matter. I am not worthless.* He took his hand and faithfully pressed it into its stickiness. Fingers extended over his hand, enveloping it. As it tried to pull him into it, Cullen mouthed the words again until he easily pulled his hand away from its grip. No longer did it feel as if the walls wanted to eat him. Safe? No, not safe, but for the time being, safer.

He knew as he waited for his next encounter with Claire that he'd not yet faced off with his biggest fear. Evan Stephens. Whenever he allowed the fear of him to settle into the room, the walls undulated in deep crests and troughs like a tsunami, threatening to overcome him. He didn't think the walls could grow any darker or more menacing, but they did, and he shuddered at the thought of facing him in the mindroom.

CHAPTER 7

AT HIS DESK, DR. Morris waited for Cullen as he pored over reports. He organized them to present to Margaret. Over the last few days, she had begun to doubt whether the treatment was doing anything at all. Cullen's condition remained stable. It hadn't gotten worse, but it hadn't gotten better either, at least to an outsider looking in. Dr. Morris worried she would pull the plug on the entire operation. He needed to show her progress. He still believed the EMDR Exposure Therapy was the right move, but results are results. Cullen hadn't come out of his catatonic state, and Dr. Morris needed proof that something was better than nothing.

Dr. Morris agonizingly stared at the picture of his family on his desk. His own memories tortured him. After Jakob died, everything fell apart. His marriage. His social connections. His mental health. When his wife, Johanna, needed him most, Joshua locked himself away in his own personal catatonic state, functioning with the dealings of life, but emotionally, he could offer nothing to her. Making sure another child didn't have to go through this pain became his obsession. And because of this, she had grown resentful.

A light knock at the door interrupted him. "Come in," he announced. Margaret Hickey entered and smiled, the type of smile that wasn't genuine, but of someone with something on her mind. Dr. Morris sensed this and knew he'd better lead off the conversation. "Ahh, hello, Mrs. Hickey. I trust all is well today." Margaret tried to speak, but Dr. Morris continued. "I have very interesting information about Cullen."

"Oh?"

Dr. Morris didn't allow her to continue. "Yes! Come to the couch and let me show you." He swiftly moved from behind his desk and enthusiastically waved Margaret over. When she sat, he continued, "I know on the outside, we have seen little progress–"

"Yes, Doctor, that's what I wanted to talk to you about–"

Dr. Morris interrupted. "Let me show you what I'm referring to." He opened a folder and pulled out a chart. "As I have told you before, when we started therapy, we measured Cullen's brainwave activity to get a baseline."

"Yes, you mentioned there were changes. Is that still true?"

"Indeed. But we've seen even more changes since starting. Look here, see Cullen's activity beforehand. I don't know if you remember, but most of the activity was firing off here." He pointed to the part of the brain near the brain stem. "The goal is to get more of the brain involved in the therapy, away from the base."

"I remember you called it the lizard brain or something." Margaret noticed an amused smile cut across Dr. Morris' face. "That's not right. It's not called lizard brain, right?"

"Well, you aren't far off. It's called the Reptilian Brain. This is where the amygdala lives. Remember, that's the part of the brain for fight and flight."

"Yes. I remember."

"Well, since we've started the therapy..." Dr. Morris pointed to a graph and reported, "Cullen's activity has been off the charts, meaning we are finding more brain activity than ever before. What's even more encouraging is that when we first exposed him to EMDR Exposure Therapy, the Reptilian Brain was very active. It showed us Cullen was very much making connections with the therapy."

"But now?"

"But over the last three sessions, the Reptilian part of the brain isn't firing off with such zeal. It starts in the beginning and then shifts to the frontal cortex."

"Okay, Doctor. But what does this all mean?"

"It means that the therapy is working. When we first introduced the stimulus, the amygdala started *freaking out*," Dr. Morris proposed, using his fingers to air quote the last two words. "But now, now that he's more exposed to the stimulus, the feeling of fear and anxiety has clearly lessened and he's making sense of it through his frontal cortex. Sure, the Reptilian Brain is still doing what it should, monitoring stressful situations, but now I believe Cullen is making sense of the stimulus, thus desensitizing from the situation. He's learning to cope with it."

"This sounds good and all, but when is Cullen going to come back to me? It's been weeks and still we aren't any closer." Emotion set into her face. "This has been so difficult. I catch myself becoming irrationally angry at things. A movie. A commercial. When something happens in my day, and I can't share it with anyone. There are days I want to go over to those kids' houses and drag them outside and...and..."

"Teach them a lesson?" Dr. Morris finished her sentence.

Margaret's eyes pierced his. "Sometimes more than a lesson. I want them to feel the pain that Cullen has gone through." Tears seeped from the sides of her eyes. "Oh God, I sound like a monster. Am I a monster? You must think I'm completely clinical."

Dr. Morris' eyes turned compassionate. "Mrs. Hickey. You don't sound like a monster. You sound like a mother who wants to protect her boy. That's my opinion. From a clinical standpoint, of course." The office grew quiet. He handed over a box of Kleenex.

"I'm sure you are just being kind."

"I'm not, Mrs. Hickey." He paused for a moment. "Can I share something with you?" Margaret nodded. Dr. Morris took a deep breath and felt the weight of the world settle throughout his body. "I rarely talk about this. Frankly, I'd like to forget it, but as you will find out, that task is truly impossible. It's a story I wish I never had to tell. I believe I told you we lost my son." Margaret pressed her lips together. "Cullen reminds me of my boy. Jakob was a cheerful kid. The kind that had such a zest for life that every time he entered a room, it lit up with his infectious disposition. And, oh my goodness, he saw the positive in everything. He did struggle with Attention Deficit Hyperactivity Disorder. With ADHD, he struggled to keep up in school and organization, but he was working through it. I'm sure it drove his teachers crazy. We tried medication, which he didn't like. But despite all of that, he always had a great attitude about things. That all changed once he entered sixth grade. Some people enjoyed his positivity, and others didn't. He never understood it. None of us did. We found that during that year, we had to give him strategies to deal with the meanness of kids. I remember his mother telling him, 'If people don't like you, it's their problem.' I agreed with her, but it just got worse. The more he tried to ignore them, the more they persisted.

"One day, later that year, he came home with a black eye. So, we did what any parent would. We called the principal of the school and told her what happened. Sure, she brought the boy in who did it and turns out because they both were fighting, they both received two days of detention. I tried to tell her that Jakob wasn't fighting. He was protecting himself, but with no evidence, it was better to send a message to both boys and anyone else. Reluctantly, we accepted it.

"When he came home a second time with more bruises, I didn't call the principal. I gave him some tips to defend himself. Gave him permission to strike back if provoked and strike first if he felt threatened. We knew there would be consequences at school, but if it sent a message to that kid, then we'd accept it. Turns out, it didn't take long for him to use his new skills. That Friday after school, he struck that bully. Unfortunately, he either didn't have too much power behind his punch or he held back, but that bully didn't like it. He beat my boy up pretty good."

Margaret, completely enthralled by the story, whispered, "I'm so sorry. What happened?"

"Well, you know how kids are constantly recording things on their phones? Well, someone posted a video of Jake's punch and labeled it *Baby Punch*. It wasn't long before the video spread throughout the school. On Monday, my wife and I demanded a meeting with the principal.

"What we didn't know was they had tormented Jake the entire day of school. Kids called him Baby Punch, taped signs to his backpack saying Baby Punch, and slipped messages into his locker. He waited for us after school so we could meet with the principal. When I went into that meeting, Jakob was waiting in a chair just outside the office. I could tell something in his eyes was different."

Margaret nearly gasped. "I've seen that look before."

Dr. Morris nodded, and his eyes pained with emotion. "That evening, we tried to give him strategies and love and anything else we could think of. But it was no use. The next day, when he came back from school, there was another altercation at the bus stop." Margaret's eyes poured with tears. "My Jakob went home and swallowed a bottle of pills. When I came home, I found him. He took his own life." Dr. Morris stared off beyond the walls of his office. "Mrs. Hickey, my boy died alone. He felt he'd run out of options. They demoralized him to where it was easier to disappear than to face the problems. We, no, not we. *I* failed my son. With all the college degrees I've earned, there's none for parenting. It's easy when things are going as planned, but as you know, when you witness your child become a shell of who they are, you feel so–"

"Helpless."

"Yes. Helpless. You see, Mrs. Hickey, I made it my mission to help kids like my son, like Cullen. So, they have the tools necessary to stand up to kids like the ones who drove my poor Jakob to do what he did. I hope you have a better understanding about why I'm so passionate about helping Cullen."

"I understand better now, Dr. Morris. Your story is so devastating. It hits home. I pray you will find peace."

Dr. Morris didn't respond, other than to nod. "I believe Cullen will return to you. I understand the need for urgency, but he will return in his own time."

A light knock at the office door announced Cullen's arrival. The orderly, familiar with the routine by now, rolled Cullen into the room and settled him next to the couch.

"Hi, Cullen. How are you today?" Dr. Morris chatted, moving past the seriousness of the conversation he'd had with Margaret.

"He looks good today. I mean that seriously," she marveled. Then to Cullen, she continued, "Hello, dear. You certainly have some color in your cheeks today."

Cullen responded by looking around the room and yet at nothing particular at all. Inside his mindroom, Cullen felt at ease hearing his mother's voice. Something told him that changes were on their way. After having Claire intrusively enter his room for the better part of two weeks, he didn't fear her visits any longer. The walls had behaved differently in the last few days, as if knowing what was coming next.

CHAPTER 8

IN THE DAYS THAT followed, the feeling of anticipation swirled and spiraled inside the mindroom walls, as if looking forward to regaining any strength Cullen had taken from them. Claire's memories delivered a deluge of emotions and pain. But it would seem that consistent exposure lessened her bite. Anxiety still loomed, but by facing his fears, Cullen felt the hope that one day he could escape his mindroom.

But Cullen knew the inevitable was coming, and his new hope would be put to the test. Claire had been just the pre-game; the warm-up act. The actual struggle would be in facing Evan Stephens.

The light pressure on Cullen's head let him know Dr. Morris was ready for his next session. The familiar words filled the room, "Rest assured that you are safe, even though some images you will see will be unpleasant and some will not. It is best that you continue to follow the light and breathe deeply. There is nothing else for you to do."

That last sentence took up space inside the room and resonated off the walls. *There is nothing else for you to do.* Like there ever was anything that could be done. *Just take it. Know your place. The quicker it's over, the sooner you can get on with your life.* These words had become his mantra.

Cullen didn't have to wait long before the walls came to life. He attempted to control his breathing but found his lungs uncooperative. The walls knew it. They pulsed even before the lights came. Like a funhouse, the walls slowly crept inward towards Cullen and trapped him with little room to move. Then the light came, and in the tight space, brightly illuminated the tight quarters, moving from right to left. Cullen didn't want to look at the light. He didn't want to follow it because he knew what that meant. But like a moth to a flame, he couldn't resist. His eyes obeyed.

For what felt like hours, Cullen waited, tracing the light. From behind him, he felt the air breathing heavily on his neck. "Whatcha looking for?" When Cullen turned his head, nothing was there. "You'll never find it, you know." Cullen tried scrambling from the tight space and found the confining walls didn't offer any comfort. Tarred fingers extended out from the walls and pulled Cullen back into a corner, holding him in place. Suddenly, in the center of the room, an image of Evan Stephens' tall frame towered over Cullen's cowering body, and he felt himself reduced to shreds. His broad frame was an insignificant thing in Evan's shadow. "Whatever you're doing here won't work," Evan's voice rang through the room, though his mouth didn't move.

On the walls, images flickered like a television struggling to turn on. Whatever he was going to be shown, he was sure he didn't want to see. "Wake your power," a voice chimed directly into his right ear. In his left ear, he heard, "Know your strength." This pattern continued while he waited for the walls to decide on a memory to show.

When it finally settled upon one, Cullen knew it right away. He heard the wall growl as an image of himself walked through the hallway towards P.E. class. Getting changed in the locker room in front of classmates was something that was new to kids entering middle school. Cullen, who was always bigger than most boys his age, was also heavier and found his weight spilled out on all sides. To top it off, because his body seemed to mature faster than most other boys, acne came with it. He became an easy target. Evan's target. It started off with just making fun of the zits that boiled to the surface. And because Evan was "the popular kid," his friends felt obliged to join in.

On this particular day, Cullen had ignored Evan's remarks, making him angry. He got into Cullen's face. "You got something to say to me?" Cullen didn't respond. "Hey fatty, don't think because you're bigger than me that I'm afraid of you."

Cullen responded, "I-I don't th-think you're afraid of me. Th-That would b-b-be ridiculous."

"What did you call me, you stuttering turd?"

"I d-d-didn't call you anything. I was s-s-saying the idea of you being afraid of me was r-ridiculous." Some unintended spit came out of Cullen's mouth and landed on Evan's cheek.

"Oh, no you didn't! Did you just spit on me?" Evan yelled.

"N-N-No, it was an ac-accident. I'm s-s-sorry," Cullen pleaded.

"That's alright. I get it."

"Y-Y-You do?" Cullen was cautiously relieved.

"No, you idiot!" Evan pushed Cullen against the lockers and spun him around, so the front of his shirtless body pressed against the cold steel. To the crowd that gathered, Evan called out, "Get your phones out. I want to keep this as a trophy." As the students did so, Evan reached under the fat that guarded Cullen's waistband and grabbed a fistful of underwear.

Cullen pleaded, "N-No. Please, Ev-Evan, don't d-d-do this."

Inside the room, as Cullen watched the scene play out, the messages played louder, alternating in his ears, "Wake your power. Know your strength. Wake your power. Know your strength." Another figure appeared, and Cullen wondered if it was Val. He didn't want her to see him this way. But it wasn't Val. It was a teenage boy he didn't know. He lipped the words, "Wake your power. Know your strength."

I don't know what that means!

Cullen felt the cold of the steel on his chest even as he watched the scene unfold. He knew what would come next. As Evan yanked at his underwear, Cullen could feel the material part through his butt cheeks, putting enormous pressure against his privates. He felt his anus rip, and he was sure there was blood. Cullen felt a scream building as Evan pulled harder. He jerked the underwear up repeatedly until the elastic waistband tore from the cotton fabric.

Cullen screamed, "NOOO!"

From inside Dr. Morris' office, Cullen's backside lifted from the seat of the wheelchair as his scream filled the room. He grabbed at the armrests and ripped the screws through the metal holes meant to hold them in place.

"What's happening, Doctor!?" Margaret screamed.

"I'm not sure. He's having a reaction to the stimulus!"

"Stop the therapy!" she pleaded.

Dr. Morris tapped the keyboard and deactivated the program. The lights on the headset dimmed and powered off. Margaret and Dr. Morris breathed heavily. Dr. Morris stood up and pulled the headset off Cullen. Mrs. Hickey struggled to pry the armrests from Cullen's hands, but they wouldn't budge. His eyes, bloodshot red and veiny, returned to staring at nothing like the first day he was transferred to St. Mary's.

"What happened to his eyes?" Margaret demanded.

"Mrs. Hickey. I'm not sure." He quickly pulled out his penlight and shined it into his eyes, but they didn't attempt to track the light. "I can't tell what's happened."

Margaret felt a rage boil inside of her. She thought she was one step closer to getting her son back. Now, it appeared as if Cullen had taken steps backwards. "I knew I should never have agreed to this...this fake science!"

"Mrs. Hickey, this was only a setback. We are still on the right course."

"Enough, Dr. Morris." Her eyes burned into his. "Enough."

"But what about the readings I've shown you? There is indeed progress."

"Enough," she whispered, harshly. "Dr. Morris, I understand you want to proceed, but nothing you do here is going to bring *your* son back. This experiment is over."

Dr. Morris thought about speaking, but his mind swirled with wild thoughts, none of which would be constructive. After a moment, he pleaded, "Mrs. Hickey, I'm sorry this happened. I wish I could say this was something normal, but we are in uncharted territory, and I still hold true to the feeling that we are on the verge of something amazing. Please."

"I'm sorry, Dr. Morris. I can't."

He slowly dropped his head and drew his lips in tightly. "I understand."

Just then, the armrests loosened from Cullen's grip and crashed onto the glass table. Dr. Morris and Margaret quickly spun their heads to look at Cullen. "I think my son needs some rest." Cullen's bloodshot eyes stared straight ahead, absent once again.

CHAPTER 9

INSIDE HIS MINDROOM, CULLEN'S nightmare continued. He could still feel the pressure from his locker room wedgie. The wall continued to hold him captive and, slowly, like a snake eating his prey, it enveloped him in its blackness. Cullen gasped for breath and tried with all his power to free himself but was helpless. Sticky, black hands like zombies clawed their way out of their graves, grabbed Cullen's legs, and pulled him into a dark hole that opened in the floor. He fell for what felt like forever.

Down

Down

Down...until...

He landed hard on his back. When he tried to get up, the black hands held his body in place. His eyes searched frantically. Even though he knew he was still trapped inside his mind, this place was a different place than his mindroom. A deeper, darker place. When his eyes adjusted, he heard the heavy steps of people walking closely around him. When he turned his head, shadows darted past him, and he could feel the wind from their legs. "Why do you let him do that to you? All of those sayings won't mean a thing if you don't believe them yourself," echoing voices called in this place.

What am I supposed to do? I'm powerless.

"You aren't. Didn't you hear? Know your strength. Wake your power."

I've heard them, but I don't know what that means. What's my strength?

Another, more familiar voice whispered and taunted, "That's because you don't have any. You're worthless." Cullen recognized Evan's voice.

"That's what they want you to believe," the other voice urged.

Who's they?

"All of those who brought you down into this hole," the voice pointed out.

"Me," Evan's voice growled, resonating off the walls.

They will never accept me.

"They don't accept you because they don't respect you."

"Ha ha ha! What's to respect? He's nothing. Awkward. Listen to him speak. It's embarrassing," Evan mocked. "He can't even get himself out of this. He lets us occupy his mind."

See what I mean? I don't have the strength. I'm powerless.

The unknown voice whispered in Cullen's ear, "Listen to me, Cullen. That's what they want you to believe."

Well, I can't say that I don't believe them.

"Enough of this self-loathing. Lift your arm, Cullen. You have the power to do so. One finger at a time," the voice bellowed.

Cullen tried with all his might to move his hands, but they wouldn't budge. *It's no use. I can't do it.*

"Told you he was useless," Evan's voice bit.

"If you don't start believing you have the power inside of you, then you never will," the mysterious voice called out.

Just then, the floor hummed and rumbled. A pulsing light moved across the ceiling of wherever he was. Cullen tried to track the light, but fear overtook his body. Dr. Morris' voice called from somewhere else, "Cullen, I'm here. Track the light. I know you're still in there and you want so desperately to come out."

Dr. Morris sat alone in his office, wondering what went wrong. The territory was uncharted, but he hoped that this was something that was normal. He'd lost Mrs. Hickey's confidence. As a result, she grew even more overprotective just when he'd won her over.

He pored over the charts, outlining the day's therapy session. Cullen's heart rate had become elevated, as well as every other reading. Something caught his eye. During the episode, most brainwave activity jumped to the Reptilian Brain. These readings were off the charts, which would explain the bump in strength. To have ripped the screws right through the holes of the wheelchair must have been because of a sudden uptick in adrenaline. He wondered if Cullen had tapped into something more controlled than primitive. Right before Dr. Morris had deactivated the programmed session, the brain shifted back to the frontal cortex. He must have faced a fight-or-flight situation which was triggered by the images, but Cullen's brain had shown enough control over that situation to where he was actually thinking about it and not reacting.

You're in there, aren't you? Dr. Morris concluded that his patient was certainly processing information, regardless of how terrifying it was. The EMDR Exposure Therapy had to be working.

He knew he had to find out, but the question was whether he *should*. Margaret Hickey expressed she was no longer interested in continuing therapy. To move forward against her wishes would be unethical, and he risked losing his license and would likely face malpractice lawsuits. All his years of hard work and dedication were at risk. On the other hand, he felt he was on the cusp of a breakthrough. To use EMDR Exposure Therapy to help those in a catatonic state was unheard of. Had Cullen tapped into something that very few could ever do at an unconscious level? Imagine the possibilities! What if Cullen could channel moments of incredible resilience? He knew he had no baseline for Cullen's abilities, but this was something that couldn't go ignored.

Deciding to act, Dr. Morris grabbed the headset and rushed to Cullen's room. He had to roll the dice. This would be his secret, and his secret alone to keep. He hadn't thought about whether Cullen's condition would worsen. There was no time for that type of thinking. He had to get better. If this worked, this would help tortured children everywhere. There was no turning back. He couldn't have what happened to Jakob happen to Cullen or anyone else.

No one would question him about what he was doing in Cullen's room since he was still Cullen's psychiatrist. Getting caught was his biggest fear. There would be no explaining that away. Knowing visiting hours at St. Mary's ended at five o'clock, he would have to continue his therapy after hours.

Once inside his room, he checked Cullen's eyes. They still looked off into the distance. By himself, Dr. Morris struggled with Cullen's much larger body to a seated position and propped him up against the wall on one side and with pillows on the other. He positioned the headset on his head and prompted the computer to activate the program. The headset hummed quietly as it turned on.

When Dr. Morris got brainwave readings and vitals, he waited for Cullen's eyes to react. When he didn't respond, he spoke to him, "Cullen, I'm here. Track the light. I know you're still in there and you want so desperately to come out."

Cullen tried to focus on the light, but fear prevented his eyes from finding it. "It's right there, Cullen. Focus on the light," Dr. Morris' voice echoed.

"Don't let fear stop you. Never again," the voice inside the room spoke.

"He won't do it," Evan's voice mocked. "He's a coward."

I'm trying. I'm trying. Cullen stuttered inside his thoughts.

Like quicksand, the sticky black surface consumed him deeper.

"Look at the light, Cullen. Before it's too late," the voice in his mind begged.

"Cullen, listen to the words," Dr. Morris called.

He listened. For the moment, he only heard the hum of the room and Evan's low, sinister chuckle. Then, faintly, he heard it. "Wake your power. Know your strength." As the floor crawled over his face, he whispered the words. Suddenly, his eyes tracked the light. Inside, he slowly dragged his body from the floor. *Whoever you are. Help me up.*

"I can't. This struggle is yours and yours alone. You can do this."

Cullen heard Dr. Morris' voice, encouraging Cullen, "That's it, Cullen. Follow the light."

With all his strength, Cullen freed his right hand and then his left. He screamed as his body released, which resonated inside his room at St. Mary's. Inside his mind, he stood up as his eyes locked with the light. Next to him, the image of Evan filled the space, but this time, it didn't tower over him menacingly. For just this moment, Cullen and Evan stood eye to eye as the room circled. Fear didn't paralyze Cullen. The messages resonated in each ear, "Wake your power. Know your strength." From the corner of his eye, he saw another image inside his mindroom.

Was that you? The voice that was trying to help me?

The boy smirked. His athletic build confidently stood in front of Cullen. His muscular arms crossed his sturdy chest. It was the type of assurance Cullen had only dreamed of having.

Thank you.

"Start helping yourself, Cullen. Believe that you have the power. Don't let them win."

Where's Val?

"She'll be back."

What's your name?

"Call me Zeke." He smirked at Cullen and, without warning, the lights went out. When Cullen opened his eyes, he found himself out of the hole and back in his mindroom.

Dr. Morris removed the headset from Cullen. Clicking on his penlight, he examined Cullen's eyes. "There you are, my boy." Cullen's green eyes followed the light back and forth. Dr. Morris sighed with relief and sat next to Cullen on the bed. "We're going to help a lot of children. I knew you were in there." He patted Cullen on the shoulder. "Let's get you to bed, shall we? We have a lot of work ahead of us." Dr. Morris helped Cullen to lie down. Before turning out the light, Dr. Morris turned to look back at Cullen. "I'm glad you came back to us."

CHAPTER 10

"HOW ARE YOU TODAY, Cullen?" Dr. Morris asked cheerily as he took his penlight and checked Cullen's eyes. "Sorry, I haven't been here the last couple of days, but I've been busy." He lifted a small suitcase onto the bed, spun the combination wheel, and popped the locks open. "Yes, I've been very busy," he mused cheerfully.

From the suitcase, he hoisted a VR headset, different from the one originally used for Cullen's therapy. He'd purchased a new virtual reality headset with high-definition video and built-in headphones. "This here, Cullen, is going to be quite the upgrade for your therapy. Meet *Jakob*. I named him after my son. You two have so much in common, Cullen. I bet you two would have been friends. Like you, they bullied him. Misunderstood him. Never gave him a chance. And I'm sure you have a lot to offer, just like my Jakob did." Dr. Morris held the headset up and admired it. Prominently displayed, Jakob's name shone in red vinyl lettering against the bright white plastic. "I added some upgrades to the programming that will be most beneficial for your therapy."

Over the course of the last ten days, Dr. Morris had continued Cullen's therapy by gradually showing images of Evan instead of exposing him all at once, which nearly caused a setback. Dr. Morris had been so encouraged with how Cullen handled the stimulus during the therapy with Claire's images. But because Evan was truly the head of the snake, a more gradual approach would be necessary. He also upgraded the programming and included more affirmation phrases and other images to help with the therapy.

Margaret Hickey returned to the hospital each day. Although she had been less confrontational, she didn't agree to Dr. Morris' urging to continue the EMDR Exposure Therapy. She argued that she was concerned with Cullen's well-being and that exposing him to the monsters in his world was doing more harm than good. "And besides," she added, "I've been really praying about this, and I feel a breakthrough is on the horizon as his brain heals." When Dr. Morris told her he'd continued with therapy on a "much smaller scale" through just conversations, one sided, of course, she consented as long as she could be present. So, Dr. Morris had Cullen brought in each day and used the penlight to track his eyes and talked him through positive affirmations for his therapy. It was just theatrics, of course, and wouldn't be enough for Cullen, but for Mrs. Hickey, it was. So, he continued the charade.

Now, with the newly upgraded headset in hand, Dr. Morris was ready to take Cullen's therapy to the next level. His brainwave scans had shown a steady level of improved activity over the first days. After using kid gloves, he felt Cullen was ready to face Evan in full force.

"Here you go, Cullen. Let's try this on for size. I think you will find *Jakob* a bit more comfortable as well. It's got built-in headphones with cushioned pads." He squeezed the headphones, smiled, and fitted the headset over Cullen's head. "The best part of this new headset, Cullen, is that it is wireless. I uploaded the program straight into the headset. I don't need my laptop any longer." He sat back and admired the way *Jakob* looked on Cullen's head. "Are you ready to take this up a notch, my friend? This is between the two of us. Remember that for me," Dr. Morris winked.

Cullen sat on the floor listening to Dr. Morris. He felt the pressure on his head. He sensed this session would be different. Recognizing this, he braced himself. Over the past sessions, he'd dealt with Evan's presence more and more in the memories. New phrases were introduced, and he'd learned to lean on them. The therapies had encouraged him to know his worth. Although he wasn't sure what his worth was, he'd started to believe that it was something more than the nothing he'd been told he was. He'd spent days listening to the phrase, *Know your strength.* Cullen knew that strength wasn't a thing he was known for. But now, something stirred inside of him that wasn't there before. *Wake your power* was another phrase. Although he hadn't the foggiest idea what power he had, he knew it lurked beneath the surface and screamed to come out.

New phrases were introduced. *You are your power* and *Stand up for yourself.* For every image of Evan that showed up on the right side of the room, the image of Zeke showed up on its left saying the new phrases. When memories filled the black walls, Cullen still found them frightening, but with each passing day, he found himself less afraid, and Evan's words carried less of a blow.

The mindroom buzzed, and the walls came to life. Cullen expected Evan, but the walls reacted less menacingly. The familiar announcement that started each session was different. Now, a boy's voice filled the room with different instructions. "Hello Cullen. My name is Jakob. Don't be afraid. We will face your fears together. Remember to follow the light and breathe deeply." When the light shined, the high definition of the new headset caused Cullen to squint. He forced himself to track it and within seconds, Evan materialized in the middle of the room. Cullen listened for the new words. "You are your power. Stand up for yourself," alternated in each of his ears.

Evan's image moved towards Cullen, but as Cullen thought about the words, the image stopped. On the left side of the room, Zeke stood with his chest puffed, nodding his encouragement towards Cullen.

Then, a memory clearly pixelated on the walls. Cullen blinked and the movie of this memory jumped from the walls and played out three dimensionally inside his mindroom. It was a memory Cullen knew well. One that happened near the end of eighth grade. Cullen had been walking in the cafeteria with a tray full of food. To get to the table where he and a couple of other kids who dared to be seen with Cullen sat, he had to walk past the table where the popular kids ate. Normally, they would just make comments or threats as he walked by, but this day was different. Evan had fashioned part of a rope with some kind of weight attached on both ends. As Cullen passed the table, he tossed the rope towards Cullen's ankles. The rope spun around both of his legs, tripping him, and he ended up sprawled across the floor. His food ended up all over his shirt and face. Then, to add insult to injury, the popular kids, laughing and taunting, poured drinks and food on top of Cullen. He struggled to get to his feet, but he slipped and slid across the floor. Of course, every phone in the cafeteria recorded the humiliation. Once again, it ended up all over social media. The caption read: *We hogtied a pig!!* Evan and his crew got detention and were forced to apologize, but they were just empty words. Cullen knew that. Heck, the principal knew it, too.

That's the way this memory should have played out, but with the new VR set on his head, Cullen found he could control it. While he was on the floor suffering the indignities of having food poured all over his body and listening to the taunts of pig noises, Cullen looked up at Zeke. "C'mon Cullen, you are your power," he urged. Instead of finding reasons to stay down, Cullen sat up and reached for the rope around his ankles. With one pull, he shredded it apart and freed himself. He could feel the milk, pudding, and salad dressing pouring down his face and body as he stood up. He picked up the lunch tray and glared at Evan. Not the Evan from the memory of the day, but the one that was in the room with him. He squared his shoulders and for the first time since entering his mindroom, Cullen found his voice without a stutter. "Evan, I take back my power." Then he snapped the tray in half in his large hands. Evan backed up to the wall and melted into it. A broad smile broke across Zeke's confident, reassuring face before disappearing, too.

Cullen tracked the light as it dimmed and turned off signifying the end of the session. The walls of the mindroom continued vibrating with a dull hum. A smile crept across Cullen's face as he approached it. They acted differently. The blackness of them subtly changed to a deep purple and then to what he could only describe as the colors of a sunset when the sun was at its lowest. Lavender and orange. For the first time, fear didn't dominate Cullen's thoughts.

Then a voice infiltrated the room from outside of his mindroom. "Well, Cullen, that was a banger, wasn't it?" Dr. Morris asked.

I don't know what that means, but if it means good, then yes.

"This is extraordinary. This is the first time your brainwaves and your heart rate have remained steady. What are you doing in there?"

The thoughts came almost instantly. *I think I'm getting better. For the first time, I feel like I'm worth something.*

As if reading Cullen's thoughts, Dr. Morris put his forehead against Cullen's. "I think it's time to come out of there, my friend." He pulled away from Cullen and looked into his eyes. They continued to search about the room. Dr. Morris curled up one side of his mouth. "I thought for a second there...ha, ha, nevermind. When you're ready, we'll all be here."

Cullen listened to Dr. Morris while watching the new colors of the walls in his mindroom dance about. *I feel like I'm close*, Cullen thought to himself.

CHAPTER 11

A WEEK LATER, *JAKOB* had displayed a very humiliating memory of a school talent show. Evan, Claire, and his buddies performed an awful performance in which they used Cullen as the target for all of their antics.

During the improvisation, they never mentioned his name, but all the students in attendance knew who they were mocking. They depicted him as a bumbling ogre that terrorized a fair maiden, played by Claire, of course. His stutter was grossly exaggerated, and they insulted the lumbering way he walked. They defeated him the same way he'd been "hogtied" in the cafeteria that day. But in this memory, as the "actors" on stage stabbed and killed the ogre with toy swords and daggers, shock waves rippled through the audience. All eyes shifted onto Cullen who, despite his size, felt small in his seat. Sensing this, Evan stood at the edge of the stage, extended the play sword into the air, and summoned an Old English accent, "The ogre is dead! And it is I, Prince Evan, who's defeated him. Never shall he wa-wa-walk these g-g-grounds again." The last words served as a dig at Cullen's stutter.

A few of Evan's goons clapped and chanted, "Evan. Evan. Evan." This was enough to get the student body to chant and clap along.

That was how the memory was supposed to end, but in Cullen's mindroom reality, it ended differently. He heard the words play in the room, *Enough is enough, stand up for yourself.*

In the memory *Jakob* presented, Val with her radiant blue streaks and Zeke, whose confident smile shone through his teeth that stood out against his dark skin, flanked Cullen on either side. For the first time, they spoke the words instead of just being a voice inside *Jakob*. Val declared, "Today is yours, Cullen." She popped a bubble with her gum.

Zeke nodded to Cullen. The usual pleasing smile erased from his face. "Enough is enough," he urged. "Stand up for yourself."

"B-But how?" Cullen questioned, realizing he could now speak inside the therapy session. With this also came his stutter.

The two represented a symbol of strength and spoke to him without the rehearsed lines of his therapy. Val smiled and responded, "This is how you get back and get out."

"Get up there and take charge. Show them that you won't take it any longer," Zeke insisted.

Cullen's eyes flitted about. Doubt filled him.

"Look Cullen, you don't want to be trapped in here forever, do you? Take a stand," Val noted, trying to convince him.

"Will you c-come with m-me?"

A smile returned to Zeke's face again. "Nah, man, this is your fight. You gotta do this on your own. We'll be right here."

Cullen took a deep breath. "H-Here goes." He stood up and squared his shoulders as the laughs and jeers went on in the auditorium.

During therapy from inside Cullen's hospital room, Cullen took a deep breath and did what he hadn't done on his own in all the time at the hospital. As Dr. Morris' eyes were fixed on the laptop monitoring Cullen's vitals, he felt a shadow fall over the room. When he looked up, Cullen towered over him like a skyscraper blocking out the sun.

Back in the memory, Cullen swallowed hard and shuffled down the aisle toward the stage. Before ascending the stairs, he looked back at Val and Zeke. They both nodded, willing him the confidence to proceed.

When he got to the stage, everyone saw Cullen, except for Evan, who was still basking in the glow of acceptance from his peers. He walked towards Evan, who was pumping the sword in the air. When everything became quiet, he shouted, "What's going on? The ogre is dead!" He spun his head around to see Cullen looking down on him. "Well, look what we have here? The ogre isn't–"

Cullen ripped the sword from his hand. "No more, Evan." Cullen realized his stutter was no longer present.

"What are you going to do about it?" Evan mocked. Some others on the stage, including Claire, stood behind Evan.

"NO MORE, Evan! And I mean it," Cullen growled.

The mindroom shook violently. The walls echoed, "Wake your power. Know your strength."

Evan, with just an inkling of fear behind his voice, asked, "What are you going to do about it, you turd?"

The colors of the walls battled for dominance. The sticky black fought to overtake the purple and orange the walls had become in the last week. It swirled and pushed in waves over the purple and orange like stormy seas, but the vibrant colors didn't budge. Instead, it just advanced upon the black until there was little left.

On the stage, Evan pushed Cullen with two hands. When Cullen didn't budge. Evan laughed nervously. "This changes nothing."

Cullen raised the fake sword overhead. "I won't let you do this anymore." Then, he brought the sword down and it cut through Evan's image, and he disappeared. Confused, Cullen blinked his unbelieving eyes. Then, he turned to the audience and shouted, "No more!"

Val and Zeke beamed as the room gradually brightened, and the memory inside *Jakob* faded. The light Cullen tracked slowed to a crawl and then, too, disappeared.

Dr. Morris looked up at Cullen after deactivating the therapy session. He remained standing. Dr. Morris was undecided about what to do next. He asked, "Cullen? Everything good in there?" He pulled the chair from the desk in the room and climbed it. He carefully removed *Jakob* from Cullen's head and placed it on the desk. With his penlight, he examined his eyes. They hadn't changed, but standing was a development he hadn't expected.

He climbed down from the chair and helped Cullen back to the bed. "This is a big day, my friend. We are very close now." Cullen blankly stared around the room. "I don't know what happened in there today, but I bet it was good."

Inside his mindroom, emotions washed over Cullen. He cried. Not tears of sadness, but of hope.

CHAPTER 12

Margaret Hickey poured herself her second cup of coffee to go with a morning cigarette. She'd quit smoking when she'd found out she was pregnant with Cullen. It wasn't necessarily an hourly habit like her parents, but she did it more than she liked to, mostly during social interactions with friends. Becoming a mother was as good a reason as any to kick the habit. But ever since Cullen transferred to St. Mary's, her nerves had been a wreck and every little thing set her off, so she picked up the habit again.

She leafed through a magazine, not really reading anything. Her thoughts consumed her. She reflected upon her failed marriage and wondered in what other areas she'd failed. *Am I a good mother?* She wondered to herself. She had been Cullen's sounding board and had encouraged him to advocate for himself when they picked on him and intervened when necessary. *Is that what a good mother does? Did I miss the warning signs?* She knew Cullen was a target for bullying, but in the last half of eighth grade, she had heard nothing that told her it had gotten worse. She hated herself for letting him go to Wilderness Camp. He wanted to go, and she couldn't hold him close forever. Independence had to come at some point, and Wilderness Camp seemed to be the perfect place.

What Cullen needed, she thought, was a male role model. Someone to teach him what it was like to be a man or at the very least teach him to defend himself. She never felt qualified in that department, and it wasn't until recently where she felt like she found her voice. Her mind raced to Cullen's father, Bruce, and wondered what he would think of his boy. The last time he'd seen him was three years ago when he showed up at fifth grade promotion. Bruce may have been a coward regarding matters of the heart, but he knew how to stand up for himself. Cullen could have used some advice. Instead, he remarried and disappeared out of their lives.

Her mind shifted to Cullen. She wondered if stopping the EMDR Exposure Therapy had been the right thing to do. There *was* progress, right? Dr. Morris had assured her of that and believed that it was going to work. But to see Cullen's eyes revert to their vacant stare felt like a step backward. Sure, that was only temporary, but it worried her. That wasn't the part that scared her the most. Cullen had always been a passive boy. He wouldn't hurt a fly. As a mother, she admired that a boy who was so large could be so gentle. Sometimes, however, deep inside, she wished he would stand up for himself. Show others that he wouldn't be pushed around. But since Wilderness Camp, there had been two instances in which Cullen's strength made her unnerved and both times had been when he wasn't conscious.

She thought of that poor teacher's hand. Ms. Saunders had been a terrific advocate for Cullen in middle school. She was the one teacher he could trust. She had a soft spot for him. But what Cullen did to her hand, shattering every bone with his grip, scared Margaret. She was sure that Cullen wasn't even aware he'd even done it and would be mortified when he found out.

Even after all Ms. Saunders had gone through—the casting and months of rehabilitation—she still called Mrs. Hickey weekly to check in on Cullen.

Then, during therapy with Dr. Morris, to watch her son rip the armrests from the wheelchair without being conscious or even breaking a sweat was unnerving. It was unexpected, and truthfully, terrifying. So, she stopped the EMDR Exposure Therapy to protect her boy. Was Cullen really able to benefit from the therapy she settled upon? She found no encouragement in it. Dr. Morris asked him questions, repeated positive affirmations, and tried to help Cullen with visualization. It didn't seem enough. At least with the other therapy, she could see brain scans and other readings. She doubted whether it was even helping him. After a few sleepless nights, she resolved to tell Dr. Morris that she was thinking about giving his alternative therapy another go.

Her cell phone buzzed against the table, sending it dancing across the wood. It was Dr. Morris. She clicked the green button and answered, "Good morning, Dr. Morris. This is certainly an early phone call. Everything okay?" Her eyes widened. "Yes, doctor. He's awake?! Oh my God, I'm on my way. Thank you, Dr. Morris."

CHAPTER 13

IN HIS ROOM, CULLEN slept. Since EMDR Exposure Therapy, dreams had invaded his mind. He normally didn't dream, but when he did, they came in terrors, often an extension of the torment he received at school. At the beginning of therapy, the same scary dreams he had over the last few years came more frequently, but the more he'd received therapy, the more he could exert some level of control over them.

The events from the last session played in his dreams on repeat. Although his body slept, the walls came alive inside his mindroom without the use of *Jakob*. It wasn't the high-definition visual he'd grown used to throughout his therapy, but it was vivid enough to feel real. Instead of participating in the memory, he watched himself stride to the stage and take the play sword from Evan's hand. This time, when he brought the sword down, Evan's hand blocked it. Confused, Cullen watched as everyone on stage surrounded him. Their expressions changed into angry, demonic-like faces: bloodshot eyes and black, uneven teeth, dripping with saliva.

They took turns shoving him around within the circle. The audience laughed and teased. Evan peered at Cullen where he watched the horror unfold. "This is what happens when you think you have power and strength. But guess what, Cullen? You have neither!" Evan growled.

The scene shifted, and Cullen found himself in a cemetery. He forced himself to look at his shoeless feet, muddied and covered in grass cuttings. Those from the stage now stared at him with solemn, darkened eyes and stood behind headstones. Using the dim light of the moon, he searched through the foggy darkness at the graves. He gasped when each one read his name: *Cullen Hickey*. Chiseled in the granite and marble displayed different dates of his death. "Wh-What is this?" he asked into the fog.

Claire's image cut through the mist. "These are the dates when you died."

"B-B-But, I'm not dead," his stutter returned.

"Aren't you?" Evan mocked. "These dates represent pieces of you that died over the last few years."

"Right here?" Claire pointed at a headstone that was over-grown with dewy moss. Cullen recognized the girl who stood behind it. "Do you remember when we convinced you that Montana Myers was *totally* into you? Then you came to the Third Street Park that day to meet her, but she wasn't the only one there. It was *so* cute when you brought her that carnation," Claire mentioned with sarcasm. "Remember that? Instead of going on a date..."

Montana spoke from behind the headstone, "...a little piece of you died that day. How would you ever think that someone like me would ever be into someone like you?"

All the ghoulish kids laughed maniacally and then abruptly stopped, once again fixing their evil gazes upon Cullen.

Of course, Cullen remembered that. His heart, which had been so hopeful, broke when all the kids came to the park and laughed at him. Inside the mindroom, Cullen watched himself tear up and ride off on his bike, dripping in slime.

"Aww Cullen. Are y-y-you g-g-gonna cry again?" Evan mocked ruthlessly. "If that brings a tear to your eye, then you'll remember this." He walked over to another grave and stood by it. A few of his classmates flanked each side of the headstone. "Remember when I convinced you to give us the answers for the science midterm last year? Oh, you were so against it, but I promised that if you did us a solid, we wouldn't pick on you as much."

"But if I d-didn't, you ww-would bring the p-pain."

"That's so me to say that!" Evan bent over in laughter. "And then, after the midterm, I told Mr. Badgley that you were cheating off my test. Oh my God, it was priceless when he confronted you about it. That big stupid face was like *duh*." A tear dropped from Cullen's eye. "Another piece of you from that day is buried right here, Cullen." Evan stomped his foot on the loose, soft soil like he was crushing a bug.

"Wh-what do you w-want from me, E-Evan?" Cullen asked, staring over the dozen graves. Each one with a different story to tell.

"Turn around, big guy," Claire sang.

Cullen spun around. Before him, an empty grave hungrily waited for another piece of him. "What's th-that for?"

Cullen panicked. Inside his mindroom, Cullen watched the scene unfold and tried hard to warn himself, but somehow, he'd lost his power to control anything. Instead, the nightmare took over him.

"That's for you, stupid. Did you think it was for me?" Evan asked while the others howled. "Check out the headstone. Today's the day we bury the rest of you. After today, you will never leave this place. Stuck forever in this nightmare."

Cullen, standing at the foot of the hole, struggled to read the headstone. As the fog cleared, he could read his name. Under it were the words, *Died November 15, 2019*. Cullen spun around and desperately asked, "Wh-What's t-t-today's date?"

As the last word fell from his lips, Evan shoved Cullen into the grave. Cullen landed with a thud. Hands emerged from all sides. Their dirty, grubby fingers pulled him into the soft soil. As the dirt covered his body, he looked up and could see the others around the perimeter laughing at him. Evan stood at the edge and waved at him with his lips pouted.

From inside the mindroom, Cullen ran to the walls and yelled at himself, "Get out of there! Come on, Cullen. Get out of there!"

A voice from behind startled him, "He can't help himself. He's trapped in that nightmare."

Cullen twisted around to see Val and Zeke standing side by side. "Wh-What d-do I do?" he shouted.

Zeke stepped forward. "Go in there and save him."

"Save yourself, Cullen," Val urged.

"How?"

"Go after him. If you don't, you'll be trapped here forever. You'll never see your mother again. Are you going to let them win?" Zeke begged.

The walls were alive again, transferring between orange, purple, and black. He knew what he had to do. Cullen ran straight towards the wall with as much speed as he could. He dove headfirst. The wall had expected him and swallowed him. When he came through on the other side, he found himself in the graveyard. He approached the group of kids who still surrounded the grave. Cullen found his voice without a stutter, "Move out of my way!"

The kids twirled around, and their shocked faces told him they weren't expecting him. They looked from the Cullen who came from nowhere to the one being ingested by the grave and back again. "How in the world?" Claire questioned.

Cullen covered the space between them in two enormous steps. "What do you think you're doing?" Evan threatened.

Cullen ignored them, pushed past the group, and jumped into the hole. With his hands, he desperately clawed at the ground, scooping handfuls of dirt out of the hole. *Wake your power. Know your strength.* His thoughts swirled in his mind like torrents of snowflakes. Finally, his hand found the buried Cullen's hand. He embraced it and pulled, but the grimy hands from the grave fought back, forcing Cullen to let go. Then, with both hands, he grabbed at the hands holding Cullen's body down and, one by one, plucked them like pulling weeds from a garden until there weren't any left. Then he found Cullen's hand again and pulled him from the dirt. Both Cullens sat in the grave. Their eyes locked.

Cullen, who was pulled from the grave, stared in astonishment through his dirt-streaked face. "How? Wh-What is g-g-going on?"

The other Cullen took a deep breath. "There's a lot that I don't even understand. But look, we need to get out of this place."

"B-But how?"

"You have to start believing that you ...," he paused. "*We*, Cullen. *We* have to believe all this stuff *Jakob is* telling us. If we don't, we're going to be trapped in here. Forever."

"But I'm af-fraid to go b-back out th-there."

"What about Mom? She's waiting for us. We have to get back to her." The dirt-covered Cullen nodded his head. "Whenever you are feeling overwhelmed, remember—"

"Th-that we're w-w-worth it."

"Yes. Yes, we are. Are you ready to get out of here?"

"W-Will it w-work?"

"We won't know unless we try." Cullen stood up and reached for the dirt-covered Cullen and hoisted him up. When they looked up from the hole, the teasing kids vanished. Val, with a large bubble appearing from her lips, and Zeke, arms folded, smiled down on both Cullens.

When they were out of the grave, they looked across the landscape of the nightmare. A menacing voice filled the room. Evan. "You're not going anywhere!" he barked.

The dirt-covered Cullen answered, "Yes, w-we are. We're g-getting out of h-here."

"I-Is th-that wh-where you're g-g-going?" He mocked before shifting his voice back to normal. "I don't think so. You're a prisoner here. My prisoner. There *is* no way out." Each kid crept out from behind the headstones towards the Cullens, surrounding them. "There's no escape. I mean, even if you manage to get out, there's no escaping us. We're going to make your life a living hell."

Evan stepped forward and grabbed Cullen's dirt-covered hand. "Let me make this easier for you. You're *not* leaving!"

Cullen tried to pull his hand away, but it wouldn't budge from Evan's grip. "L-Let go of m-me, Evan."

"That's not going to happen." Evan leered at him. Claire stood by, smiling smugly.

Cullen struggled to free himself. He looked back at the other Cullen. When he moved to help, Zeke's arm held him back. He shook his head and expressed, "He's got to do this himself."

Cullen turned and shouted to the other Cullen, "You've got this. Wake your power!" By now, Evan's grip had twisted Cullen's wrist so that his huge frame bent over. "Come on, Cullen. You can do this!"

Feeling a surge of power, he balled his free hand into a fist and, with all his strength, swung upwards. Evan's image shattered like a pane of glass, littering the ground in a million pieces.

In amazement, he looked down at his fist. "I did it. I freed myself."

"Your stutter, Cullen. It's gone," Cullen called to the other.

The victorious Cullen smiled at the image of himself. "How do we get out of here?"

Cullen from the mindroom looked around. "I guess the way I got in." He pointed.

They walked to the edge of the nightmare where the wall met them. They each put a hand to the wall and pushed through it. After taking one glance at each other, they stepped through. The black nightmare tried to hold both of them back but wasn't strong enough to.

In his room at St. Mary's, where he had spent the last three and a half months, Cullen finally woke up.

Chapter 14

CULLEN SAT ACROSS FROM Dr. Morris in the staff cafeteria. In front of him, a bowl of chicken soup waited to be eaten. While in his catatonic state, he'd been spoon fed his meals, which mostly consisted of oatmeal or anything else that was mushy. Cullen stared, mesmerized as the steam danced over the bowl. The act of feeding himself felt foreign.

Dr. Morris silently observed him. The father in him wanted to offer help, but the psychiatrist's side of him sat fascinated as this boy who'd been so lost inside of himself tried to make sense of the simplest of things.

"Cullen," Dr. Morris addressed, the father in him winning over his indecision. "Is there something I can get you?"

Then, as if seeing Dr. Morris for the first time, Cullen smiled weakly. "Did you say something?"

Dr. Morris smiled. "Yes. I asked if there was something I could get you."

Cullen slowly scanned the table, trying to make sense of things. "It's funny. I feel like I've just woken up from the deepest sleep," Cullen groaned in a tired voice.

"That's because you have, my friend. You have."

"But it feels like I'm still not awake. Like I'm sleeping awake."

"You've been mostly asleep for quite some time. I imagine it may take some time to feel like yourself." He met Cullen's eyes, noticing how different it was to have them to focus on one thing at a time. "I think your soup may be cool enough to eat. Why don't you try some?"

Cullen picked up the spoon and examined it as if using it was a completely new concept for him. He ran his finger along the cold metal and down along the belly. Finally, he gripped it by its handle and scooped a small portion of the chicken soup. Slowly, he put it to his lips. The taste reminded him of how hungry he was. A slight smirk broke across his lips. "This is good." He ate another spoonful and then another and another.

Dr. Morris chuckled, "Slow down. There's plenty more where that came from. No need to rush through it."

A dribble spilled down his chin, and he wiped it with his sleeve. He placed the spoon back on the table. "You're Dr. Morris, right?"

Dr. Morris tilted his head and smirked. "Yes, Cullen. I'm Dr. Morris. It's nice to officially meet you. We've been concerned about you."

"Where am I?" Cullen glanced around at other people sitting at other tables. "I know I'm in a hospital or something."

"That's correct. You are at Saint Mary's." Dr. Morris purposely left out that it was a psychiatric hospital.

Cullen put his head down for a moment as curls fell over his eyes. "What happened to me?"

"Do you recall anything? Anything at all?"

Cullen pinched his eyebrows. "I was at a camp. Wilderness Camp."

"Yes, Cullen. That's correct."

He pulled back the hair from his eyes. "I was being chased."

Dr. Morris pressed his lips together. "That's true."

Cullen shook his head. "I never understood why things like that happen to me."

Dr. Morris shrugged. "The world is hard to figure out," he responded.

Just then, the door to the cafeteria flew open. "Cullen!" Mrs. Hickey raced across the cafeteria towards her son.

Cullen's head turned towards her familiar voice. He tried to stand, but found his legs lacked the strength to get up quickly enough to meet her. Instead, her arms fell over his large body, which made hers look tiny in comparison. "Cullen. My God. I knew this was going to happen soon. Oh, thank God." Tears absorbed into Cullen's hospital gown. Margaret unloaded three months of love onto him. She could feel his body was different. Bigger, but skinnier. The time had taken its toll on him physically, but it was the mental scars that she was more worried about.

"Hi, Mom," Cullen responded slowly.

"Oh, my goodness," she responded, wiping the stream of tears flowing down her cheeks. "Your voice. It sounds like a man's voice. Let me look at you." As she looked into his eyes, she was relieved they focused on her instead of all about the room.

"He's still getting his bearings, Mrs. Hickey," Dr. Morris smiled.

"Oh, Dr. Morris." She ran over and embraced him from behind as he sat.

He laughed heartily and patted her hands. "I'm so happy for you both."

"Thank you, Dr. Morris. You were a big part of this." He smiled appreciatively.

Cullen watched curiously. "How long have I been here?" She stared at him, confused. Cullen noticed and asked, "What's the matter?"

"Cullen. Your stutter. It's…It's gone," she commented with bewilderment. Cullen retraced his words and a small smile moved across his lips.

Dr. Morris responded, "I remember you mentioning something about his stutter. Well, would you look at that? This is certainly something unforeseen."

"It certainly is. He's struggled with stuttering ever since he was a child. Oh, my goodness," Margaret beamed cheerfully.

Cullen cleared his throat and tested this new discovery. "So, how long have I been here?"

Dr. Morris and Cullen's mother looked at each other. He nodded towards her, letting her know it was okay. "Sweetie. It's been a long time."

"How long?"

"Three and a half months."

Cullen's eyes searched the room for understanding. His mind raced to comprehend the time he'd lost. "Three months? How could that be?"

"Cullen. You've been through some trauma," Dr. Morris stated.

He looked at his mother. She beamed with compassion in her eyes. "Was I in an accident? Did I hit my head?"

"Not exactly, sweetie."

"Then what happened?" Cullen coughed out.

"We're still trying to work out the details, Cullen. The trauma seems to be more psychological," Dr. Morris responded.

"I don't understand."

"You see, Cullen. We don't really understand either, but from a clinical standpoint, we think that your mind seized," Dr. Morris attempted to explain.

"A seizure?"

"No. Not a seizure. When you were at that camp, the kids there bullied you. Do you recall that?" Dr. Morris waited, but Cullen didn't respond. "Sometimes, when the mind experiences an influx of negative impulses, it struggles to know what to do with all that stimuli. Your brain has to decide whether to stand and fight or run away. As I understand what happened, you were being chased, so your brain ran. However, they cornered you. You wanted so badly to keep running but couldn't. Your brain didn't know what to do, so to protect itself, it seized up. It did the one thing it could to protect itself, like a goat or an opossum. Your brain just shut down. It just so happens that when this happened to you, it took some time to bring you back to us."

"Yes," Margaret beamed. "And here you are."

Cullen sat silently. Lost in a fog. He scanned his mind, but only fragments of memories were present like puzzle pieces. He figured it would take some time. Had it really been three months? Cullen shut his eyes and tried to see what he could remember. "I remember hearing things."

"Hearing things?" Dr. Morris wondered.

"Yes. I could hear..." he closed his eyes and tried to call forward memories. "Voices."

"Voices?" Dr. Morris questioned. "Care to elaborate?" Cullen closed his eyes again.

Dr. Morris glanced at Margaret and lipped, *"This is a good thing."*

Faintly, Cullen could hear mumblings, but knew he had to go deeper. He pulled himself further in until finally he came to a door. Purple light pierced around the edges of it. As he reached for the cold handle, his hand trembled. When he pushed it open, he peered into the room. *His* mindroom. Had there been a door there all along? The thought of becoming trapped in there again sent shivers through him. The walls sensed his presence and came alive. Inside the humming, Cullen could hear the voices. "You are worth it," Cullen said slowly.

"Yes, Cullen," Dr. Morris acknowledged. "Anything else?"

The walls rippled as affirmations whispered and echoed inside his mind.

"Wake your power. Know your strength," Cullen repeated.

A smile developed across Dr. Morris' face. The EMDR Exposure Therapy. Cullen *could* hear the words he programmed into the headset. Inside him, he knew he had to tell Mrs. Hickey that he continued the therapy, and this was likely part of the result. When he glanced over at her face, he could sense her confusion.

"Cullen. Where did you hear these words?" his mother asked.

Dr. Morris answered instead. "Mrs. Hickey, these are the phrases I built into the EMDR Exposure Therapy, to offset the negative images we subjected Cullen to. Of his aggressors. Plus, I used them in his therapy sessions after we stopped therapy. You heard me use them."

Her eyes darted around the room. "So, he was listening," she declared in wonder.

Dr. Morris beamed inside. His assumption had been right. "Is there anything else you can tell us?"

Cullen, his eyes still closed, imagined walking to the walls and placed a hand upon them. They reacted like water, rippling in tiny waves until they bounced off an edge and returned to him.

"Sometimes there were others. Some wanted to hurt me and others didn't..." his voice trailed off.

"Like who, Cullen? Who wanted to hurt you?" his mother asked.

Cullen swallowed hard. "Evan and Claire." He flexed his hand.

"Do you remember them there?" Dr. Morris asked, excitement edging in his voice.

"Yes."

"You said there were others. They didn't want to hurt you?" his mother pressed.

"No. They seemed like...friends."

"Thank you for this information. I think–"

"There was something else. Another voice," Cullen said.

"Someone else? A friend?" Dr. Morris asked.

Still thinking inside his mindroom, Cullen recalled, "I think. It's hard to explain. He didn't interact, he was just there."

"We're listening, Cullen. Did he have a name?" his mother asked, reaching for his hand.

Cullen opened his eyes and looked at Dr. Morris. "Jakob," he blurted out.

Dr. Morris' eyes widened as he silently swallowed hard. "Jakob," he whispered to himself so that no one could hear. Then, deciding to act quickly, he advised, "Well, Cullen. We certainly have a lot to unpack and there's no rush doing it all today. Wouldn't you agree, Mrs. Hickey?"

"But–," Margaret started. She wanted to ask who Jakob was, but after mulling over what Dr. Morris said, she agreed. "Never mind. Yes. Oh, my goodness, this certainly has been a big day. I'm so excited to have you back, Cullen." She hugged him again.

Dr. Morris waved over to an orderly who came over. "Donovan, can you please take Mr. Hickey back to his room? I'm sure he's exhausted." He looked at Cullen, who gave him a quick nod.

"Of course." Donovan helped Cullen into a wheelchair.

"Is it okay if I go with him?" Margaret asked.

"I couldn't imagine better therapy for both of you than to spend a little time together," Dr. Morris suggested. "Cullen, go get some rest."

Cullen pressed his lips together in a faint smile, and Margaret smiled at Dr. Morris before heading out of the cafeteria.

Dr. Morris' smile evaporated from his face. Jakob. To hear his son's name uttered by Cullen made it feel like he was still alive, a presence that helped Cullen to face his demons. Demons he couldn't face when he was alive. Dr. Morris smirked at the thought of his little boy helping Cullen.

CHAPTER 15

MARGARET HELPED CULLEN BACK into his room. Her heart hadn't stopped pounding from the moment she received the phone call. She'd been living every parent's nightmare. Parents do everything in their power to protect their children. Margaret felt she had, but no matter how much she tried to protect Cullen, it never got better. Guilt hung around her neck, slumping her shoulders every time her boy struggled. That weight had anchored her down over the last three months.

When Margaret helped Cullen from his wheelchair, she not only noted how much weight he'd lost, but how tall he'd grown. She could tell when she hugged him, but now he towered over herself and the orderly. She figured him to be at least six feet, four inches tall. "Can I get anything for you, sweetie?"

Cullen sat on the edge of his bed and looked at this mother through curls that spilled down his face. "I think I'm good. Just tired and need to rest."

"Are you?" she asked.

Cullen shot a confused look.

"Good. Are you good?" she wondered.

He paused, seemingly taking inventory of his emotions. "I feel different, a good different. I mean, I'm still trying to make sense of everything. Most of it felt like being caught in a storm."

"And the other part?" She sat on the bed next to him.

"The other part felt like…like spring sun after a brutal winter."

Margaret smiled, tight-lipped. "Well, it looks like you've unleashed a bit of a poet inside you." She squeezed his knee and stared longingly at her son. The feeling of having him back was better than what she imagined. "I'll tell you one thing. As soon as you get out of here, we're going to get those locks under control. You need a haircut in the worst way." They both chuckled.

"When do you think that will be?"

"Until you come home?" Cullen shook his head. "I'm not sure. I'll go talk to Dr. Morris. In the meantime, you rest. I'll be back tomorrow." She kissed him on the cheek and feebly tried to wrap her arms around his large shoulders. "I love you."

Cullen smirked and watched his mother get up from the bed and gather her things. "I love you too."

Margaret looked back and smiled genuinely for the first time in months. She felt Cullen's words breathe life into her and lessen the weight from around her neck.

With her renewed strength, she was determined to find out what was next for Cullen. She marched to the opposite side of St. Mary's to Dr. Morris' office. Since she'd been a fixture at the hospital the last three months, nurses and orderlies offered their congratulations and well-wishes.

"So exciting to see Cullen's returned to you," a nurse congratulated.

"Our family has been praying for you since Cullen came to us."

"You must be so relieved."

Each comment added inches to her smile, which stayed with her when she approached Dr. Morris' office. She knocked lightly.

From inside, she heard Dr. Morris say, "Come on in." He stood from his desk when he saw Mrs. Hickey. "Ah, hello there." His smile matched the one still stretched across her face. "How is Cullen? Is he getting some rest?" Margaret nodded. "Good. Good. His body will need some time to heal."

"Yes, Dr. Morris. He's doing great. I can't thank you enough for all the work you put into his recovery."

"You're welcome. Say what you like, but it was a mother's love that really brought him home."

Margaret beamed. "Speaking of that, how long before I get to take him home?"

"Please come sit down," he suggested, pointing to the couches. "I think Cullen should stay a little while longer before we consider releasing him. Given all that happened to him, it's important that we do two things. The first thing is to unpackage everything that's happened to Cullen before he experienced the trauma and while he was in his catatonic state."

"That makes sense. And the second?"

"I think it's of utmost importance that we give Cullen tools so that something like this doesn't happen again. We have to ask: what can we do for Cullen so that he doesn't relapse?"

Margaret gasped inwardly. She was ready to come in and suggest that she would like Cullen home as soon as possible, but Dr. Morris' words made complete sense. The thought of Cullen slipping back where he was for the last three months terrified her to her core. "We certainly don't want that."

"Agreed. This will take some time. I'm guessing with adequate progress, another two or three weeks and then continuing therapy for several months after he's discharged from the hospital."

"Gosh. That's longer than I'd hoped, but I understand."

"Yes, Mrs. Hickey. We all want what's best for him."

"Do you think he will return to us? Normal?"

Dr. Morris checked his glasses against the sunlight permeating into the room. "Normal? I hope not."

Margaret shot a concerned look.

Dr. Morris leaned in with wonder edging on his voice, "Normal isn't going to work. Normal tells us that things would be status quo. That means Cullen goes back to facing the monsters without being prepared for how to beat them. No, Mrs. Hickey. I don't think normal is good enough. Cullen needs to be better than that." A sly, excited smile set onto his face.

Margaret digested Dr. Morris' words. She would've settled for normal, but it would be nice for Cullen to have those tools. As she looked around the room, thinking about what kind of world waited for Cullen out there, post-trauma, something caught her eye. On the countertop of the built-in bookshelf rested *Jakob*. "Is that what I think that is?"

Dr. Morris' body tensed. This was a careless move, and he knew he wasn't quite ready to confess he'd been using it with her son. He'd played this scene out dozens of times, and each time ended with Margaret Hickey furious with him. He decided to let the situation develop organically. Not ready to deny and not ready to confess. "Ah, yes, it is," he answered coolly.

Margaret walked over to the bookshelf. She fingered the lettering that spelled out Jakob. She whispered the name to herself. "This one is fancier than the other one."

"I've made some upgrades," Dr. Morris answered. On the inside, his heart thumped.

Margaret continued to stare at *Jakob*. She wondered if she had pulled the plug on Cullen's therapy too early. Fear had taken over, and her motherly instinct to protect her son kicked in.

Yet still Cullen returned to her without the EMDR Exposure Therapy.

Or had he? An unsettling thought cloaked her.

"That's funny, Cullen mentioned the name Jakob."

"Yes, he did," Dr. Morris agreed. He swallowed hard.

Margaret spun around with *Jakob* in her hand. "Wasn't that your son's name?"

"Yes. I named it in memory of him."

The thought which cloaked her a second ago tightened its grip and constricted her chest. "Dr. Morris, how does Cullen know your son's name?"

It was the question he was expecting and wasn't sure how to answer. He knew at some point he may have to come clean, but he wasn't expecting to so soon. He exhaled, "Because, Mrs. Hickey, I've introduced Cullen to *Jakob*."

"What do you mean?"

Just then, the phone rang. Relieved, Dr. Morris answered, "Give me one moment." He rushed to answer the phone. "Dr. Morris here. He is? Yes. Okay, I'm on my way." He hung up the phone and addressed Margaret. "It appears that Cullen is calling for me. Care to join me?"

Not satisfied to end her interrogation, she asked, "What did you mean when you said that you've introduced Cullen to *Jakob*?"

"Mrs. Hickey, I promise I will explain everything to you. Let's go see what Cullen wants."

"Doctor."

"I promise–"

"I demand an answer. How does Cullen know your son's name?"

Dr. Morris exhaled sharply. He stared at her for a moment before confessing, "Because I used *Jakob* on Cullen. I've continued the EMDR Exposure Therapy with him."

She shook her head as if his words were a whack against her skull. "You continued against my wishes?" she whispered in exasperation.

"Yes, I did," his voice softened. When Margaret didn't fill the awkward space between them, he decided to.

"Mrs. Hickey, I know you are probably furious with me." Her eyes filled with tears. "I understand. Please, let's go see Cullen. I want you to see something."

Knowing in her mind that she'd questioned her own decision to end the therapy, she nodded her head apprehensively. "Fine. But you are right. I am furious," she bit as a teardrop escaped her eye.

"I understand. Can we see Cullen now? May I have *Jakob*?"

She looked down at *Jakob,* touched the letters once more, and handed the device over.

CHAPTER 16

DR. MORRIS AND MARGARET walked into Cullen's room and were surprised to find Cullen's silhouette staring out of his window, filling its frame. "Cullen, I understand you needed something," Dr. Morris started as he approached him.

Cullen didn't respond. He continued to watch the sky transition from day to night. Rain pattered against the window. He pressed his hand against the cool glass and held it there.

"Cullen? Is there something we can get you?" his mother asked, concerned with his lack of acknowledgment.

Cullen rubbed the condensation between his thumb and two fingers. "You know," he started, "when I was in that other place, I didn't have a window." He drew three stick figures and a square around them on the glass.

"Other place?" Dr. Morris inquired.

Without turning, he responded, "Yes, the other place. It wasn't much bigger than this room. No windows. No doors. Just four walls."

Margaret's eyes shot a sideways glance at Dr. Morris, and her eyebrows furrowed in concern.

Dr. Morris asked, "Cullen, where is this place you are referring to?"

Cullen's hands continued to explore the glass with his fingertips. "My mindroom." He slowly turned around. "And the walls. They were alive," he reveled in wonder.

"Alive?" Margaret asked.

"Yes. Moving and swaying, like black quicksand, but alive. Sometimes I felt it wanted to consume me. Pull me in. Keep me there."

"Keep you there?" Margaret gasped the words out.

"Yes." Cullen turned back to the walls and pressed both hands against them. He caressed them in circular motions. "They watched and reacted to my every move and thought."

"How scary that must have been for you," Dr. Morris empathized.

"Scary?" Cullen questioned, insulted by the minimized term. "More like terrifying."

"I can only imagine," he responded. "Was it like that all the time?"

"Much of the time...until the lights came."

"The lights?" Margaret asked.

"Yes. The therapy."

"Cullen, how did you know the lights were associated with the therapy?" Dr. Morris asked, curiosity dripping from his words.

"While I was inside my mindroom," he said, pointing to his head, "I could hear you and Mom talking about it. Shortly afterwards, the lights started."

"So, you could hear us?" Margaret wondered.

"Yes. It sounded as if you were in another room. I could always hear, but the words were muffled. But when the lights came, the words were clearer. Like coming from inside the room. With the voices came the images. With the images came the memories. With the memories came the fear."

Margaret drew a breath in sharply.

Dr. Morris held onto *Jakob* as if it were alive.

Cullen moved to the corner of the room and placed his hands on both walls. "Then a strange thing happened. The more I experienced the fear, the less frightened I became. The walls became less intimidating, and the colors changed to the colors of a butterfly. Vibrant. Beautiful. And the others, too. I drew strength from their words."

"Others? The ones you mentioned before?" Dr. Morris asked.

Margaret glared at the device in Dr. Morris' hands.

"Was one of them named Jakob?" Dr. Morris asked.

"No, not Jakob. Jakob was different. The others were...people. A boy and a girl. Teenagers. Zeke and Val. Their faces are still blurry, but they helped me face my fears."

"Fascinating," Dr. Morris whispered to himself. Then, to Cullen, he inquired, "You mentioned Jakob was different. What did you mean by that?"

Cullen's hands froze on the walls before dropping them to his side. He spun around. "Jakob was just a voice. Something present in the room, but not a person."

"A presence?" Margaret asked.

"Yes. I never saw him."

"What else do you remember about Jakob?" Dr. Morris hung on Cullen's response as if the answer would expand beyond the clinical.

Cullen's eyes closed, recalling his time in his mindroom. "Everything seemed to get better when Jakob arrived."

A tear dropped from Dr. Morris' eyes as he held the VR headset tightly to his body as if it was his son.

Margaret stared at Cullen with her mouth agape. She *had* been wrong about the EMDR Exposure Therapy. Emotion swelled into her eyes as she glanced at Dr. Morris. She was angry with him for going behind her back, and she would need to deal with that. But he'd been right the entire time. And for that, she couldn't hold it against him.

Cullen looked at the VR headset in Dr. Morris' grip. "Is that *Jakob*?"

Dr. Morris, realizing how tightly he held it, looked down at it. "Yes, Cullen."

"Can I hold it?"

Dr. Morris looked at Margaret for affirmation. Margaret shook her head slowly.

He handed *Jakob* to Cullen. His large hands caressed the sleek, white surface of the headset and ran his fingers over *Jakob's* name. With both hands, he held the headset so that he was face to face with it. He pressed his head against the white plastic.

"Hello, *Jakob*," he called out without a stutter.

Dr. Morris and Margaret stood silently outside of Cullen's room, each holding captive their own thoughts. Dr. Morris, elated at Cullen's words, waited for Mrs. Hickey to speak. He knew she was upset with him. No, not upset. Furious. His inner thoughts tried to put himself into her shoes, knowing he would be angry if the roles were reversed. But they both walked in similar shoes. Both watched the silent torment of their children as they felt their options run out. For Jakob, they did, and Dr. Morris wanted desperately to make sure Cullen's didn't. He had hoped that

Mrs. Hickey would understand his decision to continue with the EMDR Exposure Therapy. He waited like a child sitting in the principal's office.

Margaret slowly spun around to face Dr. Morris. Her conflicted eyes met with his. One part of her wanted to scream at him, tell him he was forbidden from seeing her son, and report him for some kind of malpractice or breach or whatever. She wasn't less angry at him, but seeing Cullen changed the way she thought about things. It was because of Dr. Morris that Cullen had returned to her. Deep down, she knew if her son were to continue to get better, he would need his help. She exhaled sharply, "Dr. Morris. I'm so incredibly upset with you right now."

"I understand, but–"

Margaret put up a finger to silence him. "No buts, Dr. Morris. Hear me out." He dropped his head like a scolded child. "I'm upset with you. You should have told me you were continuing therapy." Dr. Morris opened his mouth to speak, but she fired him a warning glance. "You should have told me," she whispered harshly. He nodded. "But I have to admit that Cullen came back to me because of you. Because of the therapy." She paused and pointed to the device in his hands. "Because of *Jakob*." A tight-lipped smile crept across her face. The two stared at each other for several moments. "Well, aren't you going to say anything?"

"Oh, I wasn't sure I could speak yet," he laughed nervously. "Mrs. Hickey, I was completely out of line, and I should have made more of an effort to persuade you. It was incredibly unprofessional of me. I wouldn't blame you if you reported me. No level of apology would suffice, but I do sincerely apologize. If you'll have me, I would like to continue Cullen's treatment. I believe we are on the verge of something tremendous. I'm very hopeful–"

"Yes, you can continue, but no more surprises."

"No more surprises," Dr. Morris smiled and patted *Jakob* as if he was bestowing approval upon his own son.

CHAPTER 17

FOR THE NEXT MONTH, Cullen received more therapy. *Jakob* presented Cullen with more images, and with the images came more memories. As each one manifested itself, Cullen found a new confidence building. Fear no longer crippled him. The anxiety would always be there, but Cullen learned how to face it. New phrases. *Show them your strength. Don't believe their lies. Your wounds are temporary. You are loved.* He recited the words and experienced the memories. Along with the EMDR Exposure Therapy delivered through *Jakob*, Cullen also received daily sessions with Dr. Morris.

"Cullen. I think your time here at St. Mary's is ending," Dr. Morris announced.

He looked up from his seat on the couch and wondered, "Do you think I'm ready?"

"You can't stay here forever," Dr. Morris mused. "It's time to get out into the real world. Use the tools you've gained. You're better."

Cullen took inventory of his emotions. "But what about my therapy?" he asked, stuttering slightly.

"You and I will continue to meet once a week or so for the next couple of months."

"And what about *Jakob*?" Cullen questioned.

"Well, I'm glad you asked. Your mother and I have been talking about how we can continue not only our face-to-face therapy but continue EMDR Exposure Therapy as well." He reached for a case on the side of the couch and brought it to his lap, unsnapping the locks. He stared with pride at its contents. Then, he spun the case around to show Cullen.

Cullen's eyes widened. "Is that for me?" Dr. Morris nodded. "But you won't have it anymore."

Dr. Morris chuckled, "Don't worry about that, Cullen. I'm already working on a new one. This one is special for you. You've made a unique connection with this one. The original *Jakob* is yours."

Like a kid at Christmas, Cullen picked up *Jakob* from the case. "Thank you, Dr. Morris."

"If there was ever a kid in the world that deserves this, it's you." He smiled at Cullen. "I've upgraded the programming with some new sayings. Also, the images are enhanced for a better experience."

"Better experience meaning scarier?"

Dr. Morris chuckled, "No, no, no. Let's hope not. The images may seem slightly more realistic and the audio is improved, but that's it. I will continue to upgrade it when needed."

"Ok. Well, I look forward to it. Thank you, Dr. Morris." Cullen took a deep breath as he rubbed his hand along the sleek design.

Chapter 18

CULLEN CAME HOME FROM the St. Mary's Psychiatric Hospital on a cloudy, chilly December morning. With Christmas days away and winter break providing two weeks off from school, Dr. Morris thought it a wonderful opportunity to transition Cullen out of St. Mary's and back home. To help with the change, Cullen had spent the last three weekends at home and returned to the hospital during the weekdays. When Cullen was home on weekends, he would practice activating *Jakob* and continuing with the EMDR Exposure Therapy.

He and his mother would venture out into town. As part of his recovery, they parked outside the middle school where he received much of his bullying. One Sunday afternoon, Cullen mustered enough nerve to stroll outside the campus. As he walked around the closed school, he repeated the affirmations he learned, reminding himself of his worth. Doing this each weekend helped with the anxiety that simmered under the surface.

Once he became acclimated, they drove by his new high school. In his mind, Cullen constructed scenarios he could be involved in and rehearsed strategies on how he would get himself out of them. The optimist in him pictured himself getting involved and making friends.

Initially, Margaret's heart swelled when Dr. Morris suggested it was time for Cullen to return home full time. To finally have her son home was so exciting. She'd essentially lived by herself for the better part of the last six months. Although she was ready for some normalcy, doubt crept its way in and cast a shadow that blocked out any optimism. Doubts that Cullen would be safe. Doubts that she would have the tools to help him. Doubts that she would be able to control herself if the cycle perpetuated itself again. When she expressed her concerns, Dr. Morris assured her that just because Cullen was being discharged, his therapy wouldn't cease. She found relief in his reassuring words.

Something else happened over the last couple of months. Margaret found herself not only comforted by Dr. Morris' words, but she also found solace in his company. It wasn't something expected, it just happened. Any anger and frustration she had felt about Dr. Morris' omission about continuing the EMDR Exposure Therapy had melted away. She wondered if it was right to have feelings for her son's psychiatrist. Still, she caught herself catching one last look before she left his office and sensed that he struggled to maintain a professional relationship, too. There was no rush to force it. If she had learned one thing in her life, it's that it was better to just let these things develop organically. Besides, Cullen was the priority.

Cullen pressed his head against the cold passenger side window. His eyes followed the passing bare trees as they zipped by.

Left to right. Left to right. It reminded him of being inside his mindroom whenever he used *Jakob*. He scanned for images beyond the trees, but of course, none came into view. One thing about living at St. Mary's is he knew he was safe. Fears were something he faced, but as he gained strategies on how to face the likes of Evan, Claire, and others, he wasn't sure how ready he would be in the real world. Hiding was no longer an option. He would have to take on whatever the world threw at him. That was part of growing up. Besides, he held out the hope that maybe things would be different in high school. He hoped that the few inches he'd grown might deter people from thinking about taking him on. *Keep dreaming, Cullen.* Despite feeling this way, he hoped.

Cullen felt anxious as his mother steered the car into their driveway. He'd been back at the house for the past several weekends, but this felt different. This felt permanent. There would be no unpackaging of thoughts and emotions when he returned to St. Mary's. Although Dr. Morris would continue his therapy, it wouldn't be every day. He became more comfortable using *Jakob*, but the device would serve as a way to face his fears, not necessarily understand them. Still, he again reminded himself, this was real life, and he had to live it.

The cold air bit at Cullen's cheeks when he stepped out of the car. The gray skies dusted the air with flurries. "Looks like we're going to get some snow," his mother noted. It was an obvious observation, but one rooted in making conversation after a contemplative car ride.

Cullen studied the sky and caught a snowflake on his tongue. The act made him smile. "If there's enough snow, maybe we could go sledding."

"That sounds like a plan."

Once inside, Cullen settled into his room. He placed *Jakob's* carrying case on the dresser where two picture frames sat. One with him and his mother at his birthday party a few years back. The other picture was of the last time he'd seen his father. After fifth grade promotion, he'd disappeared out of his life. Cullen didn't respect his father, but like most things in his life, he hoped for a relationship one day.

Pushing those thoughts aside, he snapped open the case and carefully pulled Jakob out. Sitting on his bed, Cullen cradled the VR headset on his lap. A flutter of uncertainty flooded his head, and he gripped Jakob tighter. "Promise me that you'll help me through this?" Cullen asked.

CHAPTER 19

Cullen would need to return to school. There were two choices of high schools in the district, and Margaret and Cullen discussed at length which one to attend. If things were normal, Meadow High School would be where Cullen would go. This is where most of the students from his middle school would end up, including Evan and Claire. So, it was a simple decision to attend Arlington High School. That meant a longer commute in the mornings and afternoons, but Cullen and Margaret thought a fresh start would be best for him. Margaret met with school administration and voiced concerns for her son. Although she wanted to request full supervision, she knew it would be counter-productive to Cullen's reintroduction and therapy.

On his first day, Cullen peered out of the car window. He repeated the phrases he'd heard from *Jakob*.

Margaret interrupted his thoughts, "You know, we could just go get breakfast and then catch a movie."

Cullen gave a side smile. "I can't run forever."

"I know. I know." She looked at her boy and smiled. It felt like it was just last year that she could hold him in her arms. Now, she couldn't even get her arms around him. "I'm glad we got that mop on your head trimmed. Those curls were unruly. And, I must say, you look very handsome. Those girls are going to have a hard time looking away." Physically, Cullen changed during his time at St. Mary's. He'd grown several inches, lost weight, and his face transformed from boyish looks to a teenager with some scruff outlining his chiseled jawline.

"Mom, seriously? You're embarrassing."

"Oh, stop. I'm just saying it to you. No one can hear me."

"I know." Cullen rolled his eyes and shifted his attention to the world outside. Mostly unfamiliar faces walked by the car, laughing and high-fiving friends excited to see each other after winter break. High school was a whole new world. As a freshman, he and all the other newbies knew they would be at the bottom of the barrel. Cullen's advantage? He was always at the bottom. It was safer to stay in the car and avoid it all, but he felt he had to prove to himself that he could handle whatever was thrown at him. The bell announced the sound of the start of the day. Cullen's head whipped towards his mother. A crimson color filled his face.

Recognizing his apprehension, she reassured, "You've got this. You've already been through hell. How much worse can this be?" Cullen gulped. "Look, you are worth it. If there was anyone who deserves to be loved, it's you. Your heart is kind. Your mind is sharp. You've got this. Now, go out there and reintroduce the world to Cullen Hickey."

"That's dorky," Cullen laughed.

"Well, maybe that's what the world needs. A little dorkiness." She crossed her eyes.

"Okay. Here I go."

"Go get 'em."

Cullen chuckled. "Okay. I'm outta here."

"Wait!"

"What? Kiss your momma." She pointed to her right cheek.

Cullen rolled his eyes and leaned down to kiss her. He opened the door. His enormous frame towered over the Nissan Sentra. He took a step forward, looked back at the car, and gave a small wave.

Margaret Hickey watched her boy get out of the car, and her eyes instantly swelled. Fear overwhelmed her. She didn't want him to go. She wanted to keep him safe at home. The idea of homeschooling entered her mind but knew her knowledge of high school English and math was limited. Besides, if she were to continue to be the good mother she knew she was, she was going to have to let her baby leave the nest and pray he would figure things out. He wasn't a baby any longer, so she recognized this was the right move. Still, she worried and would continue to do so for the rest of the day.

Chapter 20

Cullen felt butterflies stir his inside. He muttered some affirmations to himself and took one giant step towards starting over. Everything felt foreign, like stepping into a different world. School was school, but after spending so much time at St. Mary's and home, he wondered if he could learn the ropes. Arlington was much bigger than he expected.

The school was a beehive as students moved about to catch up with friends and rush to class. *The students.* It dawned on him that he hadn't thought about the students yet. A nervous flutter pushed at him. Deep inside, he knew he wouldn't see kids like Evan and Claire. Still, his mind wondered who would be here to take their place. He recited the words from *Jakob* and calmed himself.

As he walked up the concrete steps, he felt the stares penetrating his skin, and he hoped their glances were more rooted more in curiosity than anything else. He jammed his thumbs under the straps of his backpack and adjusted its weight. It was then he realized how much smaller nearly everyone was. He knew that he had grown a little, but to what extent he didn't understand until now.

When he reached the top of the stairs, a familiar voice called him, "Hello, Cullen."

He felt his body stiffen. He looked to his right and found Ms. Saunders looking at him. Awkwardly, he answered, "Umm, hi."

"Don't tell me you don't remember me." She smiled her familiar, pleasant smile.

Cullen shook his head. "No, I mean, of course I remember you." He remembered Ms. Saunders and her kindness from middle school. His stomach fluttered as he recalled during one of his therapy sessions, Dr. Morris informed him of what he'd done to her hand. He stole a glance at it.

"Ms. Saunders?"

"Yes. You remember."

"Why wouldn't I remember? You were like the only person who was nice to me."

"Oh, I didn't mean that. It just feels like last school year was so long ago. I worried you wouldn't remember me." Cullen watched as she flexed her hand, and he wondered if she remembered what he'd done to her. How could she not?

"So, what are you doing here?" he asked flatly. "I mean, you were at middle school last year."

"I took on a new position," she pointed out. "A counseling position opened up here at Arlington, so I jumped at it."

"That's good, right?" Cullen asked.

"Of course. And guess who's on my list?" Her eyes sparkled.

"Me?"

"Yes sir. I get to spend the morning helping you get acclimated. You know, show you around."

Cullen felt conflicted. One part of him was grateful that a trusted face could show him around, but another part of him wondered if he would stick out amongst the other students. He decided it was better to have an ally early on. A thought washed over him: Was Ms. Saunders here because of his mother's intervention? Someone to watch over the kid who was in the crazy house? The thought made him cringe.

"Shall we go for a quick tour of the school? Arlington is so big. I almost thought about using breadcrumbs to find my way back to the office," Ms. Saunders chuckled, looking up at Cullen. She waited for him to smile back before continuing. "Let's go this way. Do you have your schedule? If not, I have one right here." She pulled the blue folder she had tucked under her arm. He noticed the label. *Cullen Hickey* typed clearly on the top of the folder. She waited for Cullen again. He fished the wrinkled piece of paper from his coat pocket. "Ah, there we go." She tucked the folder under her arm again and reached for his schedule.

"May I?"

Cullen handed it over.

"Let's see. So, you have Mr. Heineke for first period for English I. You'll like him. Super nice."

Cullen noticed Ms. Saunders flexing her hand as she extended her arm.

"Let's go this way. What we'll do is take a tour and show you where all your classes are and explain what days you have which classes. It's overwhelming, but you'll get it. You're smart."

As the two walked down the hallway, pockets of students grew quiet. Their attention shifted towards Cullen and Ms. Saunders. Cullen noticed many of them pointing towards him, and he wondered if they knew what he'd been through. Or, perhaps, how his height made him stand out. He recited more affirmations in his mind.

A second bell sounded in the hallways and all the students scrambled to their classrooms. Ms. Saunders paused in the hallway and spoke to the students as they walked by, "Alright ladies and gentlemen. Let's get moving on. I see you, Billy Sparks."

Ms. Saunders smiled at a teen who was messing around in the hallway.

"Right away, Ms. Saunders. I'm going," the boy said, stealing a glance at Cullen.

"Thank you." She directed her attention to Cullen again, noticing his concerned face. "You okay?"

Cullen looked down at her. "Yeah. It's j-just…" he stopped talking as a flutter of nervousness took over him and, with that, his stutter.

"Cullen. They aren't staring at you in a bad way. You're the new kid. I mean, not new-new, but still a fresh face here at Arlington. Sure, you are going to recognize some faces, but most of the kids will be new to you, just like you will be new to them. Besides, I'm not sure if you noticed, but you've grown quite tall." She measured her hand at the top of her head and then brought it up towards Cullen's, only reaching around his chin.

Cullen closed his eyes for a moment and took a deep breath.

"Shall we continue?" Cullen gave a nervous smile. "Okay, then. Let me show you where your first period is." The two walked side by side, deep into the halls of Arlington. "Here we are. Room 116. Mr. Heineke's room. You will report here every morning and stay here for English, which you will have every day."

Ms. Saunders showed Cullen where the rest of his classes were. Admittedly, Cullen felt overwhelmed at how much bigger Arlington was than middle school. He wondered if he'd be able to find his way. He knew he could count on Ms. Saunders to guide him, but he hoped he could find some friends to help. "Finding classrooms is pretty easy. If the classroom starts with the number one, it's on the first floor. If it starts with two, it's on the second floor."

As they approached the office, Ms. Saunders slowed her pace and turned to face Cullen. "So, Cullen. Are you ready to go to class?"

Cullen thought about all he faced inside his mindroom and how much he'd learned from *Jakob*. He was told that he had value. He learned by facing his enemies that he could overcome obstacles. He knew that as much as those memories felt like reality, they weren't...real.

"Ready? It's more like ready or not."

"You've got this. Is it going to be perfect? Absolutely not, but each hiccup is a chance to grow. You're going to do great. You want me to walk you to Mr. Heineke's class?"

"No. I've got it."

"Yes, you do. Now go on and jump in."

Cullen adjusted the backpack on his shoulder and drew in a deep breath. He watched as Ms. Saunders turned and walked down the hallway. Part of him thought he should offer some kind of apology for what he did to her hand. The guilt tore at him. He decided that once he got settled, he would talk with her about that day. Even though he'd been told about what happened, there was still much more he wanted to know.

Chapter 21

Standing outside the classroom, Cullen closed his eyes and pictured himself with *Jakob* on his head. He imagined the light on the walls and pretended to track it with his eyes, listening for the words and searching for the memories. Of course, there was nothing. His mind conjured up the sayings and assured himself that he was going to be okay. Nothing *Jakob* had ever shown him could prepare him for walking cold into a brand-new class with a bunch of kids he didn't know. As he opened his eyes, a reflection from the classroom window caught his eye. A girl stared at him through the reflection. When Cullen spun to see her, she was gone. He couldn't put his finger on it, but something about her was so familiar. Shrugging it off, he knew he had bigger things to think about.

After a deep breath, he mustered the courage to walk in. When he opened the door, the room grew instantly quiet. The social buzz of the classroom instantly changed, and Cullen immediately felt awkward especially as every eye focused on him. His body filled the space of the doorway.

The teacher looked up from his desk, and an easy smile broke across his face. "Good morning. You must be Cullen. Welcome to Arlington. I'm Mr. Heineke." He looked up at the class and noticed his students staring. "You all look like deer in headlights. You know, the look right before they get crunched by a car?" He put his head down and used his hands to mimic pretend antlers on his head. Then, he lifted his head with antlers still in place and stared off into the distance, a surprised expression on his face as he pretended to stare into headlights of an oncoming car. This got a laugh out of the class and helped to ease some of the tension.

"Well, Cullen, I'm not big on assigned seats and stuff like that. You're in high school, so I trust you could find a seat. But, let me warn you. Choose wisely. They're a motley group."

Some students laughed. Others rolled their eyes.

"Seriously," one girl called out. "Thanks for the weird introduction, Mr. Heineke. Way to sell us out." More laughs. "You can sit over here. There's a seat open in our pod."

Pods of desks, set up in groups of four, filled the room. An empty seat rested next to the girl.

"Well, Cullen, there you go. Thank you, Lori," Mr. Heineke chirped.

She gave a bright smile towards Cullen, which made him feel both awkward and delighted. He gathered himself and prayed to God that he wouldn't do anything to embarrass himself. Mission accomplished. He pulled the chair back from the desk. When he sat down, he filled the seat and towered over the desk. Lori introduced herself and then the other students at their pod. "This is Chandler."

"Sup," Chandler bobbed his head. Not disinterested, but not going out of his way, either.

"This beautiful lady is Tasha."

"Hey there. Welcome to Arlington."

Cullen smiled and prayed once again that his grin didn't come across as creepy. If it did, nothing gave any sign.

"Okay, everyone. Put your journal away and let's shift gears just a little. So, now that we're back from Winter Break, it's time to consider the topic for your personal narratives," Mr. Heineke's voice sang, and his students reacted with groans. "Hey. Hey. Hey. Knock it off. Don't make me call your parents and tell them awful things about you." Some kids snickered. "The topic will be *Who I Am*."

"Mr. Heineke. I already know who I am. Why do we need to write an essay about this?"

"Thank you for that, Chandler. Don't look at this as just another assignment that your ogre of a teacher is making you write. This is a great opportunity for you to take an introspective look at your life. We are all humans. We are all children of the Earth. But when was the last time you stopped for a minute, put your phones down, and thought about what makes you the person you are?" He walked by a desk and picked up a student's phone. He looked at it dramatically. Then he brought it over his head. "Guys. We are so busy letting this object tell us what to think and what to like so much that we have forgotten who we really are...inside." Mr. Heineke dramatically dropped his hand to his chest.

Cullen looked around the room. His speech captivated every student. Cullen too. He knew why Ms. Saunders spoke so highly about him.

This assignment made Cullen nervous. He was just figuring himself out and hadn't the foggiest about who he was. He knew the person he was in middle school, but he hoped to be something different in high school.

The rest of the day was better than expected. Lori, Tasha, and even Chandler, spent some time showing him around and introducing him to others. Lori shared Spanish and math with him. Tasha and Chandler were in his history class. For science, all four found themselves together again. For the first time, Cullen felt what it was like to be a normal kid.

CHAPTER 22

Cullen shifted in his chair at Dr. Morris' office. Although he knew that his mother and Dr. Morris had been seeing each other more and more outside of the hospital, Dr. Morris insisted on continuing Cullen's therapy at his office on the other side of town. Something about keeping home and therapy a separate place. He hadn't told Dr. Morris much more than his transition to school being smoother than expected. But this month, he had much more to report. When Dr. Morris walked in, Cullen felt something flutter and couldn't wait to tell him everything.

"Cullen," Dr. Morris bubbled with enthusiasm in his voice. "How are you doing?"

"Dr. Morris, you just saw me the other day. You know, when you picked up my mother for dinner?"

Dr. Morris laughed. "Yes, Cullen. But we haven't chatted about how things are going? For you. At school."

"I know. I'm just giving you a hard time."

"Well, I have noticed that you've been much more confident lately. A little pep in your step. What's happening with you?"

"Things are good. Much better than I expected. The change of scenery has been a good thing."

"Any bullying?"

"No. None. Occasionally, we poke jabs at each other, but nothing that I can't handle or maneuver my way out of."

"Friends?"

"You know I have friends, Dr. Morris," Cullen laughed. "We've talked about them at the house."

"Yes, Cullen. But on the record. How are your friendships?"

"You know how I've spent the last few years. Wishing for friends. I've pictured myself in situations and what it would be like."

"And how did you imagine it?"

"Fun. Exciting. Awkward. But that's what growing up is all about, right?" Dr. Morris shook his head. "But having friends is so much better and far less awkward than I expected. And..." A wide, sheepish smile broke across his face. "I think I have a girlfriend." His eyebrows danced.

"Oh really? Does your mother know?"

"No. I mean, she's not really my girlfriend, but I think we're pretty close to it."

"That's great news. What's her name?"

Cullen closed his eyes and swooned as her name danced from his lips, "Lori. She's everything I imagined in someone who would be a girlfriend. She's smart. Sassy, most of the time. She's, like, so pretty."

"Are you surprised that someone pretty would like you?"

"Yeah, well, look at me."

"I am looking at you. You look like a handsome teenager with something to offer to people."

"I'm not. I'm not attractive and way, way out of shape."

"Cullen. Stop this nonsense. I don't know what you see in the mirror, but you've changed a lot since you first came into St. Mary's."

He put his hand to his belly to feel his weight. "I know I've changed, but it's hard to accept it."

"Cullen, you look pretty fit. I bet your clothes hung off of you like curtains when you got home. Your next phase of therapy needs to be surrounded by improving your self-image." Cullen looked uncomfortable, and Dr. Morris pivoted. "So, having a potential girlfriend sounds very exciting. I'm happy for you."

Cullen shifted upright in his seat. "It is. I get all sorts of butterflies whenever I'm around her."

"Good for you. It's our secret. That's news a boy should break to his mother whenever he's ready." He chuckled. "So, I already know the answer. But with everything going in the right direction, does doubt ever creep in?"

Cullen looked around the room as if he was going to find the answer somewhere hiding in its corners. "Yes, it does. I wonder if it's a dream. Wonder when it's going to fall apart. I keep waiting for something to go wrong."

"Is there any sign that it will?"

Cullen shook his head. "No, but it doesn't stop me from…" His voice trailed off. "It feels like someone who's dieting. The person starts off strong. They lose weight. And for a while, the person does great. But they know, deep down, that if a situation arises where they feel tempted, that's all it would take to crush the diet."

"You seem to have an odd amount of information about this," Dr. Morris chuckled.

"That's kinda how my mother describes it. Don't you say a thing about it. She would kill me. I get some kind of doctor-patient confidentiality, right?"

"You do. So, in this scenario, you are waiting for something to happen. Not necessarily a temptation for you, but for others?"

"Yes."

Dr. Morris took a moment to scribble some notes down before continuing. "Well, let's explore that some more. So, what are you going to do if that happens? Let's say you face it again. My assumption is you haven't seen Evan or Claire at this point."

"No, I haven't seen them at all. Being at a different school has helped." Cullen stood up and walked over to the window. "I don't like to think about that."

"But don't you think you should have some strategy?"

Cullen put his hand to the window and closed his eyes. "Wanna know something strange, Dr. Morris? When I was trying to find my way out of my mindroom, I met myself."

"Care to elaborate?"

"Besides hearing the voices of the two we had talked about, I met myself. Like I came face to face with *me*. Originally, I couldn't tell which one was the real me. But I came to understand they were both me. I know that sounds weird, but in the end, I realized one was the sick me and the other one was the person I was supposed to be. The healthier me helped to guide my path out. The person who entered my mindroom and the person who exited are not the same person. I mean, of course, it's me, but...different. The person who went in was this cowardly...thing. A thing that wouldn't stand up for himself. Didn't understand his value. Couldn't string together words because of his stutter. No one wanted to be around that Cullen. But the Cullen that came out? He's different; a little more confident. He's evolving into a person who knows how to deal with situations. Sure, he's insecure as hell, but recognizes that feeling that way is normal."

"Interesting, Cullen. That's some solid self-awareness."

"When I dragged myself out of there, I felt as if I was crawling over the carcasses of the Cullens that had been. As I pulled myself over their bodies, I absorbed that pain and knew that I had to become someone different." Cullen leaned against the window and let his breath fog up the glass. He drew in a sad face and a smiling face with his finger. "So, when you ask me about having a strategy in case things go bad, I don't like to. I know that as long as I stay the Cullen that came out of my mindroom, I'll be okay because that Cullen is much more confident."

Dr. Morris scribbled more notes. "You said that you know that both Cullen's are you. What happens if the sick Cullen comes back?"

"I'm hoping that it doesn't."

"That's not much of a strategy."

"For now, it'll have to be."

"Okay. So, are you still using *Jakob*?"

Cullen spun around to face Dr. Morris. "Yes. It used to be every day, but in the last few weeks, I've used *Jakob* every couple of days."

"It's probably good to reduce the number of days anyhow. Who knows, Cullen? With your intuition, maybe you have a career waiting for you in psychology."

Cullen smiled and sat down again. He reached into his backpack and pulled out a sketchpad. "I almost forgot to tell you. There's been a recent development. Want to see what I've been doing while I've been using *Jakob*?"

"Of course." He reached across the table and took the sketchpad.

As Dr. Morris leafed through the pictures, Cullen remarked, "This idea came to me around the second week I came home. I always liked to doodle, but I wasn't very good at it. Just sketched anime characters and stuff like that. The images inside *Jakob* are so vivid, I felt compelled to draw them. So, whenever I use *Jakob*, I put this sketchpad on my lap and make sure my sketching pencil is nice and sharp. As the images unfold, I sketch and sketch until the session is over."

"Cullen, how do you sketch these and use *Jakob*? Your eyes are watching whatever is inside in VR goggles."

"My hands just do it, Dr. Morris. When I'm done with the session, it's just there."

"It's just there? You mean, you aren't looking at the sketchpad? Doing this while using *Jakob*?"

"Yes." He saw Dr. Morris' expression change. "Is that bad?"

"No, Cullen. How could this be bad?" he scoffed. "It's extraordinary!" Dr. Morris studied each drawing. One drawing stood out to him. It showed Cullen looking at himself as if he were in a mirror. One Cullen stood taller and leaner than the other. The other Cullen looked much like Cullen when he came into St. Mary's, out of shape and a little shorter. The two mirrored each other with hands on hips. In the shadows, three other images stood as onlookers. One was an athletic teenager with his arms folded, and his skin shaded dark. Another was of a girl dressed in a black leather jacket, her hair shaved up to a part and brushed to the side. A tuft of hair fell across her forehead. Her confident smile revealed a small gap between the top two front teeth. Between the sketches of the boy and girl, the shadow of a smaller figure stood.

"Cullen, I'm assuming these two figures looking in the mirror are images of you, but who are the others?"

Cullen took the book from his hands. "The boy's name is Zeke, and the girl is Val. Those are the two that showed up in the mindroom. The ones that I told you about."

"And the smaller one in the shadows?"

"I don't know who that is, but he's been showing up ever since I started using the new *Jakob*. I know he's there, but he never really emerges from the shadows."

Dr. Morris took off his glasses to clean them.

"May I have a look again?" Cullen passed the sketchpad over. Something drew his eyes to the faceless image. He didn't understand what it was, but there was something.

Pushing the thought back, he added, "Cullen, these drawings are amazing and the fact that you are doing this without even looking at the pad is simply outstanding. Do you mind if I observe you one day?" Cullen shrugged his shoulders. "Thank you. I'd be very interested in seeing your entire process. Besides that, I have to say Cullen–and I think you would agree–things are going well." Cullen shyly smiled. "Keep doing what you're doing. Use *Jakob* at least three days a week. Continue sketching. I bet they help you make sense of what you see. Let's meet again soon."

Just then, Dr. Morris' phone buzzed. He looked at the text message and chuckled, "That's your mother. She wants to know if I'd be able to take you home instead of you taking the bus."

Cullen smirked. He knew this arrangement was going to be strange and take some time getting used to.

As he put his sketchpad into his backpack, Dr. Morris praised, "You know, Cullen. I'm very proud of you."

"Thanks, Dr. Morris."

CHAPTER 23

THE COLD AIR SWIRLED around Lori and Cullen as they walked along Watkins Bridge. The two had been spending lots of time together, and Cullen found himself thinking about her all the time. He hoped the feeling was mutual. As they walked, he snuck a peek at her and, to his delight, their eyes met.

Cullen blushed and looked ahead at Tasha and Chandler, who had been inseparable since middle school. Chandler picked up Tasha from behind and spun her around as she squealed. Things for Chandler seemed to come easy. The star basketball player. In fact, the only freshman on the varsity team. He was also a student body leader for the freshman class. Cullen liked Chandler. He treated Cullen like one of the guys, giving a ribbing from time to time, but nothing malicious.

Tasha was pretty cool too, but sometimes she could be shallow. Cullen cringed when occasionally she would make a petty comment about the way someone dressed or looked. Sometimes her words hit a little close to home. But overall, she was nice and accepted him.

When Cullen and Lori reached the middle of the bridge, they stopped, leaned against the bridge, and looked down at

Watkins River. The icy, clear water rushed and swirled over the boulders. The frigid spray of the water chilled the air. "You know they named this river after Charlie Watkins?" Lori said, without looking away from the rushing water.

"Yeah, I know that. I'm a *local*," Cullen laughed. Referring to yourself as a "local" was the joking way the townspeople referred to themselves whenever tourists would come looking for things to do and see.

"Do you know the story about him?"

"Other than his family settling this town? I know that he and his family started the mill back in the mid-1800s and put the town on the map by discovering gold."

"Geez, you *are* a nerd," Lori laughed, touching Cullen's arm and letting it stay there.

Cullen was thankful it was cold because his cheeks were already red. "Like I said, I'm a local."

"Legend has it that Charlie Watkins' wife and child were gravely sick with some kind of disease. I don't know what it was." Cullen knew it was enteritis but didn't dare answer. "Anyway, mother and baby die. Charlie is so distraught that he goes crazy. He insists his wife is still alive. And if she's alive, then the baby must be too. He'd come out to this very spot right here because he swore he could hear his wife calling to him. He spent hours searching the shoreline because he believed she was there, calling out to her and often muttering to himself. One day, while he's drinking at a local bar, he tells some buddies that he's planning on joining his wife. That it was the only way they could be together."

Cullen wondered, "How could he do that?"

"Well, his buddies wondered the same thing. He stumbles out of the bar that night and walks over to this very spot. Climbs up right here on this ledge. A crew of friends follow him. His buddies call out to him and try to talk him down. But he's not coming down. He confesses his love for his wife and baby and jumps headfirst into the icy water below."

"No way. Did he survive?"

"Nope. They found his body two miles downriver. Some say that's the real reason they named this bridge. They named it after him. Watkins Bridge. This spot is called Lover's Leap. Legend says if you listen carefully, you can hear Charlie, his late wife, and their baby crying." They both listened.

Without warning, Chandler crept up behind them and screamed, causing Cullen and Lori to jump and end up in each other's arms. "You are such a jerk! You scared me to death!" Lori yelled and took a swing at Chandler. Cullen laughed. Chandler ran after Tasha, leaving the two there alone again.

"So, why did you tell me this story?" Cullen asked.

"Because sometimes when you like someone, it makes you do crazy things."

"Oh really? Like what?" The two locked eyes. Cullen felt his stomach tighten into a knot.

"Like ask you to the Winter Formal." Lori bit her bottom lip.

Cullen felt every cell in his body jump for joy. He wanted to play it cool but was certain he couldn't pull it off.

"That would be awesome! I-I've," he felt himself stutter and took a deep breath. "I've been wanting to ask you, but to tell you the truth, I didn't know how. I'm not very smooth with this type of stuff."

A smile broke across her face. "That's one of the things I like about you, Cullen. You don't even know how amazing you are." Cullen could feel his heart pounding. "So, is that a yes?"

"Yes! Of course. I'd be honored, as long as I don't have to dance." They both laughed. Lori climbed up on the metal girder, so she was eye level with Cullen and kissed him on the cheek.

"Aww, you guys are so cute." Cullen and Lori spun around to find Tasha with Chandler draped over her shoulders.

"Shut up," Lori shouted at her and giggled.

Cullen floated to the bus stop. Never in his life had he felt this way. He didn't know if this meant he and Lori were boyfriend and girlfriend, but it didn't matter. Only in his wildest dreams did he think he could feel this way, but this was better, way better than he ever imagined it. Butterflies stirred in his belly, and he hoped they would never go away. He was going to Winter Formal with what he thought to be the prettiest and best girl at Arlington.

As the bus approached, a dark thought crept in. He tried to push it out, cast some light on it and scare it away, but he couldn't. It consumed his mind. What if this was another Montana Myers incident? He scanned his bus card and stepped on slowly, contemplatively.

He plopped into his seat as the memory pulled forward. He didn't need *Jakob* to bring this one out. It was one of the more painful memories because that day he felt his hope crushed.

After days of talking with Montana Myers, she had asked, "Cullen. Do you want to hang out with me at Third Street Park after school?"

"Are you s-sure you w-want to?"

"Why would I not?"

"Because you and Cl-Claire are b-best friends and I'm not s-sure if you noticed, but she h-hates me," Cullen stuttered. Saying her name upset his stomach.

"Sure, we're friends, but she doesn't get to say who I like."

"You l-like me?"

"You're so cute. Of course, I like you. That's why I want you to hang out with me. C'mon Cullen, please?" she begged.

"Okay. Wh-What time?"

"After school. Let's say four o'clock. Don't be late. See you there." Montana smiled pleasantly and touched his arm.

The feeling he felt while riding his bicycle to the park that day was the same feeling he felt after talking with Lori on Watkins Bridge. But the day he went to meet Montana took a drastic turn for the worse. As he approached Third Street Park, he didn't see Montana anywhere. He got off his bicycle and checked his phone. Ten minutes early. The pink carnation he brought for her was safe as he leaned his bike against the fence and took a seat on one swing. Something in him stirred, and he wondered why someone who hadn't been nice to him suddenly took an interest. It was true they had been talking more and perhaps Montana had seen Cullen for something different from what Claire and Evan saw. To be given a chance was the only thing Cullen had ever wanted. Yet still, the longer he waited, the more he wondered if this was just another opportunity to humiliate him.

It wasn't long before he got his answer. Montana pulled up on her bicycle. "There you are," she crowed as she walked up to him.

"I-I was w-worried that you weren't going to sh-show up," Cullen responded, looking down at his feet.

"I said that I would be here."

"I know, but p-people are always trying to do things to me." Montana, who a second before, was looking into Cullen's eyes, broke her gaze and looked down at her feet. "Wh-What's the matter?"

"Oh, nothing. Is that for me?" she asked, pointing to the carnation.

"Yes. It's nothing. I'm not always g-good at these th-things, but with you, Montana, I don't f-feel so weird. You, like, treat me nice." He handed over the flower.

Montana's eyes filled with emotion. She stared at the carnation. "Cullen," Montana's voice cracked. "You know what? Let's get out of here. Go for a bike ride."

"Why? We-We just got here." Montana looked over her shoulder and back at Cullen. "Is something wr-wrong?"

"No, Cullen. We just need to get going. Okay?"

"Umm...sure. I guess."

Cullen righted his bicycle and moved to catch up with Montana, who was already at the gated exit to the park. Montana looked back at Cullen and urged, "Come on, slowpoke." When she turned around, she saw Evan, Claire, and a group of six other kids. One of them pulled a wagon behind him.

Montana turned around to look at Cullen with a look of desperation plastered across her face. Cullen, who couldn't see the group yet asked, "I-Is everything okay?"

"No, Cullen. I'm sorry." A tear filled her eye.

It was then Cullen saw the group, and he felt his heart drop. "You set me up? How c-could you? You're j-j-just like them."

"It's not like that."

From behind Montana, Evan's voice called out, "Well, well, well, what do we have here?" He laughed. "I didn't know you were going to be here, Cullen." The group of kids fell over themselves, laughing.

"Oh, Cullen, are you here on a date?" Claire asked in a sing-songy voice. "Did he get you a flower? I thought you liked *me*. I'm totally offended." The laughter continued.

Cullen's body grew hot. Even though he'd been in this situation a dozen times, it never got easier. He wanted to cry. To run. To disappear. He tried to square his shoulders and act like he wasn't afraid. "I'm g-going to go now."

"You th-th-think so?" Evan mocked. "You aren't going anywhere." He pulled the carnation from Montana's grasp and crushed the petals in his hand.

Cullen gasped.

"Look Evan, I just w-want to go home."

"You will. You'll get to run home to mommy when we're done with you."

"Montana. Is there something you want to say?" Claire asked, smiling without breaking her glare at Cullen.

She swallowed hard, switching glances from Cullen to Claire. Cullen noted how uncomfortable Montana looked. He nodded his head slowly at her, insisting she just get it over with already. Her eyes grew even more conflicted.

When Montana didn't respond, Claire buried her hands on her hips. "Did you hear me? Isn't there something you want to say to Cullen?" Montana's eyes widened when Claire mouthed, *Do it!*

Montana took a deep breath and shifted her attention back to Cullen. Her voice started off shaky and then conviction built in, "I can't believe you thought that this was a date. There's no way I would ever hang out with a loser like you."

Everyone laughed and chanted, "Loser! Loser! Loser!"

Cullen became sick. His head dropped. He wished he could just fade away. Just then, something exploded onto his chest. When he looked down, green slime oozed down his shirt. The group of kids, each with a balloon filled with slime in their hands, chucked them at Cullen. He tried to brace himself, but it was of no use. By the time they finished their assault, there wasn't a dry spot on him.

Evan walked up to Cullen and got nose to nose with him. "This is all you'll ever be. A loser. Now get out of here before the next thing that gets thrown at you is my fist."

Cullen wiped the slime from his eyes and picked up his bicycle. As he rode away from the chanting, Evan chucked the last slime filled balloon, and it exploded on the back of Cullen's neck. When Cullen glanced back, all the kids fell over themselves. All except Montana. She looked sad and turned away from Cullen's gaze.

As Cullen willed himself away from the memory, he thought about the dream he had before waking in the hospital. He remembered Montana Myers standing behind a headstone where Claire had told Cullen that a piece of him had died. This was the day Cullen convinced himself that no one would ever like him. He had thought Montana was into him, but after that day, he lost trust in such fantasies. So, it *was* the truth. A little piece of him *did* die that day. Right now, what scared him most was the feeling he had that day was the same feeling he had when Lori asked him to Winter Formal. She wasn't capable of doing such things, right? Not her.

As the bus passed Meadow High School, his stomach turned knowing Evan, Claire, and even Montana were there. He was happy he enrolled at Arlington, away from them, but it was inevitable their paths would cross again. Regardless of how many times he imagined scenarios, fear crept its way inside, even in the best outcomes.

CHAPTER 24

As THE BIG GAME and Winter Formal approached, an energy pulsed through the hallways of Arlington. Student-made banners hung from the walls in the hallways with a variety of sayings. *Go Arlington! Beat Meadow!* and *Cougar Pride!* and *Last Chance to Dance at Winter Formal - Get Your Tickets Today* and *Cast Your Vote for Winter Formal King and Queen.*

The Arlington players portrayed a sense of seriousness about them. Sure, they behaved normally, but if anyone were to mention the game, their game faces took over. It had been five years since Arlington had beaten their crosstown rivals, and this was the only thing on the students' minds, especially the players.

Cullen found himself caught up in the excitement, even though he didn't quite get it. He attended some games and enjoyed the revelry but didn't truly understand it. Sports had always been something for others. Despite his size, he'd never been mistaken for an athlete. His feet deceived him any time he tried. He was too slow. Too clumsy. Whenever he engaged in a game of catch, he could do it, but when it was required of him to run and catch, it was as if he were wearing oven mitts. Still, he donned the blue and gold colors for spirit week and even let

Lori paint blue and gold stripes under his eyes like the eye black baseball or football players wore.

As a tradition, the pep rally riled up the student body before the big game. The marching band and cheerleaders welcomed the students into the gymnasium. The air was thick with excitement. When the lights went dim, a spotlight shone on the locker room door, sending the student body into a frenzy. The microphone clicked on, and the student body president walked to the middle of the gymnasium. He received a nod from the cheerleader captain. "Hey, Arlington High!" The students and teachers cheered. "Tomorrow is a big day! We face that green school across the way. You might know them as Meadow High School." The crowd booed and jeered. "Well, tomorrow we'll erase five years of bad luck. Tomorrow, we will beat Meadow!" The crowd set off into a frenzy again. "Join me in welcoming the team that's going to do it. Your Arlington High Cougars!"

The locker room door flew open and, led by the Cougar's mascot, the basketball team ran between the two lines of cheerleaders. The band led the student body in the school's fight song. With basketballs in hand, the team ran onto the court, split into two lines, and ran through layup drills. The last student, star player and senior, Deshawn Michaels, took the ball and dunked it. The crowd was a shiver of sharks hungry for a win against Meadow.

Cullen stood in the crowd, cheering right along with the others. He cheered loudly as Chandler ran through his drill and made a layup. Chandler looked up to the crowd and pointed to Cullen. He felt a swell of pride overcome his body, and he cheered louder. He looked on the court and caught sight of Lori, who was with the student body officers, smiling at him. He blushed as she waved.

Because the game was against Meadow, Cullen hadn't planned on attending. When asked why, Cullen told Lori that he already had something planned with his mother that he just couldn't miss. He lied. He didn't want to risk running into Evan or Claire or anybody else who'd been his nemesis in middle school. Things at Arlington had been far better than expected. Why risk any opportunity for a setback? Cullen knew that wasn't the correct way to think about it, but his nerves flared whenever it crossed his mind. He couldn't run forever, but he hoped for some more time to solidify his friendships and comfort with Arlington. Even though his heart and mind told him to stay home the night of the big game, his affinity for Lori won out. She'd convinced him it was going to be one of the best events of the entire school year and that he'd kick himself if he missed it.

He wanted to tell her everything. The bullying. The stay at the crazy house. Everything. But he wasn't sure how to approach it.

Students packed the gymnasium the day of the big game. Nearly every student from Arlington was dressed in blue and gold. The student section, called The Blue Wave, housed the crazed Cougar fans. If there was one sport students at Arlington loved more than football, it was basketball. The student section was rowdy. On the opposite side of the court, the fans from Meadow, dressed in green and white, filled the stands. The energy was alive as both student body sections had their own organized cheers. But when the Arlington Cougar players came to the floor to warm up, the cheering was deafening.

Lori looked up at Cullen and shouted, "You see! This is why I didn't want you to miss this."

Cullen smiled and shouted back, "This is amazing!" After the crowd calmed a bit, Cullen asked, "Hey, I'm going to run to the concession stand. Do you want some popcorn and a drink?"

"Sure."

Cullen walked between students and teachers and made his way to the court. When he turned the corner at the end of the bleachers, he bumped into someone. "Oh. I'm sorry," he said. When he realized who he walked into, he felt his large stature diminish. His body stiffened and he felt his color leave him. Claire Matherson!

"Hey, watch it!" Claire, dressed in her Meadow High cheerleading uniform, shouted at him. Cullen's eyes darted back and forth. He panicked and didn't know what to say. "Hello?!" she shouted and threw her hand up. When she looked at Cullen, her eyes narrowed. "Do I know you?"

"I-I don't th-think so," was all Cullen managed, failing to keep his stutter in check. He walked past her and prayed silently that she didn't recognize him. When he looked back, she was still looking at him until another cheerleader interrupted her thoughts.

Cullen charged through the doors separating the gymnasium and the foyer. He found a wall and threw his back up against it. With his hand, he felt his heart pounding. *Just get out of here. Run.* He told himself. *Maybe she won't remember you. You've grown taller, slimmed down, and grown some facial hair. Just leave.*

As he resolved to listen to his inner voice, Lori's voice cut in. "There you are." His thoughts jumbled together, and words failed him. He looked at her with wide, panicked eyes. "Hello? Cullen? What's the matter? You look like you've seen a ghost."

He struggled with what to say. He felt as if anything that came out would be a stuttered, riddled mess. Closing his eyes, he thought about *Jakob*. He wished he could put it on. Listen to the voices. Instead, he thought of the words. *You are worth it. Know your strength*. Taking a deep breath, he said, "Yeah. I'm good. Just didn't eat much today and got a little dizzy. I need to take better care of myself." He forced a fake smile. "Maybe I should just go home."

"Are you crazy?" Inside, he cringed. "It's the biggest game of the season. Heck, besides prom, the biggest weekend of the year. Please stay?" He found himself helpless against her pleading eyes.

"Fine. I need to eat. Maybe I'll feel better if I wolf down a hotdog." She smiled. It's not what he needed, but he couldn't resist her. As she turned to lead him to the concession stand, Cullen gently grabbed her hand.

"Hey. Would you still like me if you found out that things in my past were messed up?"

"What do you mean?"

"You and I know each other, but we don't really know much *about* each other. What if you find out things about my past and are like..." he snapped his fingers and continued, "I'm outta here."

"Cullen," she took his hands, "we all have things we're not proud of. Past and families included. My family is so embarrassing. Trust me. Unless you're some kind of serial killer, I can handle all of it."

Cullen smiled, bent over, and gave her a peck on the lips. She grabbed his hand and led him through the doors, into the gymnasium, and to the concession stand. Cullen's mind still raced. He tried to make himself small, but it was of no use. If someone was looking for him, they were going to find him.

CHAPTER 25

CLAIRE CHEERED WITH THE rest of her squad. She looked across the gymnasium and watched as the person who bumped into her came back in, hand in hand with a girl. She knew she knew him but couldn't put her finger on it. Did she have a crush on him at some point? He was certainly her type. Tall. A hottie. Nope, she remembered all her crushes. Yet, this boy was familiar, and she knew it wasn't something that was positive. Just then, an Arlington student who was in charge of the scoreboard walked by. "Hey. You." He turned quickly and pointed at himself. "Yes, you. Come here. Who's that really tall kid across the way? Over there."

The boy followed Claire's finger in the direction to where she was pointing. "Oh, he's new. He transferred here at the beginning of the semester. Curtis or something."

That wasn't it. She didn't know a Curtis. "So, nothing else? You know nothing else about him?"

"Nope."

"Useless," Claire grumbled. The kid narrowed his eyes and walked away.

She ran the name he said over and over in her mouth. Then, all at once, it hit her.

Not Curtis. Cullen. Cullen Hickey.

Her eyes widened. *So, this is where you ended up. Haven't you changed?* She snickered as she waited for the Meadow's team to come to the court. Not the entire team, just Evan.

The door to the locker room flew open and out they came. Half of the crowd booed while the other half cheered wildly. Evan, last in line, followed the team to the court and ran through their warm-ups. Claire could hardly contain herself. She was bursting inside as she kept in coordination with her cheer squad while keeping a watchful eye on Cullen. *How did he end up here? Wasn't he in some insane asylum somewhere...where he belonged?* she thought.

When the Meadow team finished with warmups, they settled to the benches and Claire saw her chance. She snuck up behind Evan and whispered, "Hey!"

"Hey, yourself." He smiled. "You know Coach is going to lose his mind if he sees you here."

"Whatever. Listen. I'll only be a second. Look across the court. See that big kid over there?" Cullen was participating in some kind of cheer led by the Arlington cheerleaders.

"Yeah, I see him. He's huge. Why isn't he on the court?"

"Because that kid is Cullen Hickey." She stared across the court.

"No way." Evan took a moment to check. "So that's where he ended up."

"That's what *I* said!" Claire laughed. "Anyway, I thought you'd like to know."

"Hey! Claire. You aren't supposed to be chatting it up with my players before a game!"

She smiled sweetly. "Sorry Coach." Then to Evan she snickered, "Gosh, he's so possessive."

Evan stood up, pulled down his warmup sweats, and stared across the court. It didn't look like Cullen, at least not the Cullen he was used to. He squinted his eyes to make sure and that Claire wasn't being her dramatic self again, but it was definitely him.

A shout overtook his thoughts. "Stephens! Stephens!" Evan directed his attention back to Coach. "This is a big game. It's not how you earn time off the bench. Get your head in the game!"

"Yes, Coach! Sorry Coach!"

CHAPTER 26

CULLEN AND LORI WALKED back to the rowdy stands. He tried to put his nerves on the back burner and enjoy the moment. His past was bound to catch up with him. There was no hiding from it. That's the reason he used *Jakob*. Still, he couldn't resist the urge to search the gymnasium for Claire. Once he spotted her, he put his head down and did his best to avoid eye contact. Lori led him back to their seats in the bleachers. He looked up and watched as Claire talked to an Arlington student. She pointed a finger in his direction, and he knew she was asking about him. His stomach sank.

Then he watched the Meadow's basketball team come out of the locker room. His body stiffened when the last player exited and ran through the team's drills. Evan. He wanted to shrink. Disappear. Then, when the team sat down, he watched Claire sneak behind Evan and whisper to him and point. Cullen tried his best to not look their way, but the pull of curiosity was too strong. As she pointed at him, for a moment, Cullen met Evan's eyes as he tracked her pointed finger. This was it. Claire had figured it out, and she was telling Evan. And there was nothing Cullen could do about it.

Something from behind Evan and Claire caught Cullen's eye. Someone who looked very familiar. Although he knew the face, he couldn't recall where he knew him from. He stood with his arms crossed and smiled. Cullen felt a smile creep across his lips and looked down for a second to collect his thoughts. The referee's whistle jolted him, and when he looked back, the kid was gone.

The game held all the energy and aggression of a heavy-weight title fight. Cullen found his attention divided much of the time between the excitement of the court and the draw to know where Evan and Claire were at. For the Cougars, Chandler played much of the game and was every bit as good as any of the upperclassmen. Evan, a good basketball player himself, hadn't seen the court until later in the second half. He'd been riding the bench while the more seasoned players took charge of the team.

When Evan got into the game, he and Chandler gave a quick hug when the action stopped. *They know each other?* Cullen's stomach became unsettled at the thought. When the action started again, Evan received a pass. From the base of the bleachers, he and Cullen locked eyes. Cullen felt his body go warm. Evan curled the corner of his lips. He acted as if he was going to pass the ball to a teammate, but his pass went wide and struck Cullen on the arm, who was returning from the concession stand with bottled water. The crowd hushed for a second and then jeered at Evan.

Upon hearing the whistle signaling the turnover, he glared directly at Cullen. In an instant, Cullen heard the words from *Jakob, Know your strength*. Evan pointed at Cullen with two fingers and then pointed to his own eyes. No doubt it was a gesture telling him that he knew he was there. Cullen didn't flinch like he would have in the past. He stared back, and the crowd noticed. They cheered, "Ohhhhh!" Cullen broke his gaze first and walked back to his place next to Lori. He felt a touch of renewed strength and found himself less fearful. Oh, his heart steadily thumped, but it wasn't the type of fear that set his feet running.

Evan didn't look Cullen's way again the rest of the game after getting an earful from his coach for the turnover. Even Claire didn't bother to look at him. With the score tied in its last seconds, the intensity of the game had taken over the entire gymnasium. Fresh off a timeout, it was Arlington's possession. One of the team's biggest players caught a pass as Chandler worked his way through a screen to the top of the three-point line, clapping his hands. He caught a perfect pass, and he released the shot as the buzzer signaled time had expired. The entire gymnasium was in gasped silence. The ball hit the rim, bounced off the backboard, and dropped through the hoop. Then all at once, the student body of Arlington High School, Cullen included, charged the court. After a five-year drought, the Cougars won on a last-second shot. The players lifted Chandler on their shoulders. Cullen, close by, high-fived his friend and couldn't help but get caught up in the spirit of victory.

After most of the crowd left, Chandler came out to the basketball court to a handful of friends and family. He greeted them one by one. He received a hug from some and high-fives from others. Waiting for him at mid-court was Evan, his gym bag hanging over one shoulder. "There he is. The star of the game," he laughed and smiled at Chandler.

"Ha ha! That thing didn't want to go in." The two embraced in a hug. "How are you? Man, it feels like forever."

"Too long," Evan agreed and chuckled, looking at his feet. "I miss playing on the court with you. Travel ball was so much fun."

"It was. Glorious memories."

"Yeah. You know you can still come on over to Meadow."

"And you can still come over to Arlington," Chandler laughed.

"Over my parents' dead bodies! They bleed green," Evan bent over laughing.

"And mine bleed that blue and gold." The two high-fived once again.

"Yeah, man. We're a long way from travel ball." The two looked around the gymnasium. "So, tell me something," Evan began.

"What's up?"

"Who's that tall kid that you gave a high-five to? He a friend of yours?" Chandler pinched his eyebrows in thinking about who Evan was talking about. "Dude. That really, really tall kid. Probably the tallest kid in the entire gym."

"Oh, he's a new kid. A transfer. Cullen. He's different, but a cool dude."

Evan notched his head back in disbelief. "Cullen?"

"Yeah, you know him?" Chandler looked confused.

"I know him. He went to my middle school."

"Yeah, so? What's he a serial killer or something?" Chandler laughed.

"No, man. He's no serial killer, and he wasn't a cool dude when I knew him, either. The kid's mental. Like he had no friends."

"No friends?"

"None."

"C'mon man. You must got him mixed up with someone else. Sure, he's a little awkward, but he's alright. Nice kid."

"He's got a stutter, right?"

"Nope. See, you got the wrong kid."

"I'm not buying it." Evan shook his head, trying to put pieces together. "We used to pick on him all the time. Innocent fun. He used to freak Claire out. Stalked her and stuff," Evan mentioned and stared off beyond Chandler. He shook his head again. "If it's the same kid, and I'm sure it is, he even crushed a teacher's hand with his own hand over the summer. Broke every bone and ended up in a crazy house."

"Well, he's got the size to do that. But that dude doesn't even realize how big he is. He's really nice. Like, almost too nice."

"I hear there's a video out there from when it happened. I'm gonna shoot it over when I find it."

"Alright, man. It was good seeing you."

"You, too." The boys gave a quick hug and went on their way.

CHAPTER 27

THE AFTERNOON OF THE Winter Formal, Cullen sat on the carpet, legs crossed, in the middle of his bedroom. In his lap, a sketchpad and a pencil waited. He fastened *Jakob* to the top of his head, lowered the VR goggles over his eyes, and pushed a button on top. The pulse of light motioned from left to right. He took a deep breath and allowed his eyes to track it. *Jakob's* voice filled the headphones, "Hello, Cullen. Don't be afraid. I'm here to help you."

Hello, Jakob. It's been a few days. Cullen answered in his thoughts.

"Do your best to breathe. This will not be painful. Please track the light and take deep breaths. Rest assured that you are safe even though some images you will see will be unpleasant and some will not. It is best that you continue to follow the light and breathe deeply. There is nothing else for you to do."

See you on the inside. Cullen tracked the lights until the walls came alive.

The basketball game from the day before came into focus. He walked from his seat in the stands down towards the court and towards the concession stands. "Hey, watch it!" When he looked down and saw Claire there, his heart raced. He looked inside the gymnasium *Jakob* recreated. He stared at Claire's face, his mind racing with the memories of the things she'd done to him. When he looked behind Claire, he found Val staring at him. Cullen looked confused.

"Just ask me the question you want to know," Val smiled.

Cullen pinched his eyes. This was out of the norm. Val never really started conversations. "Were you there yesterday?"

"I was."

"In the gymnasium?"

"Yup," she responded.

"So, you saw her. Claire?" Val nodded. "How is that possible?"

The walls of the gymnasium reverberated like sound waves. Then everyone froze in place. "Cullen, I've been there since you started using *Jakob*. You've come such a long way." Still from her place behind Claire, she walked forward. "This was the moment you've been waiting for. Why didn't you say something?"

"What was I supposed to say? I was completely caught off-guard. Truthfully," Cullen continued, "the way things were going, I was hoping I would avoid her forever." Cullen chuckled uncomfortably.

"After all she's done to you? That's what you have *Jakob* for, so you will never forget."

"That's not the only reason."

"You were to learn tools to deal with these people. But Cullen, what good are the tools if you won't use them?"

"Val. It was the first time seeing her. Don't you think I should get a pass?" he laughed. Just then, the room rotated ninety degrees. Cullen peered under the bleachers to his left. In the darkness, he swore he saw something. He squinted and the outline of a person gleamed momentarily, but found his attention pulled as *Jakob* presented another memory.

Across the court, he watched as Claire talked to Evan while he sat on the bench before the game. Cullen walked across the court between the frozen players and stood in front of them as *Jakob* played the memory.

He watched Claire's mischievous smile stretch across her mouth as she leaned across Evan's shoulder. "Because that kid is Cullen Hickey," she said.

Evan's eyes, squinting, looked through the Cullen that stood in front of him, as if he were trying to read an eye chart. "No way. So, that's where he ended up." Evan's face took on the familiar devious look it did whenever he was about to inflict pain on Cullen. His stomach sank as the look sent chills through him.

"That's what *I* said!" Cullen watched as Claire, too, grinned. "Anyway," her voice echoed, "I thought you'd like to know."

Cullen remembered the memory and looked behind Evan and Claire. There stood the kid from the night before. During the game, Cullen couldn't recall who it was but here inside *Jakob*, the name came to him instantly. It was Zeke. "I saw you yesterday, too."

"Yup. So, how does this make you feel?" He signaled towards Evan and Claire.

"That I saw you? Confusing."

"C'mon, man."

"Oh. This?" Cullen flicked a finger at Claire and Evan. When Zeke didn't react, Cullen continued. "To tell you the truth, it scared me."

"How long have we been doing this? All those things we've been telling you. You've spent months in a hospital."

"I know."

"Despite all the things you heard inside *Jakob*, only one question is really important."

Cullen studied the smug, frozen faces of Evan and Claire. "What's that?"

Zeke folded his arms across his broad chest. "All those affirmations are fine and good, but they're useless if you don't believe them. So, Cullen, do you? Are you buying any of it?"

Cullen ran through the sayings. *Know your strength. Wake your power. You are worth it.* "Of course, I want to believe it. It's hard to know my worth when I've never been regarded as anything of value."

"What's that supposed to mean?"

"This isn't something that I can just get over. Yes, I believe that I'm worth it. But, no, I don't know how to wake my power. I don't know my strength. That is something that I won't know until I'm face to face with it. Right?"

"So, you just hide out until that day, man?"

Cullen laughed, "It's better than looking for it."

"But you can't run from it."

"I'm not running. Like I told Val, it's going to take time."

Then the same shadowy figure that had been lurking under the bleachers caught Cullen's attention. It moved behind Zeke, reached for his hand, and led him out of the gymnasium. Cullen studied Evan and Claire's images. Swirling emotion consumed him like a coming storm. The image inside *Jakob* blurred in the background as Evan's words echoed, "So, that's where he ended up."

The light replaced the images and Cullen breathed deeply. When the session ceased, Cullen pulled *Jakob* off his head and placed it on the floor beside him. He looked down at what he drew on the pad. Cullen's pencil lines sketched the image of Evan and Claire on the sideline of the court. Behind them, Zeke and Val stood. Zeke's hands rested on Evan's shoulders and Val's on Claire's. To the right, the shadowy figure of a child watched on.

A knock at the door broke into Cullen's thoughts. "Come in."

"So, how's it going?" Margaret asked. "Are you ready for your big night?" she sang.

Cullen smiled and shook his head. "It's a dance, mom. That's all. Not a big night."

"Oh, sure it is. After all you've been through? Things are really coming together for you. A girlfriend. Your first high school dance. Hanging out with your friends." A tear came to her eye. "This is all I ever wanted for you, Cullen. Now it seems as if things are happening."

"I know, Mom. I just don't want to get too far ahead of myself. Do you know what I can use right now?"

"What? Anything."

Cullen held the ends of the tie around his neck and begged, "I could really use help with this. I can't figure it out to save my life."

The emotion in her eyes trickled down one cheek. "Here, let me help." As she took the ends of the tie and looped them into the finished product, she confessed, "I used to help your father with his ties. I swear that man was all thumbs with this."

"How come he stopped coming around?"

Margaret shrugged and cocked her head. "Who knows? I'm guessing he's got another life now and isn't interested in the one we have. It's a shame. He would have been useful with some things you've gone through. If he could just see you now. You're a man...well, almost. You are certainly taller than him." She chuckled. "Maybe one day you two can reconnect."

"Forget him, right? If he can't see the treasures in front of him, then good riddance."

"A boy needs his father, Cullen." Silence crept in the conversation while Margaret put the finishing touches on his tie. "There you go."

"We're okay without him. Besides, you've got someone now." Cullen's eyebrows bounced.

"Oh, you stop," Margaret playfully smacked Cullen on his chest. "Dr. Morris and I are just friends." Cullen shot the *you've got to be kidding me* look, which made his mother blush a little. Margaret stuck her nose in the air and replied, "A proper lady doesn't kiss and tell."

"Ewww," Cullen laughed.

"What? You asked for it," Margaret chortled. "So, seriously, how are you feeling about tonight?"

"I'm actually excited." Cullen shifted his weight awkwardly.

"You say you're excited, but your actions tell me something different."

"It's nothing."

"Tell me. It's what I get paid for."

Cullen laughed for a second and then became serious again. "Guess who I saw last night at the basketball game?"

"Who?"

"Last night was the big Arlington-Meadows game. I saw Evan Stephens and Claire Matherson."

Margaret's eyes narrowed and her cheeks grew hot. "And?"

"And nothing. I accidentally bumped into Claire at the concession stand. She didn't know who I was, but she had that look in her eye that she recognized me but couldn't put a name to the face."

"Did she say anything to you?"

"Nothing really, but before the game started, she must have figured it out because I saw her talking with Evan and pointing across the court towards me."

Margaret felt her heartbeat faster. She took a deep breath before responding, "Anything else? I swear if they say or do anything I'll–"

"Mom. It's okay."

She bit her tongue and exhaled. "Do you need to talk to Dr. Morris?"

"Yes. Probably. It's something that will take some time to, you know, work through the feelings. I used *Jakob* and that helped."

"Okay," she gulped, shaking away any ill-feelings. "Oooh-pooh, enough of those people. Are you ready for tonight?"

"Mom, you already asked that. Yes. I'm ready." Margaret reached up and pushed some hair back onto her son's head. "It's going to be a fun night."

"I know. I just want this night to be perfect for you. You ready to go? I need to get you over to Lori's house for pictures."

"Oh, gosh. Don't do anything to embarrass me, okay?"

"Cullen Hickey. You give your mother this one night, will you?" she laughed.

"Okay. You get one night." He crossed his eyes at her.

"Doesn't matter what you do to that face of yours, it will always be so handsome."

Cullen rolled his eyes as his mother left the room. He looked in the full-length mirror at his image. Part of him still held onto the image of that fat, awkward kid who feared everything. But he had to admit to himself: he was embracing the new Cullen. As he straightened his tie, an image in the background startled him. He squinted closer to the mirror and saw the outline of the shadowy boy he'd sketched many times now. When he spun around, it wasn't there. When Cullen looked back at the mirror, only a jacket hanging on a hook was there. Cullen laughed uncomfortably to himself.

CHAPTER 28

"LADIES AND GENTLEMEN, BIG Shot Chandler is in the house!" someone grabbed the microphone and announced as Chandler, Tasha, Lori, and Cullen entered the gymnasium. The crowd roared.

"See, you worried that we'd miss something if we were late," Chandler shouted over the cheering to Tasha.

"Yeah, yeah. Whatever," she sang, letting Chandler soak in the moment. From behind them, Cullen put his hand on Chandler's shoulder and gave it a squeeze. The four of them walked through the throng of students, saying their hellos.

They put their things down on Table 13 as the music kicked in again. Tasha pulled Chandler to the dance floor and gave Lori the *c'mon girl* eyes. Lori extended her index finger. She turned back to Cullen. "You ready to dance?"

"Like, right away? We just got here."

"C'mon. It'll be fun."

"Not the way I dance. I'll probably hurt someone," Cullen chuckled uncomfortably.

Lori looked at the dance floor and met Tasha's eyes. Tasha put her hands up as if to ask, *Are you coming?*

Lori redirected her attention to her date. "Cullen. Look at these kids. Half of them don't know what they're doing except to grind up on someone."

"I definitely don't wanna do that," he teased.

"You don't have to. Just move with the music."

It was hard to say no to Lori's charm and beauty, but Cullen wasn't quite ready. "Why don't you go ahead? I'll work up my nerve and meet you out there in a minute. Okay?"

"Okay," Lori begged, pouting her lip. "By the next song you better be ready!" Extending on her tippy toes, she kissed Cullen on the lips. Then she backed away, keeping her eyes locked on him, and rolled her fingers toward him, enticing him to come to the dance floor.

Cullen smiled at her, shaking his head. He understood little about flirtation, but he imagined that the butterflies she gave him resulted from it. He playfully rolled his eyes and sat back in the white linen covered chair. As he watched the three of them dance together, time on the dance floor slowed down. Cullen closed his eyes and took a deep breath, trying to muster up the courage to head to the dance floor.

Cullen imagined himself inside *Jakob*. He'd done this before and found peace in doing so. Just then a voice whispered into his ear, "Man, if I had a girl like that, I'd keep her close."

Without breaking his gaze on Lori, he asked, "What are you saying?"

"Man, Cullen, she likes you and all you're gonna do is just sit there?"

"Zeke. I don't know how to dance."

"Man, look at these fools. None of them know how to dance. They're all just figuring this out. Like you."

"But what if they laugh at me?"

"Look, you aren't the same ol' Cullen. Say those words that brought you here. You've got this."

"You think so?"

Cullen felt Zeke's hands press down on his shoulders, even though he wasn't physically with him. "I do. You better get out there or that dude is going to move in on your lady."

Cullen watched a kid he hadn't seen before moving closer to Lori. He had that look in his eyes. The kind he'd seen in movies when someone wants someone else. Cullen wondered if he would ever master that look.

"Okay," he stood up. "I'm going in." He turned around, hoping to see Zeke there. Of course, he wasn't. Cullen walked through the crowd, towering over nearly everyone.

When he approached his friends, Lori spun around and squealed with excitement. She jumped into Cullen's arms. When he put her down, he faced the student who was moving in on his girl. The two locked eyes and the kid, realizing who Lori was with, gave Cullen a nod and walked away.

The music pulsed through the gymnasium. Cullen did his best not to step on Lori's feet. She even took his hands and placed them on her waist while she threw her arms around his neck. Their bodies moved with the music. As the beats changed, Cullen loosened up.

Back at the table, Cullen took it all in. His new friends joked and laughed with each other. He had the girl of his dreams on his arm and people that genuinely liked him. This was everything high school was supposed to be.

Then, during a lull of the music, cell phones around the gymnasium sounded off with beeps and dings. Every student reached into purses and back pockets drawn to the sounds and vibrations of social media. As they looked at their screens, a mixture of gasps and laughter crescendoed in like a wave. Some students looked around the gymnasium as other pointed fingers towards Cullen. He felt his face run hot. He recognized the glances sent his way. They were the glances of people who knew things about him that he wasn't aware of. The things that set him apart from others. The things that made him a pariah. Cullen looked from Lori, to Chandler, and to Tasha. Whatever it was they were watching pulled their faces closer to their screens, squinting as if moving closer would help it become clearer. Cullen watched as Chandler's face leaned closer to Tasha. He struggled to read his lips, but somehow, he knew he was talking about him. Lori? As if in slow motion, he glanced to his right to see her. She looked at him, astonishment plastered across her face.

He needed to see whatever it was for himself, but fear paralyzed him. His own phone chimed. Like revealing the culprit of a whodunit, he looked down at the notification. Swiping at the screen, the horror which moments ago trickled into him, now flooded over him and threatened to drown him. He battled to control his breath. On the screen, a video of Cullen at Wilderness Camp played. The video was jumpy and difficult to make out, but Cullen knew what it was. Kids circled a boy, casting insults towards him. Chanting the made-up children's song, "It's raining. It's pouring. Colon's butt is flowing. Slipped on it and bumped his head. Ate it for breakfast in the morning!" He watched in horror as the children reached out, slapped, and pinched him repeatedly. The boy begged for mercy and received none. Then the indignation as they wrapped his body in toilet paper. They shouted, "Every colon needs toilet paper cause he stinks!" and "Cover up that turd!"

Cullen felt the room become cold and quiet. When he lifted his head, he found most of the students staring at him, including Lori, Chandler, and Tasha.

A choking sensation overwhelmed him when he looked back down at the video. His body tipped over and the kids in the video laughed maniacally. The teasing intensified as they kicked dirt onto him. Then, a whistle blew. The video jumped as its videographer scattered from the oncoming counselors. Whoever filmed the video hid behind some bushes and continued to video the event.

The adults who arrived on the scene circled the boy. Cullen recognized Ms. Saunders. Until now, he'd only heard of what had happened. Now he witnessed it firsthand. The audio was scratchy, but whoever pieced together the video added closed captions which allowed the words to be displayed. Ms. Saunders' words spelled out on the screen. "Cullen, sweetie. It's Ms. Saunders. Can you hear me? Are you hurt?" She paused. "You *can* hear me. We're here for you." Then Cullen watched as Ms. Saunders tried to pull her hand away. The words continued, "Cullen, you're hurting me. Please let go." Seconds later, she screamed, "He's crushing my hand!" She screamed. No words on the screen were required, as her terrified cry needed no interpretation.

The person holding the phone comments, "Oh crap. He's killing her."

Ms. Saunders shouted, "Cullen! Let me go! You're hurting me!" Then she turned to the other adults and pleaded, "Help me!" They try to free her. The sound of bones breaking dominated the audio like the crushing of an empty plastic water bottle, drowning out Ms. Saunders' screams. With her free hand, she swung at Cullen while another adult jumped onto Cullen to help.

Bones snapping echoed.

More screams.

As a last gasp effort, Ms. Saunders demanded, "Cullen Hickey! Let go of me!" Finally, she fell backward, holding her hand, crying. "He broke my hand." Cullen laid motionless on the floor as the others focused on Ms. Saunders.

One counselor cringed. "What the hell happened? That kid's a freak!" The words stayed on the screen and pulsed. The video ended and started again on an endless loop.

Cullen didn't need to see it again. He'd lived through it once and now to witness it from a different perspective sent his mind spiraling. Nausea bubbled into his gut. Beads of sweat developed on his forehead. He didn't want to face his friends or, more importantly, his girlfriend. The mask he'd worn over the last few months had been torn off, exposing the past he so desperately tried to hide.

"Cullen?" Lori's voice whispered.

He stiffened.

"Cullen? Are you okay?" she tried again.

After spending moments collecting his thoughts, he lifted his head. His eyes waded in pools as he met hers. He tried to speak, but everything in his mind was a jumbled mess of emotions.

"Talk to me," Lori pleaded.

Snapping out of his daze, he slowly lifted his head and met the ocean of stares from everyone in the gymnasium. Panic slowly draped across his face when he looked at Chandler and Tasha. Their eyes expressed only astonishment, like someone had taken a picture of them mid-surprise. He felt a hand touch his, and he pulled away as if it were being bitten by a spider. He stared down at the hand. It was Lori's. He met her gaze. She tried to hide her surprise with a timid smile.

"Cullen. It's okay. It's me." His eyes flitted around the room. "Look at me." She gently pulled his face to hers. "It's going to be okay."

"B-But you d-d-don't understand. It w-won't be," Cullen's stutter barreled through his speech.

Noticing this, Lori's eyes pleaded with Chandler and Tasha and then focused back on Cullen. "It will be. Just take a deep breath. Do you want to get out of here?"

Cullen felt the moisture of the sweat on his forehead. "I-I j-j-just want to b-b-be alone." His colossal frame stood up and tipped his chair over, causing nervous gasps from those around him. He mustered the courage to look around the room at the eyes casting judgment upon him.

As he walked away, Lori called to him, "Cullen. Wait for me."

He spun around as tears streamed down his cheeks. "N-No. I n–need to be alone." He moved towards the doors. Students and teachers parted the way for him.

Once outside, Cullen ran around the side of the school and threw his back against its brick. Tears streamed from his face. *How? How could this be happening again? What should I do? Who posted that video?* His mind swirled like being lost in a snowstorm and found he couldn't focus on anything in particular. Phrases from *Jakob* played in his mind in distorted vibrations, taunting him. To say them was one thing, but to believe them was another. After months of rehabilitation, preparing for this very moment, he folded. He mustered the strength to look at his phone and watch it again. Tears splashed onto the screen.

A notification popped on the screen. A text from Lori read: **Cullen. Where'd u go?** Cullen put the phone down by his side. Not knowing what to say. It chimed again. **Cullen pls**

He held the phone to his chest before texting, *I can't. I just can't.*

Pls. Let's just talk about it.

I'm sry. Lori, I wish I could. U wouldn't understand.

R u sure? We don't have to talk about it. I just wanna know ur alright.

I...I. Cullen started typing but couldn't finish.

A notification popped across the screen. Cullen clicked on it. The video played again. Cullen glanced at the views. *Fifteen hundred and counting. How could so many people have viewed it already?* He scrolled through the endless comments that showed over the video.

What a freak!

Does this kid go 2 our school?

Arlington got a new badass.

CRUNCH! Damn, that gotta hurt.

I think I got math class wit that kid. Didnt know he was a serial killer.

That's just mean.

You'd think a kid that big could fight back. Instead, he crushes that poor lady's hand. Dang.

Cullen scrolled through all of them. One message buried through the feed looked as if directed at him, as if the person who wrote this knew him personally.

Get off that wall. It's time to awaken your power.

Cullen's bloodshot eyes searched the dark. For what, he wasn't sure. When he peeked around the corner, he saw Lori outside of the school, looking for him. He wanted to run to her, to tell her everything. Concerned she wouldn't understand, he did what had served him well in middle school. He ran as if the predators from the video were chasing him again. At the bus stop, he hugged himself against the cold and the indignity of the video that played in a constant loop in his mind.

He swiped his bus fare card and found his seat next to a window and placed his forehead against it. The night swept by as the light of the streetlights rushed by, illuminating pockets of the city. Cullen watched as the people on this cold night seemingly fixed their judgmental eyes on him, as if they too had watched the video.

When the bus driver announced the next stop, a trio of men jumped on. The smell of alcohol and cigarette smoke filled the bus. After they found their seats, two in one seat and the other sat across the aisle, they looked back at Cullen several times, cracking jokes. Cullen wondered if the target he'd worn the last few years was back, or perhaps they'd seen the video, knowing he'd become the latest viral sensation. Cullen met one of the trio's eyes.

"You good bro?"

Cullen sifted through the various responses and decided it was best to not engage, causing the three to murmur angrily.

"Hey. My boy asked if you were good," the man who appeared to be the ringleader asked, a tuft of greasy black hair fell over his face.

Cullen locked eyes with them. "I h-heard. S-S-Sorry. I'm having a b-bad day." Then he looked away.

"That's cool. Bet you get made fun of a lot for that stutter you got," he pointed out as the other two men laughed.

"C'mon, Daryl. Leave the kid alone," the one with the shaved head suggested.

Frustrated that Cullen didn't look up, Daryl snickered, "M-May bb-b-be if w-w-we speak his lllanguage, he'll understand."

A second ago, Cullen had wanted to hide away, but Daryl and his friends struck a nerve. He looked down at his phone, scrolled through the comments on the video, and found the comment again. ***Get off that wall. It's time to awaken your power.*** A fire stoked in his belly.

"C'mon man. Just let it be," the friend laughed.

Daryl shifted in his seat. "Man, he's just a punk. He ain't gonna do nothin' about it."

"He's just a kid. Let's get off and get some beers."

Daryl turned to his friend. "Jack, when did you get so soft?"

"I ain't soft. You know that," Jack scoffed.

"Well, shut up and show me, Jack."

Jack looked at Daryl and his other friend. "Tsk, I ain't gotta prove anything to you."

Daryl laughed. "You're just like this stuttering turd right here. Ain't I right?" he teased Cullen.

Cullen looked down at the video again and watched the comments scroll steadily past. The crunching of Ms. Saunders' bones in her hand echoed in his mind. He imagined watching the scene play out, not on the grainy video in his hand, but in high definition. Cullen squeezed his fists together each time he heard the crunching. It felt so real.

Daryl's voice became muffled as Cullen seemingly ignored him and looked away to the back of the bus. This angered Daryl. "Don't turn your head from me!" he shouted. It surprised Cullen when he looked up, and Daryl was standing over him. A large, cigarette-odored finger wagged in his face and his lips moved, but the sound continued to be muted as if from underwater.

Inside his chest, Cullen felt his heart thump loudly, but controlled—like someone who was sitting under a tree, reading a book instead of someone who was about to get into a fight. By the time Cullen had calmly put his phone into his pocket, Jack and the other guy joined Daryl, flanking him on both sides. Daryl's face had taken on one of rage and anger, as his finger waggled just inches from Cullen's nose. As muted curse words fell from Daryl's lips, a steady rage burned hot inside Cullen. Without warning, Cullen's large hand reached up and seized Daryl's finger with the precision of a cobra. Instantly, he pushed the finger back unnaturally until he felt the snap of bone vibrate through his own hand. Clarity washed over him, and he knew that this is what Ms. Saunders' bones must have felt like. Cullen twisted the wrist and continued to push the finger.

Back.

Back.

Back.

Back until the skin at the base where the finger met the palm ripped open, exposing blood and ligaments and muscle and bone. Daryl screamed, not like a man, but like a small child, and still Cullen didn't let go. Jack and the other guy tried to pull Daryl's hand from his grip.

Jack shouted, "Man, I tried to be nice!" He threw a punch that landed directly on Cullen's cheek. Instead of falling back, Cullen released his grip on Daryl's finger and snatched Jack's collar. In one movement, Cullen lifted him off the ground and dropped him into a seat. When Jack threw a kick at him, Cullen brushed it off like discarding a fly. He loomed over Jack and grabbed him by the ears with both hands. For a moment, he glanced at his reflection in the bus's window. He focused his attention back on Jack. Part of him wanted to smash his head against the glass repeatedly until either the glass shattered, or Jack's head split like a watermelon. His mind held onto reason. Cullen brought Jack's face inches from his own and screamed.

The bus came to a skidding halt, and the bus driver jumped from his seat. "You!" He pointed at Cullen. "Get off this bus!" When Cullen didn't immediately respond, the bus driver took a step towards the back of the bus but froze when he saw the blood pouring from Daryl's injured finger. Cullen still held Jack's head in his hands. The other thug occupied another row of seats. His hands covered his ears. Fear held him captive and held him as if he were a statue.

The horrified bus driver looked up at Cullen and changed his approach. "Hey, kid. Look, I know it wasn't your fault, but I can't have violence on my bus. I gotta call an ambulance to help that fella over there. You gotta get off this bus, or I gotta call the cops."

The bus driver took a step back when Cullen snapped his attention to him. "The cops? You're going to call the cops on me?"

"I don't want to, but I think they're gonna have some questions. Wouldn't you think?" He pointed to Daryl, who was still holding his hand.

"Nah, don't worry about it," Daryl gritted through the pain. "There's no need to call an ambulance or the cops. We're good here, right?" He asked Cullen.

"This wasn't my fault. These guys started with me."

The bus driver answered, "But, son, I'd say you finished it."

Then Cullen peered down at Jack's head as if he had just realized it was in his large hands. He trembled, "I-I don't know wh-what happened." He released Jack's head and stood up.

"You almost tore my damn finger off my hand. That's what happened!" Daryl shouted, trying to save face.

By now, Jack righted himself and directed his attention to Daryl. "Dude, really? You wanna piss this freak off again?"

Cullen's eyes narrowed. "I'm not," he whispered loudly.

"I don't think you're a freak. You were just worked up about that fella there," the bus driver said, pointing to Daryl.

Cullen closed his eyes, took a deep breath, and whispered loudly without a stutter, "I'm not a freak!" He walked towards the front of the bus to leave. The bus driver quickly stepped back and nearly fell into one of the seats. Cullen looked back to the thugs and the bus driver and snarled before leaving.

Cullen barely felt the chilly wind as he walked along the road. The sounds of breaking bones and screams echoed inside his head. Tears traced lines onto his cheeks. The night spiraled in his head. *The video. Has it changed everything? Am I going to return to the old Cullen?* No matter how hard he tried to shake the feeling, he'd been down this road before. Even if he was bigger than most and probably wouldn't endure the physical punishment he had in the past, this was worse. At least after a beating, it ended. Yes, there were the effects afterwards, but this would be different—never ending. Social media didn't take a break. The judgmental stares at school wouldn't end. Would the friends he'd made stay with him? What about Lori?

He'd been called a freak before, but without justification. But now? Now there was a reason, and he knew kids wouldn't let this go. He ran the image of Daryl's finger in his mind and heard the crack of the bone. *Only a freak would do that, right?* He thought about the feeling of holding Jack's head and how insignificant it felt in his large hands.

Only a freak...

As he approached Watkins Bridge, a dark thought stuck like the walls inside his mindroom. He tried to shake it off but couldn't escape it. The more it permeated into his thoughts, the more it made sense. The common denominator had always been him. Remove that and all is well. *Is the world a better place without me?* His mind raced for reasons not to but could only come up with one. His mother. But she was a resilient person and could move on, right? Life would be less complicated with him out of the picture.

Cullen traced his fingers against the cold steel of the bridge. Below, he could hear the rushing water. As he looked over the edge, the cold spray moistened his face. *This is what death must feel like. Cold. Uncaring. Complete.* He thought about the story Lori told him about Charlie Watkins. He jumped from this spot to be with his wife and child, but it was also to escape from the memories of pain. The pain of losing the one person put on the earth to love him. Charlie Watkins jumped from Lover's Leap to escape his broken heart.

Cullen climbed the cold steel and shuffled his feet on the girder. His hand held onto the metal as he looked down. The rushing water called to him. *There's no pain down here.*

"That's wh-what I want," he shouted.

Then you know what you have to do.

"But..."

There are no buts. Free yourself.

A rush of certainty blanketed his mind. He didn't want to leave, but he knew pain stalked him around every turn. Even though *Jakob* presented a chance to change the person he once was, it couldn't erase the power of reality. The only way to get away from these things was to disappear.

He shifted his feet, so the toes of his dress shoes hung over the edge of the metal plank. He nodded his head in permission to take the final plunge and end all of it.

"Hey!" Cullen stiffened and turned his head. Nobody was there. He focused his attention again to ending his life.

Once again, another voice called out from the other side, "So, that's it?"

Cullen spun around and a silhouette stood in the shadows. "What do you want? Who are you?" Cullen called out.

"That's not the question you should be asking. Who are *you*?" The silhouetted figure asked. "That's the only question that matters."

That voice. So familiar. From the other side, a female voice in the shadows called out, "So, after all we've been through, you're just going to end it?"

"What do you mean 'after all we've been through?' There's only me. After what *I've* been through? I'm done dealing with it."

"Now, you're just trying to hurt our feelings," the voice joked.

"Our feelings? Evan? Claire? Is that you? Haven't you done enough? You couldn't just leave it alone and let me have a life. No. I guess it's only fitting that you get a front-row seat to my end." He waited for a response, but only the wind answered. He turned to jump again when finally, an answer arrived.

The male voice called out, "Did you just call me Evan?"

"And me Claire?" the female asked. "If that ain't the worst thing anyone's ever called us. Right, Zeke?"

Out of the shadow, Zeke's athletic frame moved into the yellow light. "I agree, Val. Cullen, we've been through so much and now you think I'm Evan?"

Cullen's head spun. "What the–"

"Unless he's calling *me* Evan," Val laughed, moving to stand next to Zeke, a bubble emerged from her lips.

"Zeke? Val? How can this be?"

"You don't believe it's us?" Val asked, her blue streaked hair fluttered in the breeze.

"Come on down and check it out for yourself," Zeke commented.

Cullen looked at his feet. "No. You guys don't understand. It's all happening again. It's better this way."

Zeke stepped forward. An understanding smile broke across his face. "Cullen, whatcha mean we don't understand? We were in there with you, man. We may be the only ones who *actually* know what you've been through."

"No one ever told you the problem would go away. The problem is that you don't believe in yourself. What worked in the past ain't gonna work."

"It's time to awaken your power and *show* your strength," Val encouraged.

"Don't you mean *know* my strength?"

"No, we mean show your strength. Man, Cullen, look at yourself. You've got some strength up there," Zeke pointed to Cullen's head before continuing, "and there." He pointed to Cullen's chest. "Running ain't gonna work this time. Come on down, and let's talk about it."

"I don't know."

"You might not think your mother needs you, but losing you would crush her," Val pleaded.

"You're what keeps her going. C'mon down from there," Zeke suggested.

Cullen looked down towards the rushing water. "I've come this far, right?" Val and Zeke nodded their heads. Cautiously, Cullen climbed down from the ledge. He stood shoulder to shoulder with them. "I can't believe you guys are here."

"Do you believe it now?" Zeke asked.

Cullen put his hand onto both their shoulders. "I wouldn't believe it if I couldn't touch you."

"Here we are," Val smiled.

"If it weren't for you two, I wouldn't have gotten out of St. Mary's. You both gave me the power to pull through."

"Man, you had that power all along," Zeke affirmed.

Cullen thought back to the incident on the bus and wondered if that was the power Zeke referred to.

"We just helped you direct that power," Val said, patting Cullen on the chest and snapping her gum.

Cullen looked down at his chest and placed his hand on it. "I'm so confused. I just thought—"

"Don't overthink it. The important part is we've got your back." Zeke smiled that confident smile.

"Heck yeah, we do," Val laughed, extending her forefinger and pinky. "Rock and roll."

Zeke and Val put their arms around Cullen and pulled him in for a hug. "It's getting late, Cullen. I'm sure your mother is worried about you. Go ahead and get home," Zeke suggested.

"Will I see you guys again?"

"Cullen, we're here for as long as you need us to be. When the time comes that you don't need us, then we can talk about it. We've got a lot of work to do. Head home," Val reassured.

Chapter 29

As Cullen lumbered down the street, exhausted from the walk and the chill in the air but mostly from events of the evening, he spotted a police car parked in front of his home. He hastened his pace and walked through the front door. Two police officers, Dr. Morris, and his mother waited for him. When she looked up from the table, Cullen noticed her swollen eyes and quickly realized she had been crying.

"Cullen!? Oh my God." She jumped up and sprinted to him, her face enveloped with relief and anger. After a quick, yet strong hug, she barked in exasperation, "Where the hell were you? Do you have any idea what time it is? Dr. Morris has been driving around for hours looking for you! Oh, my goodness, what happened to your face?"

He felt his cheek where Jack had punched him. "It's nothing." Her actions took him by surprise. It was then that it hit him—he hadn't realized what time it was at all. Until a little while ago, time was going to cease to exist. In addition, his phone had died on the walk home. "Mom, I'm s-sorry," was all he could manage in a slight stutter.

"Sorry? It's one in the morning! Where did you go?"

Behind his mother, Dr. Morris rested his hands on Margaret's shoulders. His face didn't express anger, just concern. The two police officers let the conversation play out without interrupting, but their very presence made him anxious. "I didn't know the time," he stammered.

"Did something happen to you?" she asked.

Cullen's eyes flitted around to each person. "It seems like you already know," Cullen mumbled.

"Cullen, what your mother is trying to ask is, are you all right?" Dr. Morris added. "I notice your stutter is back a little."

Cullen looked at the ground. "Can I sit down?"

As he moved to the table, his mother added, "Lori called. She was worried sick about you because you left Winter Formal. Something about a video?"

"Yes. It was just better to leave."

"Was it bad?" Dr. Morris asked.

"Yes."

"Why didn't you just call me to pick you up? Oh my God, you look haggard. What happened to you?" Margaret asked.

"It's nothing."

"It's *not* nothing, Cullen!" Margaret cried out.

He wasn't about to mention that he'd come close to taking a dive off Lover's Leap. "I n-needed to be alone, Mom. I'm s-sorry."

"That doesn't explain where you were," Margaret agonized, fighting back her frustration.

"I took Bus 15 like I've done a bunch of times. I didn't think it was going to be a big deal." Cullen noticed one of the police officers whispering to the other and then walked out of the room.

"Not at one in the morning, Cullen!" his mother reacted.

"To be fair, it wasn't that late when I took the bus."

"Then what happened?" she asked.

"Nothing." He looked up at the remaining police officer, who seemed to have taken more of an interest. "There was a situation."

"Cullen," Dr. Morris asked, "what kind of situation?"

Cullen put his head down. "Ma'am, I think I know what may have happened." One police officer locked eyes with his partner as he came back into the room and nodded his head.

"How would you know?" Margaret asked, throwing her hands up. "Can someone tell me what the hell is going on?"

"Cullen, I'm Officer Mead and this is my partner, Officer Kowalski. You said Bus 15, correct?" Cullen gave a quick nod. "We received a call about a disturbance on that bus route earlier this evening."

"Did something happen to you?" Cullen didn't speak. "Cullen Hickey. Whatever it is, it's obviously affecting you. Does it have to do with the video Lori was talking about?" Margaret asked.

"What happened on the bus had nothing to do with the video, but while I was watching it, these guys on the bus got in my face. I was just minding my business. I tried to ignore them when one of the bigger guys stood over me. He wanted to fight. When I refused, he just got angrier. I...I had to stand up for myself." Cullen stuttered.

"Well, I know you. You didn't want to fight," his mother noted.

"I had to. After I defended myself, the bus driver kicked me off the bus."

Margaret looked at the officers. "He's just a minor. How could they get away with that?"

"Ma'am, with all due respect, he doesn't look like a minor."

"Look at what they did to his face?" Margaret shouted.

"Now, Margaret. Let the officer finish," Dr. Morris tried to diffuse her. She shot him a warning glance.

"Well, allegedly, your boy broke the man's finger," Officer Kowalski revealed.

"Well, he had it coming, didn't he? Picking on a kid," Margaret defended.

Cullen looked down at his hand and flexed it, noticing some scrapes. Blood stained the cuff of his shirt, and he covered it with his jacket and folded his arms across his chest.

"Ma'am," Officer Mead continued, "From what was reported, Cullen quite literally almost severed his finger off his hand."

Margaret peered at her son and then at Dr. Morris. Her eyebrows furrowed in concern. "Well, I'm sure he was just defending himself, right?"

Dr. Morris reached for Margaret's hand as Officer Mead continued, "From my understanding, the bus driver reported this was the case. They haven't talked to this group of people from the bus."

"Thugs. You mean thugs," Margaret spat.

Officer Kowalski pressed his lips together. "We only have the bus driver's testimony. I know there are cameras on the bus, and we are working to secure that footage."

Dr. Morris asked, "What about hospitals? I'm sure if what you say Cullen did is true then that person is going to need to see a doctor."

"Yes, sir. This is a fluid situation." Margaret folded her arms. "Ma'am, I understand this is scary. I assure you we'll investigate it. We're glad that Cullen is home safe, but given the new set of circumstances–"

"Circumstances?"

"Yes. When you called us, you were concerned that Cullen was missing, but based on this new information, we're going to need to ask him some questions. Is this okay to do?"

"Wait. Is Cullen in trouble?"

Officer Kowalski spoke, "No, Ma'am. Since officers were called to the scene, this would be helpful in our investigation."

Margaret looked at Dr. Morris, concern swelling in her eyes. She asked, "Is this something that can wait? I mean, it's late."

"It is late, but it's best to get this information while it's still fresh."

Mrs. Hickey threw her hands up in defeat. "Cullen, are you feeling up to it?"

"S-Sure, if I need to," Cullen answered.

Officer Mead asked, "Thank you, Cullen. We promise to keep it brief. So, how is it you came to be on Bus 15?"

"I was at Winter Formal. Everything was going great. Then this..." Cullen paused, trying to control his stutter and emotions. "This video starts chiming on every phone."

"Video?" the officer asked.

Margaret broke in. "Cullen has had a history of being bullied."

Officer Mead asked, "So, what was on the video?"

Tears filled his eyes. "It was a video of when I was at Wilderness Camp this past J-June. I-I was being chased by a bunch of kids and I, like, passed out."

Dr. Morris added, "If I may, Cullen. With that incident, Cullen didn't merely pass out. He fell into a catatonic state that landed him in the hospital for nearly six months."

"I see. So, this video. Do you still have it on your phone, and may I see it?" Cullen, who had plugged his phone in, handed it over. Both officers watched the video and winced at the sound of Ms. Saunders' bones breaking in her hand.

When finished, Officer Kowalski handed the phone back to Cullen, but Margaret intercepted it. As the video looped, she watched in horror as the children circled her boy. Tears spilled down her cheeks when Cullen collapsed to the ground. And when Cullen crushed Ms. Saunders' hand, she whimpered, "Those bastards."

"So, Cullen, was that you on the ground?" Officer Mead asked. He nodded. "Is this something that's happened before?"

"The bullying?" he stuttered.

"Yes."

"What about the other part?"

"What other part?" Cullen asked.

"The part where you broke that woman's hand."

"What are you asking?" Margaret asked, unbelievingly.

"I didn't mean for it to sound disrespectful. I just want to know if Cullen fought back like that before. Do you always react this way?" Officer Kowalski asked.

"This is ridiculous. How can you ask such things? He didn't even know he did that," Margaret said, exasperated. She looked to Cullen for affirmation.

"If I may, officer. As you can see in the video, this happens after Cullen falls to the ground. At this point, he's awake, but his mind has slipped into an unconscious state. He is completely unaware of what's happening. His mind is in full fight-or-flight mode," Dr. Morris offered.

"So, you say that he did that and completely didn't know it was happening?"

"Like I said before, this incident landed Cullen in the hospital for six months."

"I see. And what hospital?"

"St. Mary's Psychiatric Hospital."

"And if you don't mind me asking who you are and your relationship?"

"I'm Dr. Joshua Morris. Cullen's psychiatrist."

Officer Mead turned to him and asked, "Making house calls now?"

Margaret gasped, but Dr. Morris put his hand on hers and retorted, "Oh, officer. I think you are tinkering into matters that have little or nothing to do with what you're investigating. I think the Hickey family has been more than accommodating, considering this late hour. Wouldn't you agree?"

Officer Kowalski nodded. "Just one or two more questions and we'll be out of your hair." Margaret folded her hands across her chest. "Cullen, the 911 call came into dispatch at 8:05 this evening. So, the incident had to have happened just a little before that. Then you were kicked off the bus."

"What are you asking him?" Margaret shouted out.

"Follow my thinking here, Ma'am. I think it may be a question you have as well." She huffed. "Cullen, it's one o'clock in the morning. Where were you the last five hours?" Officer Mead asked.

Margaret sat upright in her chair as if the question the officer asked was suddenly her own. Cullen absorbed the stares of the two officers, Dr. Morris, and his mother, who all agreed. The question was a logical one, but the problem was that Cullen didn't have an answer. He knew it was late. His mother had told him the time when he first came home, but he failed to make the connection about how late it actually was. The question washed over him. He didn't remember time passing as it did. "I - I," he stammered. "After I g-got off the bus, I walked d-down to Watkins Bridge and then I came home."

"What were you doing at Watkins Bridge?" his mother asked.

"I just went there to clear my head, Mom. There was a lot to process tonight." He wasn't about to admit that he came inches from ending his own life, that all it took was one setback to send him packing. "I ran into a couple of friends, so we chatted."

"For that many hours? It's freezing out there."

"I g-guess I just lost track of time. I d-don't know what else there is to s-say."

Dr. Morris made note of the frequency of Cullen's stuttering lapses and intervened, "Officers. I think you have enough information for tonight. It's obvious he's been through some trauma. Please allow the boy to get some rest. Perhaps a good night's sleep will jog his memory, yes?"

"That's fine. I think we have all we need. Cullen, if you remember something, your mother has my card with my contact information. I'm glad you're home safe. Thank you," Officer Mead said.

Margaret and Dr. Morris escorted the officers to the door. "So, is Cullen going to be in any trouble? For the incident on the bus?" Margaret asked, concerned.

"I don't think so, Ma'am. From the accounts of the bus driver, he was just defending himself. But..." the officer stopped herself.

"But what?" Margaret said in an exasperated whisper.

"We've never heard about a person ripping off the finger of another person. And I can see where this question could be offensive when I ask this, but does Cullen have...aggression issues?"

Officer Mead's question took Margaret aback. "No. Cullen's never, and I mean never, hurt anyone in his entire life. If you knew what that boy has been through..." her voice trailed off.

"Thank you, officers. If we have any other information, we will reach out." Dr. Morris opened the door and escorted the officers through the threshold. "Thank you again."

Margaret gently closed the door and pressed her back against it and exhaled. She gazed into Dr. Morris' eyes and begged, "Please tell me that this isn't starting all over again."

He took her hands into his own and smiled. "You didn't think Cullen was going to go through the rest of his life without an incident, did you?"

"Well, I had kinda hoped so," she said, smiling faintly. "Is it too much for a mother to ask?"

"No, it's not. The reason Cullen's gone through all this therapy is so that it would prepare him to be ready for situations like this."

"But that video. Oh, my goodness, to watch the event that sent him to the hospital just sickens me. And, that poor teacher." Margaret took a deep breath. "Poor thing. Who would post that video?"

"The question isn't who would do such a thing, but why? What purpose would it serve?" Dr. Morris wondered. "Shall we check in with Cullen?"

When they moved into the kitchen, Cullen wasn't there. "Cullen? Where'd you go?" Dr. Morris called out.

"Poor kid is probably exhausted. I'm going to push for a therapy session with him tomorrow to help him sort out some of these emotions?"

They walked down the hallway towards Cullen's room. Margaret lightly knocked on the closed door. When there was no answer, she opened the door a crack, expecting to see Cullen sprawled into his bed. Instead, in the dark room, he was sitting on the floor with his back to the door. His shoulder rose and fell with each deep breath. *Jakob* rested on his head. Dr. Morris smiled. He turned to Margaret and whispered, "I guess he's already started his therapy." He closed the door.

Chapter 30

Cullen watched the images materialize inside *Jakob*. He wasn't sure what *Jakob* had meant to show him, but the weight of the video and the incident on the bus clung to him like a burr. What made it worse was, in a moment of weakness and defeat, he wanted to end his own life. If it hadn't been for Zeke and Val, Cullen would have been dead. Period. Kaput.

Finally on *Jakob's* walls, the scene on the bus appeared. Cullen expected it, but what was unexpected was that Cullen, who usually watched himself in a memory, watched through his own eyes. As he moved his head around, he could observe his surroundings. He peered down at the video that was leaked to everyone. *Leaked*, he chuckled to himself. This wasn't a leak. This was a flood, and Cullen wasn't sure how to brace himself against it. The clarity of the high definition nearly catapulted him back into the situation again. The thugs, he remembered. He forced himself to look up and sure enough; they were there. He watched as an agitated Daryl stood up and stalked over to Cullen. In the bedroom, he felt his heart pulse quickly and reminded himself to slow down his breathing.

He was only acutely aware of what Daryl was saying when he looked at the back of the bus. The shadowy figure of a boy, the same one Cullen had sketched from the gymnasium, watched, and Cullen couldn't remember if he was there before. He called out to him, "Who are you?"

"The question of who I am doesn't matter. Who are you, Cullen?"

"Who am I? I'm scared."

"Why? You are strong. Get off that wall. It's time to awaken your power."

"That was you? I saw that in the comments from the video." The boy pulsed through the shadows. "I've heard these words a thousand times, but now that the moment is here…I'm not sure how to."

The size of the boy didn't change, but the surrounding shadow grew disproportionately around him, threatening to spread throughout the bus. Within the shadow, screams resonated. Not from the boy, but from the shadow itself as if it was alive. Cullen recognized the screams as his own. Years of torment cried out to him.

"You know the power is there. Use it."

"On him?" Cullen asked, pointing to Daryl.

"On all of them." The darkness around the boy swirled.

Cullen looked away from the shadow and calmly put his phone into his pocket, and he focused on Daryl's finger that was inches from his face. Then, as if time slowed down, Cullen reached up and seized his finger. As he bent the finger backwards, he watched Daryl's expression change from angry to surprised, and it finally settled on suffering. The sound of bone snapping felt satisfying as its vibration resonated in his own hand. Time returned to normal as Cullen twisted his wrist and applied more pressure to Daryl's finger. A blanket of helpless fear draped over Daryl's face. As Cullen applied more pressure, he took satisfaction in seeing Daryl's pained grimace. The walls inside *Jakob* vibrated with energy. The shadowy figure smiled his approval. Cullen applied more pressure until he watched the skin open like a zipper. Daryl's scream filled the space.

Behind him, he heard Jack say, "Man, I tried to be nice." Cullen felt the connection of the fist on his cheek. He watched the terror in Jack's eyes as he realized it would take more than a punch in the face to do any good. That's when Cullen watched his own arms lift him up and toss him as if he were throwing a pillow onto a couch. He brushed off the feeble kick and grabbed Jack's head, which felt so insignificant in his large hands. Cullen looked at his reflection in the window and didn't recognize himself. Then *Jakob* replaced Cullen's image with the shadowy boy. The words, *Do it. Wake your power*, echoed inside the bus.

Inside Cullen's mind, chaos ensued. He wanted to finish Jack off, but Jack wasn't the issue here. He wrestled to show mercy. Picking up Jack's head to his own, Cullen screamed, not only at Jack, but at the boy's image before him.

The memory shifted focus to the moment before he left the bus. "I'm not a freak!" he declared. The shadowy boy figure now stood in front of Cullen, who still viewed the world through his own eyes. "You're not done yet, are you? You are not a freak."

As if in a trance, Cullen followed the boy behind some bushes in front of a home where he lay in wait. "There." The figure pointed to a metal trash can lid. Cullen didn't want to pick it up, but his body obeyed. He felt the cold metal in his hands.

From behind the bushes, Cullen watched as Daryl, Jack, and the other guy departed the bus. Daryl wrapped his hand in some kind of cloth. He could hear them. "What the hell was that?"

Jack responded, "I hit him with all I had, and he didn't even flinch. Told you we should have left that kid alone."

"I didn't realize that freak was going to tear my damn finger off. Light me up a cigarette, will you?"

Freak.

"You better get that thing taken care of," Jack pointed out.

"Yeah, my girl's house is just a couple of blocks from here. Gonna have her take me to the hospital."

"Whatcha gonna tell the doctors?" the third guy asked.

"Can't tell him some lunatic nearly tore it off?" Daryl laughed, wincing in pain. "I'll tell them I hurt it while I was building something. Who knows? I'll come up with a story."

Lunatic.

"Want me to walk with you?" Jack asked.

"Nah, it's cool. It's not far from here, brother."

"Alright. We're heading this way," the other guy spoke.

Inside his bedroom, Cullen sketched feverishly on the pad in his lap. During all the time he spent with *Jakob*, he'd experienced many uncomfortable memories that he wished would stop. However, he knew it was necessary to become stronger and to face his fears. But this...this was unusual. This fear he wore differently.

Inside *Jakob*, he watched from his own eyes as Daryl walked away from his friends. With the metal trash can lid tightly gripped in both hands, Cullen followed him. Just a step ahead, the shadowy figure led. "I don't want to do this."

"After what he did to you?" the boy chided in a childish whisper, filling the space inside *Jakob*.

"He got what he deserved."

"Did he? He called you a freak and lunatic even after what you did to him. It doesn't sound like he learned his lesson. Tsk. Tsk."

Daryl turned down an alley, and after a car passed, Cullen crossed the street and followed him.

"This is not what I want to do. I've made my point."

"Don't you want to know your real strength?"

Daryl stopped for a moment to relieve himself against a telephone pole. "Look at him. Eww. He's an animal." As Cullen closed the gap quickly, he could see his breath fog up in the chilled air. He watched as his hands lifted the trash can lid over his head, aimed towards the unsuspecting Daryl.

At the last moment, Cullen turned his head. He ripped *Jakob* off, ending the session. His chest heaved and sweat spilled down his face. When he looked down at the sketch pad, he gasped. The pencil marks revealed a battered Daryl. His right eye closed, and a gash etched just above the eyebrow. His left, fear-stricken eye opened wide. As the figure standing above him appeared to be bringing down the metal trash can lid, Daryl extended his left hand, exposing his severely damaged index finger. Watching in the background, the shadowy boy looked on. He'd sketched the boy in other sessions, but this time, the pencil lines which made up his face more clearly detailed his features. He'd never seen this face before like the way Zeke and Val's faces had come to him.

Terrified, Cullen threw the sketchpad aside as if something were crawling on it. He scoured his mind but didn't remember hunting down Daryl. Couldn't recall the shadowy figure. He wondered if it was a dream. No, it couldn't be. But it couldn't be real either. *How could I not remember this?*

CHAPTER 31

ON MONDAY MORNING, DR. Morris snuck into Cullen's bedroom after he'd left for school. The day before, he'd tried to have a meaningful session with Cullen and came away with a burning feeling he was hiding something. "So, Cullen, how are you feeling about what happened this weekend?"

"About the video?"

"The video. Winter Formal. Whatever comes to mind."

"I'm angry, if I'm being honest. I don't understand why this keeps happening to me," Cullen questioned, his stutter improving from the day before. "What have I done so wrong that life keeps dumping on me?"

"I'm sorry you're feeling this way." Cullen nodded. "I wish I had answers for you, but this will pass. You are strong." Cullen rolled his eyes. "Want to tell me what that was about?"

"That's all I've been hearing inside *Jakob*. Inside my head. But who cares about strength and power when you can't use it?"

"Use it?"

"Those people think nothing of unleashing hell onto me by any means necessary. Perhaps if I stood up to one of them, it would stop. Maybe..." Cullen paused and folded his hands together tightly so that his knuckles turned white. "Maybe if I showed people how strong I could be, then…" his voice trailed off.

"Like what happened on the bus last night?"

"I just reacted. His finger was right in my face. He was going to do something to me if I hadn't done it. They could have hurt me."

"I understand. I'm not here to judge. Is that what you mean about showing your power?"

"Mostly."

"Cullen, don't you think the power and strength comes from here and not there," Dr. Morris illustrated, first pointing to Cullen's head and then to his hands.

"Dr. Morris, what good was that going to do last night? That guy looked at me as a weak, meaningless piece of garbage. Please help me understand what good thinking I'm powerful would have done in that situation. To show the world that I can take a beating? No, I disagree with that. From now on, that guy will think twice before picking on someone weaker. I'd say that I made my point."

Dr. Morris smiled at Cullen's flippant joke about the incident. "How are your sessions with *Jakob*?"

Cullen adjusted uneasily. Dr. Morris noticed as his right foot pushed the sketch pad under his bed, and mentioned, "Fine. They're helpful whenever I'm stressed out."

"Did you use *Jakob* last night?" Dr. Morris knew the answer but wanted to know how truthful Cullen was willing to be.

"I did."

"And?"

"And," Cullen stuttered more frequently, "it was f-fine. I could reflect on what happened, but I don't feel any less fr-frustrated."

"How are the sketches going?"

Cullen looked down towards the floor and back up again. "Some days they're there and others not so much."

"And last night?"

Cullen shook his head slowly. "Nothing," he lied and chuckled uncomfortably. "It was probably because I was so tired. A lot to process, you know."

Dr. Morris nodded as a faint smile crept across his lips. "There sure was. Okay, Cullen. Let me know if there's something you want to talk about. I'm here for you."

"Okay. I will. I'm still working through the emotions. I'm worried about going to school tomorrow."

"Thinking about taking the day off? I'm sure your mother wouldn't disapprove."

Cullen shrugged. "I'm not sure. Part of me never wants to return, but I know in reality, that makes little sense."

"Atta boy," Dr. Morris smiled. "Have you heard from Lori?"

"She texted me a few times. Well, more than just a few times."

"And?"

"And I didn't answer back, other than to tell her I'm fine."

Dr. Morris pursed his lips. "You know, it says something that she's concerned for you. Looks like you've got someone in your court."

"And?" It was Cullen's turn to press.

"And it's good to have someone on your side. Furthermore, you're going to want to keep her there. Answer the girl." With that, he stood up and moved to the door.

"Dr. Morris."

"Yes, Cullen?"

"Have you ever felt like you've done something bad, but weren't sure what to do about it?"

Dr. Morris nodded. "Have you done something bad, Cullen?"

"Hypothetically speaking."

"Hmm. I guess I would have to analyze what the cost would be to myself and those around me. Hypothetically speaking, of course." He noticed the concern in Cullen's eyes. "I will say this, Cullen. You are never wrong to do the right thing." Cullen nodded and Dr. Morris left the room.

Dr. Morris felt guilty about looking in Cullen's room without his permission, but his curiosity loomed greater. Searching under the bed, Dr. Morris retrieved the sketch pad. He leafed through the drawings and noted how each was growing more and more detailed. *What is it you're hiding?* Upon turning the last page, Dr. Morris found what he was looking for. His heart pounded as the detailed picture revealed the violent scene. The man in the drawing, battered and bruised, unnerved him. However, it was the drawing of the boy in the shadows who looked on that caused Dr. Morris to pull the pad closer. His eyes widened. He walked to the window and opened the blinds to get a better look. In disbelief, he dropped the sketch pad and brought his hands up to his mouth. A tear escaped his eye. "How? How could this be?" he whispered out to nothing. He switched the light on the desk on and mustered the strength to look at the drawing again. "There you are," he cried. "My boy. My Jakob."

CHAPTER 32

CULLEN FELT THE STARES. They burned through him like an ant under a magnifying glass. They judged him. Most of all, they haunted him. The students parted for him like a plague as he walked up the stairs, where he found Ms. Saunders waiting for him. He'd known that his mother had emailed her over the weekend, so it wasn't a surprise that she wanted to talk. What surprised him was that she was smiling. "Good morning, Cullen." He pressed his lips tightly. "I heard you and I were stars in a movie together." Cullen closed his eyes in a heavy, unbelieving blink. "Let's go talk about it."

Cullen followed Ms. Saunders through the door. Side-by-side, they walked towards her office. He struggled to not make eye contact with the kids in the hallways, but his eyes pulled in their direction. One kid called out, "Hey, Ms. Saunders. You gonna be okay?"

Another chimed in, "Let me know if you need a hand." Which was followed by sporadic, uncomfortable laughter. Ms. Saunders shot a look in the boys' direction, and they quieted.

They entered the office, and she directed Cullen to a seat and found her way around the other side of her desk.

"So," Ms. Saunders smiled uncomfortably.

Cullen cocked his head. "So."

Ms. Saunders let out a chuckle. "Well, I'm as surprised as I'm sure you were to see that video." Cullen curled up one side of his mouth. "It occurred to me we never talked about what happened at Wilderness Camp."

"Truth be told, I really wasn't in the condition to talk about it."

"True, but we've had these last couple of months to talk it over and we haven't. That's on me. I'm sorry."

He drew in a deep breath and asked, "Does it hurt?"

Ms. Saunders looked at her hand and flexed her fingers. "Truthfully? It's really not that bad. Every once in a while, especially when it's cold, it gets kind of tight. But that's all. I've got full use of it."

"That's a relief. Ms. Saunders–"

"Don't say it. There's no need to."

"I need to. I'm sorry. Of all people, you have always been the nicest to me. I-I didn't know wh-what was happening," Cullen fought back his stutter.

"I understand, Cullen. There's really no reason to explain. It's me who should apologize to you. I didn't know what was happening until one of the kids told us. I wish I'd been there to stop it."

"Where was everyone?"

"I don't recall what the circumstances were, but one kid got hurt and we went to check on her at the infirmary. We were gone for only minutes." She dabbed some tears away with a Kleenex. "I came by several times to see you at St. Mary's."

"My mom told me. I bet I was terrific company." The two shared a chuckle before the veil of awkwardness returned.

"So, about that video. I'm not sure we'll ever know who took it, but do you know who sent it?"

"I had hoped this was all in the past, but it turns out that people are the same wherever I go. I saw Evan and Claire for the first time since last school year at the basketball game on Friday."

"Okay. Did they say anything to you?"

"Actually, nothing," Cullen realized. He'd regained more control over his stutter. "I nearly knocked over Claire near the snack bar."

"I bet that felt good." Cullen cocked his head. "You know, to almost run her over."

He smirked. "It was weird because she acted like she didn't know me."

"I'm not sure if you noticed, but you've changed. A lot."

"So I'm told. She looked at me like she might recognize me, but I got out of there before she could. And then, right before the game, it looked like she figured it out. As Evan was sitting on the bench, she told him I was here. I tried so hard to blend in, but it was too late. My guess is that it was he who posted that video. I'm not sure how, but everything was going great until then. It seemed to have gone viral in minutes."

Ms. Saunders closed her eyes for a moment. "Gosh, Cullen. I hate this, but you're going to get through this. I'm going to be here for you."

Cullen twisted his mouth as if he wasn't really buying it. "You know something, Ms. Saunders? I wonder if it would just be easier if I weren't here."

"Cullen, what are you saying?"

"I'm not talking about that," he lied. "When I was in the hospital, I was aware of everything around me. Like I was there, but not really. While I was inside my mind, I got to face off against my past. No matter how much Evan and Claire and those other idiots tormented me, I realized it wasn't real. To be honest? I started to feel safe there. I know that sounds so weird, but once

I started to gain control of it, it wasn't as bad. It was only my mother's beckoning that pulled me out."

"And now?"

"Now? I'm still not comfortable in my own skin, but I felt like I was getting better. Then, in one fell swoop, it all crashed down onto me. To those kids out there, I'm a freak now. The kid who crushed the teacher's hand. The fat kid that let smaller kids crush his spirit. I thought things were different. I had a dream last night that I found the door that led back to the room in my mind, and I went back in. Back to safety."

"Cullen, you don't know that people feel that way about you."

"Ms. Saunders, you're kind, but you're wrong. Did you see the way they looked at me? There's chum in the water."

"What about Lori?"

"I haven't spoken to her since."

"Why?"

"Because now she knows about me. About my past."

"So, you haven't told her anything?" Cullen shook his head. "Don't let this defeat you. Rise up. You're only assuming the worst here, and I don't blame you, but this can be different."

"I hope so."

"Will you promise to come to me if things get hairy out there?"

"Sure."

"C'mon. Let's get you to class."

"Thanks, Ms. Saunders." She stood up and gave Cullen a hug.

In the hallway, eyes judged him. Fingers pointed. Students snickered. This felt different. In the past, students would say things to Cullen. Hurtful things. Hateful things. But they hurled no insults. Cullen expected people to walk by and throw a shoulder into him. Kids, although staring and whispering, made a wide pass around him. Perhaps the emergence of the video made students react differently. *Fear?* Cullen wondered. That wasn't what he wanted, but at least, he figured he wouldn't endure any of the physical trauma. But he wasn't sure he wanted to be feared, either.

As Cullen closed his locker door, Lori was there. A combination of hurt and anger filled her eyes.

"So, you ghosted me all weekend? After what happened?"

"I-I," Cullen stammered.

Lori punched him in the arm. "Is that all you have to say? I was worried sick about you. The very least you could have done was talk to me."

"I was embarrassed. I didn't know what to do or say or…" Cullen worked to control his stutter. "There were things in my life that are different from the way they are now."

"You mentioned that Cullen, but is this what you meant?" He nodded. "Well, whatever it is, maybe it's different now."

"What if it's not? You don't know what I've been through."

"Well, I'm here. If you just let me in."

"Look, Lori. You are the best thing to happen to me in a very long time. I'm shocked every day that you want to be with me, but I'm afraid. Afraid that you'll find out everything and see me the way other people see me."

"How is that, Cullen? How do others see you?"

He closed his eyes and took a deep breath, thinking about being inside *Jakob*. "Like a nothing," he gritted out in a whisper. "A nobody. A target for people to dump on."

Lori gasped quietly. "Is that how you think I see you?"

"No, but if you ever did, it would crush me." A tear formed in his eye. "Look at everyone. This is how they see me. Take a good look, Lori."

She turned to face the kids chatting by lockers. The students in the hallway. Some teachers, too. Some averted their eyes when she looked at them, while others turned to whisper to their friends. Then she looked at Cullen. "Just because they're staring doesn't mean any of those things. They saw a stupid video and are curious. There will be a few jerks who will say something, but I think they're just waiting to see how you react. High school stuff. Show them that none of this bothers you. You can explain to those who actually care about you, but you don't owe anyone anything. What I'm sure about is that I'm here for you in whatever capacity you need me to be." She reached out her hand. Cullen, surprised by her action, smiled shyly and took her hand into his. Together, they walked down the hallway to English class.

Tasha and Chandler were already seated when they walked in. The class fell into an audible hush at the sight of Cullen. Mr. Heineke noticed the silence that fell over the room and looked up from his desk. Casually, he greeted, "Good morning, Lori. Good morning, Cullen." Then he turned to the rest of the class. "Oh," he joked. "I spent the entire year praying that I could ever get the class this quiet and look, my prayers have been answered." This broke the tension, and Mr. Heineke winked knowingly at Cullen. "We have a few moments before the bell rings. It would be far too much of an imposition for me to expect it to remain this silent. Go forth and be merry."

Cullen and Lori sat in their pod with Chandler and Tasha. The awkwardness was a thick fog. "How's it going, guys?" Lori asked.

"It's going," Tasha remarked. "I'm still recovering from the weekend. You missed so much, girl. Partied too hard. Stayed up too late. And slept too long yesterday."

"It was an interesting one," Chandler noted, looking back and forth between Lori and Cullen.

"You didn't go to the party?" Cullen asked Lori.

"Wasn't in the mood," she confessed, pressing her lips together to say that it was okay.

Chandler looked at Cullen. "You cool?"

He nodded sideways and gave his shoulders a little shrug. "I've had better weekends."

Chandler turned his mouth sideways. "I bet."

The bell rang, and the class started.

CHAPTER 33

MR. REID WAS A teacher on campus that everyone seemed to like. It wasn't because he was a better teacher than most. He was the teacher who many considered the "cool" teacher because instead of mentoring and molding young minds, he tried to fit in and be one of the kids. Say the cool things. Do cool stuff in class while letting kids coast on into the next grade. He'd even given social media a whirl and friended all the kids from his classes. The problem with Mr. Reid was that he was getting on in years, and what worked in his late 20s and 30s wasn't working as well now. Most kids found humor in Mr. Reid but that waned as he entered his mid-40s. Students still liked him, but not as the cool teacher. To some, he took on more of that creepy uncle vibe. When Cullen's video emerged over the weekend, Mr. Reid looked at it as more of an opportunity to gain rank among his students.

Later in the afternoon, Cullen, Lori, Chandler, and Tasha strolled down the hallway. It seemed as if some time with friends helped Cullen. Although things were awkward, the four spent most of the day together. When you hung out with Chandler, most people thought that if it was cool with him, then it was cool with them.

Mr. Reid stood just outside his classroom and greeted his students like he did every day. Most kids reluctantly took part in the handshakes he developed. For some, it was a firm handshake. For others, it was the standard issued high five. Not too strong, but loud enough to let the others know he was still relevant.

As he saw Chandler, he cheered, "There's Mr. Big Shot!" He pretended to shoot a basketball in his direction. Chandler smiled, enjoying the notoriety. "No seriously, that was clutch, my man." He high fived Chandler as he walked into the classroom.

"Thanks, Mr. Reid. I had my teammates to help."

"Spoken like a champ."

As Tasha and Lori walked in, Mr. Reid gushed, "Well, if it isn't Arlington's best dressed ladies!" He put his hands up like he was raising the roof at a wedding.

"You forgot smartest. Best dressed and smartest ladies in the school," Tasha pointed out.

"Oh," he shouted. "Someone brought their A-game today."

As Cullen approached, Mr. Reid's demeanor changed. Still friendly, but different. "Well, someone had an interesting weekend," he announced loudly. Some kids in the hallway snickered. When he saw Cullen's expression change, he joked, "I'm just kidding. Up top." He put his hand up for Cullen and waited. Instead of walking past him, Cullen decided to let it go and put his hand up to accept Mr. Reid's high five. Before their hands clapped together, Mr. Reid pulled his hand down and teased, "Not too hard, alright?!" The few that heard it laughed.

Tasha turned around and sneered, "Not cool, Mr. Reid."

"I'm just kidding. Right, Cullen? You know I'm just kidding." Cullen just walked past him.

"Alright everyone. Last week, we finished the unit on the muscular system. Who can remember Mr. Reid's five cool facts about the muscular system?" He clapped after the words, *"cool facts."* Some hands flew into the air. "Alright, let's see. Timothy."

"Muscles make up like 40 percent of a person's total weight."

"Oh yes! Who's got another?"

"Miranda."

"The butt muscle is the body's largest muscle."

"Boom. Another."

"Yes, Chandler."

"The hardest-working muscle in the body is the heart."

"Speaking of heart. How fast was your heart beating on that last shot? Because mine was thumping away, my man!"

"Nah, Mr. Reid. My heart rate stays nice and even. Cool as a cucumber."

"Oh please," Tasha teased.

"Okay, next one! Go, Amanda Duffy."

"The ear contains the smallest muscles in the body."

"What? Speak up. I can't *ear* you." Mr. Reid laughed at his joke while the class groaned. "Okay, okay. They can't all be winners. Who's got the last one?"

Cullen raised his hand. "Oh, Cullen. Give us what you got, but please be gentle."

Cullen, put off by the joke, felt his heart pound, and he regretted putting his hand up. His stutter creeped into his response. "The j-jaw muscle is the strongest m-muscle by weight because it can ex-exert up to two hundred pounds of force on the teeth."

"Easy for you to say," Mr. Reid attempted to joke about the mouth, but it came out as if he were making fun of Cullen's stutter. A few of the classmates chuckled, but more out of feeling uncomfortable with the attempt. "Tough crowd today. My apologies for how that came out." Cullen glared at him.

"Okay, for today we are going to work on understanding the skeletal system. What good are muscles if they have nothing to hold them up? Who can tell me how many bones there are in the human body?" A few hands went up. Mr. Reid pointed to students who called out their answers. "Some of you are really close. There are two hundred eight bones in the human body. There are five primary functions of the skeletal system. Movement. Support and protection. Production of blood cells. I think that one is the most surprising for people. Attachment of muscles. And, finally, for the storage of minerals. Bones are composed of minerals. They store calcium and phosphorus in bones. So that's why it's important to eat calcium-rich foods like dark green, leafy veggies and milk. If the events of this weekend taught us one thing, it's making sure our bones have enough calcium to keep them strong."

Pockets of students "ohh-ed" as Mr. Reid attempted a burn to sound cool.

He laughed, "Oh, come on. Can't you take a joke? What's next? Are you guys gonna chase me down the hallway?" Some of the class laughed uncomfortably. Mr. Reid relished in the moment.

Chandler didn't laugh. Tasha didn't laugh. Lori didn't laugh. When they looked at Cullen, his hands, white-knuckled, gripped the edges of his desk. His red face didn't show embarrassment. It displayed something else. Inside, his heart raced, heating his blood. Cullen, like a volcano, was on the edge of an explosion. A smile still across Mr. Reid's face, looked at Cullen and noticed the change. "It's okay, Cullen. I was just joking with you. In my experience, I find that if you make light of a stressful situation, it helps to understand it."

Cullen curled the corners of his lips into a snarl and stood up. He tightly gripped the desk in his hands. "Everything is always just a joke with you, isn't it?" he growled without a stutter. "I'm tired of having to see the lighter side of things." He picked up the desk, which sent Mr. Reid cowering in the corner of the room. A couple of students took out their phones to record.

Chandler stood up, too. Not to record, but to talk to Cullen. "Whoa, dude. C'mon man. Put that desk down. How about you and me go for a walk?"

"We all will, Cullen," Lori pleaded.

"It's easy for you," he pointed out to Chandler. "Everyone likes you. No one would dare throw shade at you."

"Look, you're getting worried about a teacher who's still trying to hold on to his glory years, if he ever had any. Don't let him get to you. He's nothing." Mr. Reid, still cowering, nodded his head.

"Cullen, you don't want to do this. Come on. Let's get out of here," Lori begged.

"That's just it. What if I want to? What if this is the only way to get people to stop?"

"Look, we saw what he did. You've got witnesses, right?" Chandler asked the students, looking around. They shook their heads. "Let's go for a walk, alright dude?"

Cullen put the desk down and took a deep breath. "I want to be alone right now." Cullen grabbed his backpack and hurried out of the room.

Once Cullen left, Mr. Reid stood up and nervously confessed, "Whew, that was close. Thanks for having my back, my man."

Chandler shook his head in disgust. "I'm not your man. We ain't friends. You're a grown man. Get a clue."

"We're reporting you to administration," Lori threatened and ran out of the classroom after Cullen.

"You're what we call a real tool, Mr. Reid," Tasha bit, and she and Chandler followed Lori out of the classroom.

In the hallways, Lori called after Cullen, but he kept walking. "Cullen, please wait." He walked through the hallways and out of the front doors of the school. As Ms. Saunders was coming out of her office, Lori called to her, "Ms. Saunders."

"What's the matter?"

"It's Cullen. He just left school." Lori, Chandler, and Tasha reported everything that happened in Mr. Reid's class.

"Oh, my God. Can you call him?" Ms. Saunders asked. Lori tried, but it just went to voicemail. "Okay, relax. We'll figure this out. I'll call his mother and ask her to call me when he gets home. In the meantime, why don't the three of you report to study hall? I'll deal with Mr. Reid."

CHAPTER 34

CULLEN STORMED OUT OF Arlington. His mind raced. Being tormented by kids was one thing, but now adults? He flexed his hands tightly. He felt as if there was no escape. His *fate was* this. This *was* what he was put on this earth for. Something had to change. But how?

As he walked down the sidewalk, Cullen saw Zeke, arms folded, waiting for him behind a tree.

"Where you heading?"

"Away. Somewhere away from here."

"Whoa, whoa. Slow down. What happened?" Zeke asked, trying to catch up with him.

Cullen spun around quickly. "What happened?! He kept pushing me and pushing me. Making fun of that video from Wilderness Camp!"

"Who?" Zeke wondered.

"Mr. Reid. He wouldn't stop, Zeke. He wouldn't let it go."

"Okay, man. Let's talk about it. Take a breath."

A SnapChat notification chimed on Cullen's phone. He swiped his screen, and the video of the incident in Mr. Reid's class played.

"Oh, great!" Cullen lamented. "I knew it was going to be a matter of time before this happened!"

Zeke pulled the phone from Cullen's hand and watched. "Oh man. This sucks." He handed the phone back to Cullen. "So why didn't you throw that desk?"

"You don't think I wanted to?"

"Wanted to do what?" Val came sauntering towards them. Cullen turned and showed her the video. "Well, why didn't you?"

"Because they already call me a freak. I won't give them another reason." Cullen walked down the sidewalk again, away from Arlington. He ignored the chiming of text messages.

Zeke called out, "Yo, Cullen. Wait up." He and Val rushed to his side. "Dude. You ain't gonna like this, but you wanna know what I think?"

"To be honest, I'm not sure I want to."

"Hear him out," Val pleaded.

"Val, what difference is it going to make?"

"Didn't we help you wake up? Aren't we the ones who helped you with the courage to face your fears? We reminded you of the power and strength you have inside. So, yeah, maybe what he's got to say will make a difference."

Cullen spun to look at Val. The blue streaks in her hair had gone wild across her face. He took a deep breath. She was telling the truth. "Okay, what do I need to know?"

Zeke folded his arms across his chest. "Look, man. You running away like this ain't gonna help. You playing the victim ain't cutting it, man."

"I'm not playing the victim. I *am* the victim! There's a difference!" Cullen shouted at Zeke.

"Then what are you doing right now? You're running. *That's* playing the victim."

Cullen's eyes welled with tears. "It's better I'm not around."

Val embraced Cullen's hands into her own. "No, Cullen. That's not true, but what Zeke is saying *is*. No one promised this was going to be easy, but you've got to take your power back. They have all zapped you of it."

"Look at me, though. I'm not like you, Zeke. I don't have muscles, good looks, and confidence like you. And you, Val. You're so edgy and cool. No one would ever think about saying anything bad to you. You'd probably beat them to a pulp." Val didn't argue the point.

"It won't stop until you stand up for yourself," Zeke insisted.

"I don't know how. I'm afraid."

"You ain't gonna know until you try," Val encouraged, cocking an eyebrow.

Cullen's phone chimed again. "It won't stop. Why can't they leave me alone?"

"You're going to want to check those messages." Zeke pointed to the phone.

Cullen looked down and checked. "It's my mother." He scrolled through a few messages. "Hey, guys. I gotta run. Chat later?"

Cullen ran to the bus stop, caught the next bus, and bolted home. Once again, a police car sat in front of the house. *What the heck is going on?* he thought. He opened the door and called out, "Mom? Everything okay?"

Cullen's mother met him at the door. "Yes, Cullen. Everything's fine. I hope."

"What do you mean, you hope?"

Dr. Morris came around the corner and slipped Cullen a note. *Shhh*, it read. Cullen slowly lifted his head and met Dr. Morris' eyes.

"So, Cullen. The officers from the other night are here, and they want to ask you a few more questions. Will that be okay?" Dr. Morris asked.

"Umm, yeah, I guess. Am I in trouble? I already told them everything I know about the other night."

Margaret tightened her lips and looked wide-eyed at him. "They are probably just tying up loose ends is all." She led Cullen past the kitchen and into the living room, where the police officers waited for him.

Both officers stood up. "Hi Cullen, I'm not sure if you remember us from the other night. I'm Officer Mead and this is my partner, Officer Kowalski."

"Sure. I remember."

"That's good, Cullen. We've mentioned nothing to your mother yet. We wanted to wait until you got home. But there's been some recent developments in that bus incident from the other night. Is it okay if we ask you a few more questions?"

Cullen looked at his mother. "Sure."

"Thank you, ma'am." Officer Mead took a folder from under her arm, opened it, and pulled out several images. "Here are some stills we secured from the bus video." Officer Mead pointed to one part of the picture and then to another. "Can you confirm that this is you?" Cullen shook his head. "And these are the three men that were on the bus with you?"

"Yes," he said. His stomach tightened.

Officer Mead placed the photo on the coffee table and directed his attention to the next one. "Can you confirm this is when this man is standing over you?"

"Yes. I think his name was Daryl. That's what this guy kept calling him. This one is Jack."

"What about the third man?"

"He didn't say much, so I don't know his name," Cullen stammered.

"I see." Officer Mead put the photo down next to the first one. "Is this when you engaged Daryl?" The photo showed Cullen with Daryl's hand in his own and appearing to bend the finger back.

Cullen looked up at his mother and Dr. Morris. "Yes. He d-didn't give me much of a ch-chance. He was threatening me."

"We're not here to judge. Can't say I wouldn't have done the same thing," Officer Mead admitted.

"Can I-I see that?" Cullen asked. Officer Mead handed the photo to him. In the grainy photo, Cullen noticed a dark space at the back of the bus. His mind went back to the last time he used *Jakob* and the image of the boy he'd seen. He didn't remember seeing the image when he was actually *on* the bus, but *Jakob* had shown him that the boy was there. Had the image captured him? He didn't dare say anything.

"Is there something else in that image we're missing?" Officer Kowalski asked.

Cullen shook his head. "It's just that night was such a blur. I was...sc-scared."

"I understand." Officer Mead took the photo from Cullen and placed it on the table. "This one here appears that you have a hold of the other man. Jack was his name?" The image showed Cullen standing over Jack, his head in Cullen's hands. "Cullen, can tell me what was happening in this image?"

Cullen peered at his mother and noticed emotion in her eyes.

"As Daryl was standing over me, Jack kept trying to tell him that I was just a kid, and he should leave me alone."

"So, what happened?" Officer Kowalski asked.

Cullen put his hand up to his cheek where Jack struck him. "After I grabbed Daryl's finger, Jack punched me in the face. The next thing I know I was on top of him. He also tried to kick me a few times. But...But I didn't hurt him. I just screamed at him. I never wanted to hurt anyone."

The two officers glanced at each other.

"Is my son in trouble?"

"I'm not sure, ma'am. We're still investigating," Officer Kowalski answered.

After the officer placed the last picture on the table, he showed Cullen the next one. "And this is you leaving the bus, correct?"

"Yes sir," Cullen responded.

"And this picture. Would you confirm this is Daryl, Jack, and the other man getting off the bus as well?" The image showed a camera view from where the bus driver sat.

"Yes."

"Notice the time stamp on this picture and the one where you left the bus? There's about a five-minute difference. Did you see these three men get off the bus?" Officer Mead asked.

Cullen appeared to search his mind. "No sir. I was on my way to W-Watkins Bridge. Wh-Why?"

Officer Mead pulled out the last picture. Cullen jumped from his seat. "Argh!" he shouted

Margaret jumped up as well to get a good look at the photo.

Dr. Morris stammered, "Officer, what is the meaning of this?"

"I'm sorry to cause such a disruption, sir."

"Who is that?!" Margaret asked, disgust mixing into her words.

Officer Mead pressed her lips together before saying, "That would be the man from the bus, Daryl. His girlfriend found him unconscious a few blocks from where you and the others got off the bus."

As Cullen got the courage to look at the picture again, his last session with *Jakob* rushed into his mind. The image showed a badly beaten man. One eye swollen shut. Nose lacerated and twisted sideways. Other cuts and bruises littered his face. Inside *Jakob*, he'd witnessed Daryl's beating and couldn't be sure if he'd actually done it. All signs showed that he had, and this scared him. No, not scared him. The thought of not knowing whether he put someone in this condition horrified him.

"Is-Is he dead?"

"No. We're trying to find out who did this," Officer Kowalski said.

"And you think Cullen did?" Margaret asked weakly.

"There were those hours in which Cullen didn't know where he was. He's got a motive and certainly has the strength. Also, these images place him near the scene. With that said, we can't say for sure if it was him or not," Officer Mead confided.

"Well, it wasn't. He couldn't." Then she turned to Cullen. "Tell him it wasn't you that did this, and we can call it a day." Eyes penetrated into Cullen, awaiting his next words. His stomach hurt, and he felt his body grow cold.

"It wasn't me. I could never do that to someone," Cullen stuttered.

"You did nearly rip his finger off his hand," Officer Kowalski reminded.

"But you can tell from these pictures, they provoked my son. Would you rather come here to show us pictures of Cullen in that state? This man was obviously looking for trouble and maybe he found it," Margaret bit.

"No, ma'am. We wouldn't want that for anyone. We just want to get some answers."

Margaret composed herself with a deep breath before saying, "Officers, Cullen has been the target for bullies the greater part of the last five years. We don't know why. He's a good kid. The only thing he wants is to fit in. Be normal. Despite what he did to those men, he's never shown an ounce of aggression before."

"I understand. Perhaps Cullen has had enough of this. Perhaps he's realized his size and felt as if it's time to do something about it," Officer Mead pointed out.

Cullen listened to her paint a picture of him. *She's not wrong*, he thought. *I have had enough, and I'm stronger than I give myself credit for. If it happens again, I can't promise that I won't do the same thing.* His phone chimed repeatedly in his pocket. No doubt it was about the video from Mr. Reid's class.

"Do you want to check those?" Officer Kowalski asked. "If you need to, it's okay."

"No, it's fine." Cullen placed his hand on his pocket. "Look, I didn't do that to D-Daryl." Cullen didn't feel comfortable stating this with certainty because he couldn't be sure if he hadn't. He needed to buy some time to figure this out. "I got off that bus and just kept walking." His phone chimed again. "I don't know what happened to him."

"Okay," Officer Mead relented. "I'm sure that we can count on you if we have any further questions?"

Cullen nodded.

Margaret looked concernedly at Cullen and then responded to the officers, "I hope you find whoever did this to that man."

"Yes, Officer. And here's my card if you need to get in contact with the family," Dr. Morris offered.

"Thank you. We'll be in touch."

"Hopefully not too soon," Margaret said.

Officer Kowalski smirked, and both officers left.

Margaret pressed the door shut and took a moment to collect her thoughts. When she turned around, she met Cullen's eyes.

"What is going on?"

"Mom. N-Nothing."

"I know the answer, but I need to ask. Did you do that to that man?"

"Oh, Margaret," Dr. Morris begged. "Hasn't the boy been through enough? Of course, he didn't do that. If he says he didn't, then we have to believe him. The man was clearly a thug, who, like you said, was looking for trouble. After the incident on the bus, he probably harassed the wrong person."

"Maybe, but what I can't get my head around is why would someone who suffered that type of injury pick another fight? It sounds like Cullen did a number on that finger."

"You make a good point. Perhaps, in a bit of irony, he ran into some trouble on his way home. That area where Cullen and that crew left the bus isn't the best area."

Margaret agreed, "Maybe. That sounds more likely."

Cullen listened. He wondered aloud, "Dr. Morris, how do you know where we got off the bus?"

"Excuse me?"

"You said that area wasn't the best area. How do you know where we got off?"

"Well," Dr. Morris scratched his head, "knowing that bus route, I know it runs through the west side and that part of the city isn't the best area. So, I figured that was the case. Correct?"

"I guess so," Cullen chewed on Dr. Morris' words.

"Cullen, this doesn't answer the question. Did you do that to that man?" Margaret persisted.

"Margaret, leave the boy—"

"Don't tell me how to parent. I just need to know."

"Mom, I w-would never do anything like that, but the truth is there are hours of that n-night that I can't recall. I didn't even know how late it was when I came home."

"Isn't this concerning, Joshua?"

"Yes, of course, but it's all part of the process. He's still healing." Cullen's phone chimed again, and Dr. Morris noticed his expression change upon hearing it. "What's concerning is how active your phone has been. How do you kids say...*blowing up*? Is that right?"

"Not exactly." Cullen chuckled and retrieved the phone from his pocket. "I didn't want to check my messages while the police were here."

"Why is that?" Margaret asked.

"Because something happened again."

Margaret took a deep breath and threw her hands into the air. "What now?"

"It's easier to just show you, I guess." He handed the phone over to Margaret and Dr. Morris.

"This was today?" Dr. Morris asked.

"Yup. Science class."

"What caused this to happen?"

Cullen shook his head and felt his throat tighten. "Mr. Reid is one of those teachers that most kids like because he tries to be one of them. Personally, I think he's annoying, but I just keep my head down and roll with it. Today, he kept cracking jokes about that video from Wilderness Camp and what I did to Ms. Saunders' hand. It was one joke after another. It just got to the point where I couldn't take it anymore."

"Oh, my God," Margaret spit. Just then, her cell phone rang. She looked down and the caller-ID read *Arlington High School*. "It's the school." She answered, "Hello? Yes, this is she. Oh, hello, Ms. Saunders. Yes, he's here. Right. He's telling us about it now. Is anything going to be done?" She looked at Cullen and Dr. Morris, put a finger up to them and left the room to continue her phone call.

"I'm sorry that happened to you, Cullen. Did you have the same feelings that you did on the bus?" Dr. Morris inquired.

"How do you mean?"

"I mean, what made you stand up to that Daryl fellow? Did you have the same feelings? Like you wanted to hurt your teacher?"

Cullen swallowed hard. "Yes," he choked.

Dr. Morris patted Cullen's shoulder. "It's okay to have those feelings. I certainly understand. I was furious after they took my Jakob from me." He squeezed his hands together. "Furious."

"What did you do about it?" Cullen continued to choke out stuttered whispers.

"I did what you're doing now." Cullen shook his head, confused. "I talked about it. When my Jakob died, I had to rely on others, family, friends, and other psychiatrists."

"I have some friends to talk to about it with."

"Oh, that's good news."

"I have you, too."

"And your mother?"

Cullen peered at the doorway to make sure she wasn't there. "I don't tell her everything."

"Why is that?"

"It's so hard to watch her worry. She's been through so much. I don't want what happens to me to break her down further."

"I understand. At the very least, she should stay in the loop." Cullen pressed his lips and gave a quick nod. "Tell me something. These feelings. Do you feel them all the time?"

"No. Not all the time, but I feel them s-simmering under the surface. Wh-When I feel them, I seem to forget everything that's around me. It's a little scary."

"Explain."

"You gotta promise not to say anything," Cullen pleaded.

"I'd consider this a session."

"The last time I used *Jakob*, I saw what happened to Daryl."

Dr. Morris immediately thought of the sketch he'd found in Cullen's room. "What do you mean, you saw it, Cullen?"

"I saw everything."

"Everything?"

"Everything. I saw the person following him. Then, when Daryl least expected it, I saw the person attack him."

Dr. Morris sat up and asked quickly, "Wait, Cullen. Are you telling me you know who attacked Daryl, and you didn't tell the police?" Cullen nodded. "Why?"

"Because I think it was me," he whispered loudly. His eyes searched the room as if his mother would walk into the room at any second.

"What makes you think that?"

"Because when I was inside *Jakob*, I relived what happened on the bus."

"Like you watched it?"

"No, like I was actively part of it. Through my eyes. First person. I saw everything. My breath in the cold air. Moving through the streets—stalking Daryl. I felt the weight of the garbage pail lid in my hands. The vibration of the thud it made against his face and head. Everything. Then, when I pulled *Jakob* off my head, I saw what I sketched."

Dr. Morris rubbed his hand against his mustache and took off his glasses. After a moment, he returned them to his face. "Cullen, are you sure?"

"I'm sure about what I saw. I'm sure about what I drew. But no, I'm not sure if I actually did it. Aside from what *Jakob* showed me, I have no recollection." Cullen dropped his head. "Are you going to turn me in?"

"No, Cullen. What you are talking about is circumstantial. Until there's proof, there's no reason to alarm anyone. It will be our secret. Can I offer you some advice? Don't mention any of this to your mother. Not yet anyway."

"I wasn't planning on it."

"Good boy."

Margaret came around the corner. "That was Ms. Saunders, as I'm sure you heard. She explained everything to me. Mr. Reid is a real piece of work. She couldn't tell me if there was going to be any disciplinary action against him, but she assured me he would be spoken to. Imagine the nerve. He should have known what happened to you last summer. This is something he should have steered clear of. If he felt threatened by you, I say good. Maybe he'll learn his lesson. Ms. Saunders says that she can transfer you out of that class if you want."

"I don't. My friends are there."

"Well, how about taking a couple of days before returning? I hope they make him apologize. He's lucky he doesn't have to face me right now. I'd share a piece of my mind and perhaps a piece of my fist." Then she muttered, more to herself, "I swear they'll let anyone in the classroom these days."

"Mom, I want to go to science. Running away won't solve anything. Right? That's how I heal."

"I don't know, honey. Sleep on it, all right? And speaking of running away, no more of that. Ms. Saunders was worried sick. You should go see her if another problem comes up. You have an ally in her."

"Okay." Cullen pulled up the video again and read through the comments.

"Don't put yourself through that," Dr. Morris suggested.

"I just need to answer Lori and tell her I'm okay."

"Okay." Dr. Morris watched the last seconds of the video before Cullen swiped up and opened his text messages. "I've got a great idea. How about some ice cream?"

"But we haven't got any," Margaret pointed out. "Besides, I still need to get dinner ready and make it."

"How about I head out to the store, grab some ice cream, and be back in time for dinner. Sound good?"

"Sure."

"I'm always up for ice cream. Pick up some chocolate syrup too," Cullen called, momentarily forgetting what had transpired.

"You got it." He gathered his keys, kissed Margaret on the cheek, and walked out.

Margaret kept her gaze on the door even after Dr. Morris left. "You like him," Cullen teased.

"Excuse me?"

"You heard me," Cullen smiled. "It's okay. I like him too. Not the way you do though," Cullen laughed.

"He's been my rock through all of this. He's so calm in the most stressful situations. It's maddening sometimes. How can someone remain so relaxed when it feels like the world is collapsing?" Cullen bobbed his head in agreement. "So, how are you doing?"

Cullen collected his thoughts before speaking. "I'd be lying if I said I wasn't disappointed. Everything was going so well. I should have guessed it would end up like this."

"Oh honey, don't say that."

"Mom. Really. It's the truth. Some people are just meant to live this life. When people like Mr. Reid do what he did today, it gives permission to others to join in. It's been that way the entire time. I'm just a target."

"Cullen Hickey. Stop that right now. You're meant for so much more."

"In order to achieve that, I fear I'm going to have to..." His voice trailed off.

"Have to what? Tell me," Margaret pleaded.

"Take it back," his voice didn't stutter. It wasn't until this very moment he'd thought the terrifying thought.

"Cullen, what does that mean?"

"I'm not sure, but I can't keep living this way."

Cullen bit at his fingernails as his mother sat down and rested her head in her hands. He wondered if her mind revisited the images from Bus 15. He closed his own eyes and became unnerved at pictures of the way he towered over Jack and how small his head looked in his hands. That was unsettling enough, but the one of Daryl's battered face sent chills up his spine making him doubt himself. Perhaps, his mother doubted as well, and this made his heart hurt even more.

Her emotional eyes fixed on Cullen as she sighed, "Cullen, I agree with you. Take your life back. I've been waiting so long to hear you say this, but...but make sure it doesn't come at a cost."

"A cost?"

"Be careful. I don't want to see you or anyone else get hurt."

Cullen shook his head. Deep inside, he didn't know how her request would be possible. To get to this point, he'd been teased, attacked, and beaten. The torment landed him in the hospital and made him a hostage inside his own mind. Would it be possible? How could he undo what's been done?

"That's my hope too, Mom. Something needs to change. I'm gonna go to my room. Get some homework done or use *Jakob*."

Margaret smiled concernedly. "You can't go until you give me a hug."

"Are you serious?" Cullen laughed.

"You know I am." She moved to Cullen and hugged him. "God, you're like a big teddy bear."

Cullen rolled his eyes. "I'll be in my room."

"I'll start on dinner."

CHAPTER 35

WHILE IN HIS BEDROOM, Cullen sat on his bed. He turned *Jakob* over in his hands and wondered what it would show him. Answers? More questions? He looked down at his phone and thought about the video from Mr. Reid's class and decided he would go back to class. Cullen put down *Jakob* and picked the sketch pad from the floor. He leafed through to the last sketch of Daryl. His mind raced with frightening thoughts. *Did I do this? Could I be this brutal?* He rubbed his thumb over the picture of the shadowy boy looking on. *Who are you?*

On the floor, he rested the sketch pad on his lap. He took a deep breath and placed *Jakob* on his head. As he pushed the button, he heard something tapping on his window. At first he thought nothing of it, but it continued, so he took *Jakob* off his head and walked over to the window. Zeke and Val waved from outside. He slid the window open. "What are you guys doing here?"

"You gotta come with us, man," Zeke urged.

"Can't you use the door like normal people?" Cullen chuckled.

"We would if we were normal. Come on out."

"Where? My mother's freaked out, so I can't be gone for long."

"Oh, trust me, we won't be that long. It's gonna be a blast," Zeke smiled with confidence.

"Okay, okay. Give me a minute." Cullen picked up *Jakob* and put it in the charger, closed the sketch, and hid it under his bed. After grabbing his shoes, he darted into the living room. "Mom, I'm going to head out for a few minutes."

"Wait. Where are you going? It's almost dinner."

"I'll be back. You and Dr. Morris can eat together. Like a date or something."

"You haven't answered my question. Where are you going? And with who?"

"I'm gonna meet up with some friends. Nothing big. They just wanna see if I'm okay after today."

"Okay. Okay. Don't be too late. It's going to get dark soon. Don't forget your phone and your wallet."

"Got it. See you in a bit." Cullen closed the front door and searched for Zeke and Val. "Hey guys? Where'd you go? Zeke? Val?" Cullen walked around the house, past the thick bushes.

Val jumped out and shouted, "What took you so long?" She and Cullen laughed.

"Where's Zeke?"

"He walked down to the corner."

"So, what did you guys have in mind?"

"Oh, you'll see. Let's just say that we're going to get a little payback."

"Payback?"

"Yup!" The two walked to the corner and found Zeke leaning against a fence.

"Sup, Cullen."

"I was just going to use *Jakob* and hoped I'd see you guys there."

"Looks like you got an even better deal," Zeke teased, causing Val to chuckle as she popped a bubble of chewing gum.

"Okay, so what are we doing?"

"Taking back some of that power that teacher of yours stole from you today. Tell you what, he's really lucky you didn't throw that desk at him," Val grunted.

Cullen stopped in his tracks. "Guys, what are we really going to do?"

"Let's just call it a little retribution," Zeke smiled and made his manicured eyebrows dance.

"I don't want to hurt anybody."

"Who said anyone was gonna get hurt?" Val asked. "Unless we want to go that route."

"No. I don't want anyone to get hurt."

"You say that, man," Zeke started, "but at some point, you gotta make a stand."

"No one gets hurt. That's it or I'm outta here," Cullen insisted.

"Fine. Just checking where your head's at." Zeke relented.

"Good. So, what's the plan?"

"We found out where Mr. Reid lives," Val chuckled, exposing a chipped tooth.

"Whoa. What did I just say?"

"Relax," Zeke assured. "But you have to admit, he deserves a little payback, right?"

"Okay."

"You got money on you? We're gonna head up to Zito's Convenience Store up the block and pick up some eggs," Val laughed.

"Then we're gonna turn his house into an omelet." Zeke and Val high fived each other.

Cullen just stared at them. "I don't want to get in trouble, you guys. This idea sounds terrible."

Zeke firmly put his hand on Cullen's shoulder. "Cullen, you won't get caught. And even if you do, after what that fool did to you, you'll just get a slap on the wrist. Disgruntled teenager gets revenge on a jerk-wad teacher by egging his house. Again, he's lucky you didn't hit him right upside the head with that desk."

"Come on, Cullen. What do you say?" Val's puppy dog eyes peeked from behind her punk rock hairstyle.

"No one's gonna get hurt?"

"Cullen. You're the one in control. If you wanna keep control, that's all you gotta say. If you want to get a little crazier, you make the call. You're the captain. We're just your mates," Zeke smiled.

"That just sounds dorky," he playfully pushed Zeke's arm. "I'm in!"

"Yes!" Zeke and Val cheered and put their arms around him.

"So, where's this jerk-wad live?"

"It's already in your phone," Val pointed to Cullen's phone.

Cullen, confused for a moment, slid the home screen up and there it was, Mr. Reid's address. "That's only a few blocks from here. Let's do this before I lose my nerve."

After picking up a couple dozen eggs, the three approached Mr. Reid's house. The last rays of light held onto what was left of the day. They hid behind some bushes between the houses. "Are you ready for this?" Val asked.

Cullen nodded. "Wait a minute. Do you guys see that?"

"See what?" Zeke asked.

"The car's door is wide open." In the driveway, a white Nissan rested in the driveway. The driver's side door was opened. Cullen shushed Val and Zeke. "Listen." A sound came from the car. "The car's dinging like the keys are still in there."

"So?" Zeke questioned.

"That means Mr. Reid's gotta be around here. Like he could come out at any moment."

"Then we gotta get moving and empty these egg cartons," Val suggested with urgency in her voice. She handed Cullen an egg. "Care to do the honors?"

Cullen's eyes grew large. "Should I?" Zeke and Val shook their heads emphatically. "Okay, here goes." Cullen launched one that hit the bay window. He threw two more; one hit the front door and the other at another window.

"Think about how he made you feel. Small. Insignificant," Val yelled.

"I hate him," Cullen yelled, chucking one that made it inside the open car and splattered against the inside windshield. "I won't let him do that again to me. Take that!" Cullen threw three more eggs, two of which smeared all over the front door. Cullen's hair had gone wild as he chucked one after another until there were no eggs left.

Zeke smiled at Cullen. "Feel better?"

"I do. I really do." Cullen high fived Zeke.

Just then, someone yelled from behind them, "Hey, what are you doing? You shouldn't be doing that! Get out of here or I'm calling the police on you!"

"Oh, crap!" yelled Cullen. "Let's get out of here." They looked wide-eyed at each other and darted down the block, laughing hysterically. Once they were safely away from Mr. Reid's, the three of them bent over, panting.

Cullen looked at his two friends. "I don't know if that was the right thing to do, but it sure was fun."

"You didn't stutter once saying that, so I know you enjoyed it," Val pointed out, giving Cullen a punch in the arm, followed by a hug.

"You're right! I can't seem to get a full handle on it again. It creeps back in."

"You will. Once you gain some more confidence." Zeke gave him a high-five. "Didn't it feel great to get some control back?"

A slight smile pulled at the corner of Cullen's mouth. He pulled out his phone. "Oh crap, I gotta run. Get together again soon?" Cullen took off towards his house. His heart still pounded at the excitement of getting back at Mr. Reid. Deep down, he knew he was going to get busted for this, but Zeke was right. It would be just a strongly worded punishment. As he walked up to his house, he wished he could see Mr. Reid's face when he discovered all that mess. He chuckled, "Jerk-wad."

Before walking in, his phone chimed again. He reached into his pocket, expecting yet another comment about the video, but instead, a text from Lori waited for him. He slapped his head with his palm. *I forgot to text her.*

He looked down to read, expecting the worst, but was happy to read, **Hey Cullen. I hope ur okay. Don't let that jerk get you down. I hope to hear from u.**

She's not angry, whew, Cullen thought.

After mentally checking his feelings, he typed, **I'm sry that I didn't text u back. I was chatting with my family. I'm actually pretty good, considering.** He didn't dare mention the visit by the police.

U coming to school tomorrow?

I'll be there

:)

Cullen pressed his phone against his chest and walked in. His mother and Dr. Morris were finishing dinner. "There he is," Dr. Morris called out.

"I was hoping we would eat dinner together," Margaret looked disappointed.

"Sorry. A couple of my friends came to check on me. You know, after today."

"I know. I know. That's a good thing. See, these setbacks are just that. It's good to have friends, right?" Margaret asked, putting aside her disappointment.

"I hope I didn't miss dessert," Cullen said. He felt guilty about lying about what he was really doing but resided in the truth that his friends checked on him.

Dr. Morris pointed out when Margaret stepped out of the room, "It seems that your mood has changed."

"Yeah. It was good to talk with you and my friends."

"Good. I'm glad to hear it. I wouldn't give much concern about that fellow from the bus. If you're feeling out of sorts or need some coping, I recommend using *Jakob*."

"I was planning on it."

Cullen felt nervous about going to school the next day. He wondered what Mr. Reid would say to him and how he would react. He tried to put the day's events behind him.

Chapter 36

At lunch, Tasha, Lori, and Cullen sat at their usual hangout. Chandler plopped down next to Tasha and kissed her on the cheek. "Dude, did you hear about Mr. Reid?" Cullen stiffened as Chandler asked him.

"N-No. What happened?" Cullen felt his stomach tighten. *Did they figure out who egged his house already? Oh man, I'm dead meat.*

"He's a complete no show today. Like no one knows where he is."

"He's probably just sick or something," Tasha offered, chomping down on an onion ring.

"I don't think so. You know Sarah Schneider? Her mom's the school secretary, right?"

"Yeah. Okay, we all go to the same school. Spill the tea," Tasha insisted.

"She told me that something serious is up with him. Like really serious. Someone broke into his car."

Cullen felt his neck tense. His mind raced back to the open car door in the driveway.

"How's she know all that?" Lori asked.

"Well, when he was a no show at school today, they called his cell, and no one answered."

"So?" Tasha asked.

"Girl, you've got something going on today. All feisty and stuff. Just let me finish." Tasha rolled her eyes and smiled. "So, they called the person on his contact list. His mother. The dude doesn't even have a wife or a girlfriend. His mom is his emergency contact."

"Chandler. F-Finish the story," Cullen demanded. Sweat beaded on his forehead.

"Dude, you good? You look like you've seen a ghost."

"Yeah, you don't look too hot," Lori observed. "You sure you're okay?"

"What? Me? I'm fine. My stomach's been funky all day. Had ice cream last night and my body can't handle it," he lied. "Keep going."

"His mom doesn't know where he is. When she went over, she found the car. Eggs smashed all over it and the house. She called the cops. I guess they're waiting to hear. Crazy, right?"

"I bet he's fine," Tasha said.

"Or...now hear me out. Maybe he's dead."

"He's not dead," Cullen blurted out.

"Dude, don't freak out," Chandler laughed.

"Don't call me a freak," Cullen mumbled.

"Cullen, man, chill."

"Cullen, are you sure everything's fine?" Lori asked. "We're just talking here. Having some fun."

"Sorry. Sorry. I just...nothing. I'm going to head outside. Get some fresh air," he stuttered a little.

"Want some company?" Lori asked.

He looked at Chandler and Tasha before forcing a smile at Lori. "Sure."

"See you guys later," Lori called back over her shoulder to Chandler and Tasha.

Chandler watched Cullen and Lori walk away while Tasha polished off the last onion ring. "What do you think about Cullen?"

Wiping her face, Tasha responded, "He's different, but he's alright. Lori seems happy. He wouldn't be my first choice, but…"

"My boy, Evan, says he was a real freak show in middle school."

"That's middle school."

"It was just last year, Tasha. He said he had no friends."

"None? Doesn't seem right."

"That's what he said. He would be creepy and stare at his girl. She had to call him out."

"I mean, he can be pretty scary. That thing that happened in Mr. Reid's class was…different."

"Hmm. Remember that video? Evan told me that after that happened, he ended up in a mental hospital for months. Rumor has it that he was a total vegetable."

"That video was pretty terrifying."

"Sure was."

Tasha sat up as a thought hit her. "Who sent out that video, anyway?"

"I'm guessing Evan did. Saw him at the basketball game and he was asking about Cullen. Told me about the video, but I just figured he was gonna just send it to me. Didn't think he was going to put it on blast."

Tasha crunched on a carrot stick. "That was not cool. I mean, especially if he knew Cullen ended up in a hospital. Sounds like this friend of yours isn't all that nice."

"He's one of the boys, you know. He can give it pretty good to people. All in good fun."

"Hmm. Sounds like it." Tasha rolled her eyes.

Cullen and Lori walked hand in hand through the glass doors. Concern consumed her mind. Her affection for Cullen was strong, but she knew there was this whole other side he was holding back from her. Could it be that bad? Was it something she could help with? How would she know if he didn't open up? She decided she'd approach.

"Hey, is everything alright?"

Cullen kicked a rock by his feet. "I'm okay, I guess."

"Cullen, look at me. I won't pretend to understand what you're going through or even what you've been through, but I'd like to."

Cullen shook his head. "I don't want to drag you through this."

"Then why are we together? It's easy to be with someone when things are good. Like really easy. A genuine test of a relationship is how people handle things when things go bad."

Cullen chuckled. "You sound like a marriage therapist."

She smiled uncomfortably. "You know you aren't the only one that has issues. I'm a child of divorce. It sucks. That was what the family counselor told me when I was dealing with my parents' selfishness. It makes total sense."

"I guess it does."

"Well?"

"Well, what?" Cullen smirked shyly.

"Why are boys so ridiculous? Will you at least tell me what's got you so stressed?"

"Lori, over the last four or five years, I've been bullied mercilessly. Not just picked on. Tormented."

"I knew it had to be something like that. Kids today use that word so freely, you never know how true all of it is. But when I saw that video, I knew what happened to you had to be serious."

"It was."

"But, Cullen, you're so…big. Like who in their right mind would mess with you?"

"I wasn't always this size." Cullen noticed his stutter had quelled a bit. "It started gradually and then when kids realized I wouldn't fight back, it gave people permission, I guess."

"Why didn't you fight back?"

"The truth? Here's the most manly response you'll ever hear." Lori squeezed his hand. "I didn't fight back because I was scared. A few years ago, I stood up for myself and it didn't turn out the way I hoped it would."

"Cullen, by telling me that, it *is* the most manly thing you can do. I've never asked you to be something macho for me. Did you think just because you were one of the biggest guys in school I was like, 'Oh my, I gotta have that boy!'?"

"Oh, so I'm not manly," Cullen joked and crossed his arms.

"I'd say you're something, alright," Lori joked, reaching up and putting her hands on his chest.

"Ha ha. Anyway, it's embarrassing to be the kid that everyone picked on. The kid with no friends." Cullen grew quiet for a moment. "You know, after that incident, the one on the video? I ended up in the hospital for months."

"I'm so sorry, Cullen. It must have been hard." Cullen shook his head. "So, you say you didn't have any friends?"

"Not really. Once I became a target, it was safer to stay clear of target practice. I don't blame them. Friends just had a way of evaporating that way."

"You have friends now, right?"

"Things are a little different now. They haven't seen what I've gone through. I don't doubt they would leave too."

"Don't say that."

"Lori, it's true. Chandler's friends with this guy, Evan. This guy made my life a living hell. That's what he made of my life. Hell on Earth."

"Chandler?"

"Yup. I saw him and Evan chumming it up on the basketball court like they knew each other. I'm sure he had to say something about me."

"You sound paranoid."

"I'd say yes, but when you've been kicked around the way I have, you know things. Even if I'm wrong, it's better to be cautious than right."

"Even if they said something, you can trust Chandler." Cullen remained quiet. "What? You don't believe that?"

"I want to, but..."

"But?"

"I want to believe, I do. I'm just going to reserve my right not to answer right now."

"I don't think you have anything to worry about."

"To be honest? I'm beyond worrying at this point. I've learned a lot about myself these last few months."

"What about me? Do you worry about me?"

"I don't want to." Cullen dropped his head.

"What? I want a guy who's gonna worry about me." Lori delivered a playful punch to his arm.

"Not like that. Of course I worry, but that worry is caring. I worry because I care about you. I don't want to worry about losing what we have. You're pretty amazing. I'm scared that all of this will start again, and you'll see me the way others have in the past."

"I would never, especially since knowing what I know now." She leaned into him and squeezed him as hard as she could. Cullen's body swallowed Lori's in an emotional hug.

Their lips met briefly before they separated. Cullen blushed. Then something caught his eye. At the corner of the building, he saw Zeke, hands folded across his chest, and Val, her back leaning against the wall, arms also folded and her right boot against the wall. Cullen waved at them.

Lori spun around to see. "Who are you waving at?"

"Just a couple of friends."

"Oh. Are they upperclassmen?"

"I think so."

"You think so?" Lori laughed.

"Well, I know their names. Just don't know what grade they're in."

"Good for you. More people on your side."

"Yeah. I know they always have my back," Cullen smiled, shifting his gaze from them back to Lori.

"Well, I hope you know," Lori added, poking her index finger in the middle of his chest. "I will always have your back, too."

"I know." Lori's smile made Cullen's heart flutter. "I'm going to go talk to my friends really quick. Can I meet you inside?"

"Sure. Go hang out with your upperclassmen," she teased. She turned and walked away. Before walking in, she turned to see Cullen walk across the blacktop and go around the corner of the building.

She felt a little guilty, but something overwhelmed her. She was curious to see Cullen's friends. Moving through the hallways, past the locker rooms and the gymnasium, she crept to the glass doors that led to where Cullen and his friends were. She hid behind the wall and peeked outside the window, and she saw Cullen in an intense conversation with someone, but she couldn't see anyone because they were in the alcove that led to the outside entrance of the locker rooms. She scooted to the other side of the window to get a better look but couldn't see anything. Already feeling guilty enough, she moved back across the window, trying hard not to sneak a peek back to Cullen, but curiosity got the best of her. When she glanced back at Cullen, he was staring at her. Her heart stopped, and a warmth washed over her. What to do. *Stop*? *Go*? *What if he questions me? Should I tell the truth? Lie?* After the conversation they just had, she tried to convince him that she could be trusted. She worried this was a breach of trust.

These thoughts sprinted through her head as she kept moving. Act naturally. Answer questions later if she must. Who was she kidding? Of course, there will be questions.

CHAPTER 37

CULLEN WALKED AWAY FROM Lori, towards Zeke and Val. He looked back once at Lori as she walked back through the glass doors. As he approached them, Zeke teased, "Oh man, Val, our boy's got it bad."

"Shut up." Cullen jokingly pushed Zeke's shoulder.

"Let's head over here," Val suggested and walked around the corner of the building and by the doors of the locker rooms.

"Did you guys hear about Mr. Reid?" Val and Zeke shook their heads no. "He's missing. Like didn't show up to work today."

"So, he got sick. He doesn't strike me as the most responsible person. He didn't call a sub?" Zeke suggested.

"I'd thought that, but when his mother went over to check the house, she saw what we saw. His car door was still open today."

"Like I said, he's not the most responsible person."

"Wait, did you say his mother? His mother had to check on him? That dork doesn't have a wife? I'm not surprised." Val joked.

"Guys, you are missing the point. If Mr. Reid is missing, then something could be wrong."

"So, what if he is? It's not like you had anything to do with it," Zeke insisted.

"Umm, did you forget? We were there last night."

"Cullen, I'm pretty sure it's not a major crime to chuck some eggs at someone's house," Val tried to reason.

"Hello?" Cullen threw up his hands. "Let's say something happened to him. That place is a crime scene. We were literally at the scene of the crime last night. His neighbor saw us. I bet they would tell the police. If we get identified, we could be in big trouble," Cullen begged them to see the urgency.

"What would it matter? You did nothing but throw some eggs. You're a kid. How much trouble could you get into?" Zeke stated.

"He probably went out last night and partied like he did in his twenties. You're fine," Val reassured.

"Why do you guys keep saying I'm going to be fine, and I did nothing? You were there too. Don't forget that."

"Of course, Cullen," Zeke agreed.

Val leaned against the brick wall. "Right now, I think you have other things to think about."

"Like what?"

Zeke pointed toward the windows. When Cullen looked, he saw Lori looking at him. *What's she doing? Is she following me? No. Maybe she was just looking for me. Why go this way and not by the blacktop where they had been earlier?* These thoughts confused Cullen's mind as Lori walked past and back toward the cafeteria.

CHAPTER 38

Cullen waited for Lori outside of Mr. Reid's classroom. He wasn't sure how he was going to approach her. After the conversation they had at lunch, he thought his best bet was to be blunt. "Everything okay?" Lori asked Cullen.

"Yeah, I think."

"You think?" Lori cocked her head.

"Well, it's just that when I went to talk with my friends, I saw you."

"OMG, I'm so sorry about that. I went to look for you when I didn't see you outside. And then when I found you, I realized how creepy I looked, and I panicked."

"You panicked?"

"Yes, once I saw you, I was like 'there he is.' Then, the longer I stared, the more I thought about how bad it looked. And then when we locked eyes, I really freaked out and got the heck out of there."

Cullen laughed. "None of this would have to do with some curiosity about my friends?"

Lori's cheeks flushed. "Okay, fine. I was a little curious. I didn't know you had other friends."

"No other friends?"

"Oh, God. That's not what I meant. I meant that I hadn't seen you with any other friends than us."

"Well, I guess I totally get that. But I do have friends."

"I'd like to meet them someday. You know, if you think I'm cool enough to hang out with upperclassmen."

"Yeah, I don't think you are," Cullen joked.

"Ha. You think I'm not cool enough? I'll have you know I'm the coolest person in this school," Lori smiled.

"The entire school?"

She looked up and down the hall. "Maybe this hallway."

"The entire hallway?"

"Well, how about these two tiles we're standing on?"

Cullen noticed Tasha and Chandler walking towards them. "I'll see you inside?" Lori kissed him on the cheek.

"What's up, Cullen? Everything good?" Chandler asked.

"Yeah, Chandler. Sorry about earlier today."

"It's all good." Chandler gave a high five to Cullen and went into the class.

When Cullen walked into the room, he felt his heart race. He replayed the day before as he stared at the place where Mr. Reid had cowered. As he approached his desk, he traced his fingers over edges where he held it in his hands.

"Cullen?" Lori's voice barged into his thoughts.

When he lifted his head, the stares of his classmates pierced into him. He nodded and sat down. Chandler and Tasha smiled, but something behind their smiles bothered him. He couldn't quite put his finger on it. Putting it aside for the moment, it wasn't long before the class buzzed around the elephant in the room.

"Did you hear about Mr. Reid?"

"I hear he owed people some money, and they tossed him into a van."

"Someone told me they think he's dead."

"See, that's what I was talking about. There are some crazy rumors out there," Chandler whispered. Cullen shifted uncomfortably in his seat.

As the bell sounded and the substitute started class, Ms. Saunders knocked on the open door. "Hi there. I'm sorry for the interruption. Can I see Cullen, please?" Surprised, Cullen locked eyes with Ms. Saunders and pointed to himself. "Yes, Cullen. You're going to need your backpack, too."

There was a collective murmur as Cullen stood up. He looked down at his three friends and headed for the door.

When he reached the hallway, he stood in front of Ms. Saunders. He looked over his shoulder and saw Officer Mead and Officer Kowalski in the hallway. "Wh-What's g-g-going on? Is everything okay?" Cullen stuttered nervously.

"Cullen, just breathe. These officers need to have a word with you."

"Wh-What's this all about?"

"Hello, Cullen. Is it okay if we take this conversation out of the hallway?" Officer Mead suggested.

"Yeah. I guess. What's happening?" Officer Kowalski moved aside and waited for Cullen and Ms. Saunders to walk down the hall.

"C'mon Cullen. We can use my office." Once they started, both officers followed closely.

From behind, Lori's voice called out. "Hey, where are you taking him?"

Ms. Saunders stopped and looked back. "Lori, it's okay. This will all get sorted. Head back to class, please."

"But Ms. Saunders. What's going on? Is Cullen in trouble or something?"

Cullen turned around to face Lori. "It's okay, L-Lori. I'll text you later," he pleaded with her between stutters. Then, he lipped, "It's okay."

In Ms. Saunders' office, Cullen, the officers, and Ms. Saunders sat on chairs in a semicircle. "I've called his mother, and she's on her way."

"What's happening?" Cullen asked.

"Cullen, I'm sure you remember us."

"Yes, of course. Officer Mead and Kowalski. Can either of you let me know why you had to take me out of class?" Cullen felt his heart in his throat.

"You had an incident in Mr. Reid's class yesterday, correct?" Officer Mead asked.

Cullen looked at Ms. Saunders and back at the officers. "Yes."

Officer Kowalski asked, "Is there any reason you didn't tell us about this when we were at your house?"

"I don't know. I didn't think it had anything to do with that other thing." He looked at Ms. Saunders and wondered how much she knew.

"Cullen, were you at Mr. Reid's house yesterday?" Officer Mead asked.

Ms. Saunders' eyes widened as she expected an answer. Cullen shot her an embarrassed look and cast his eyes away. "Yes."

"Are you aware that Mr. Reid is missing?"

"Yes. It's all everyone's talking about." Then, as if struck by something, a terrifying thought crossed his mind. Flashes of the incident on the bus zipped into his mind. He still couldn't recall if he'd been responsible for what happened to Daryl. What *Jakob* had shown him shadowed him in doubt. "Wait a minute. Are you thinking I had something to do with Mr. Reid?" Cullen stammered.

"Why were you there?" Officer Kowalski asked.

"I-I was very upset about what he did to me."

Ms. Saunders interrupted, "Cullen, can you tell the officers why you were so upset?"

He nodded. "He teased me in class about the Wilderness Camp video. The one I showed you the first time you were at my house. One joke after another. He thought it was funny, but it made me angry."

"Angry enough to go to his house?"

"Yes. A couple of friends and I thought it would be funny to..." he paused.

"To do what, Cullen?" Officer Kowalski prodded.

"We thought it would be funny to egg his house. We bought a couple dozen eggs and went over and pelted it."

"What store did you buy the eggs from?"

"Zito's Deli."

"And you mentioned you went with some friends?" Officer Mead asked.

"Yes."

"Do these friends have names?"

"Zeke and Val."

"Last names?" Officer Mead asked as she took notes in her pad.

"I don't know. Look, I know what you're thinking."

"What are we thinking, Cullen?" Officer Kowalski asked.

"You're thinking I had something to do with whatever's happening to Mr. Reid."

Officers Mead and Kowalski glanced at each other. Officer Kowalski nodded. "So, did you?"

"No, I swear, we just w-went there to egg h-his house. That's it." Cullen scoured his mind for the incident. "There was one thing, though."

"What's that?" Officer Mead asked.

"His car door was open, and it sounded as if the keys were still in the ignition. I even threw an egg inside of it," Cullen stammered.

"So, you're saying when you got there, the car door was open? Which side?"

"The driver's side."

"Did you and your friends see Mr. Reid?"

"No. We didn't."

Just then, someone shouted outside Ms. Saunders' office. "Where is my son? This is ridiculous." A secretary opened the door and tried to speak, but Margaret pushed the door open and barged in. When she saw the police officers, she shouted, "This is enough! Why won't you leave my poor son alone?"

Officer Mead spoke, "Mrs. Hickey, we were just asking him some questions."

"How dare you ask him questions without parental consent!" She looked at Ms. Saunders and barked, "How can you allow this?"

"Mrs. Hickey. I don't have the power here to say they couldn't."

"What do you mean by that?" Her chest heaved.

"Mrs. Hickey, we were called here to investigate a potential situation with Cullen's teacher, Mr. Reid." Margaret gasped. "While we were talking with Ms. Saunders, it came to our attention that Cullen had an incident that happened during Mr. Reid's class yesterday. I'm sure you know about that, yes?" She shook her head. Officer Mead continued, "Because of this, we wanted to find out what had happened and if he knew anything. Nothing more."

"I know who Mr. Reid is. Fired is what he should be."

"Well, Mrs. Hickey, he's missing," Officer Mead revealed.

Margaret, shocked, stood upright. "Oh?"

"With your feelings aside, we wanted to ask Cullen about his whereabouts yesterday," Officer Mead said.

"Do you suspect foul play?"

"It's too early to tell, but the circumstances appear suspicious," Officer Kowalski admitted.

"What does this have to do with my Cullen?"

Officer Mead started, "Cullen was at Mr. Reid's house yesterday."

Margaret's face changed to shock and insult. "No. He was with us after school."

Officer Kowalski shook his head slightly. "Apparently not. He's admitted to us that he was there. So, if he saw anything, it might be helpful in our investigation."

Cullen, seeing his mother's unbelieving look, defended himself, "We egged his house, Mom. That's it!"

"How could you do that? You are in some big trouble."

"Ma'am, we've secured video from the scene. We haven't looked at it yet. It's being transferred and recorded as evidence. It's footage that was pulled from a Ring doorbell camera from a neighbor who reported the egging."

Cullen thought about the neighbor who yelled at him, Val, and Zeke.

"Well, my boy had nothing to do with Mr. Reid's disappearance." Officers Mead and Kowalski looked at each other without answering. "He wouldn't do something like that," she pleaded.

"Until a few minutes ago, you never thought he'd egg someone's house, correct? Cullen's been present at two locations where there's been foul play," Officer Kowalski remarked.

"Foul play? I'd hardly call what happened on the bus foul play."

"Call it what you want, ma'am. Like we've said before, we need to investigate all leads. Right now, Cullen is the only person we know who was at the scene. We just want to find out what he knows." Then Officer Kowalski turned to Cullen. "Do you have any other information about your friends, Zeke and Val? Cell phone numbers? Addresses?"

Cullen's eyebrows dipped above his nose. "Actually, no. I don't. I met them this past fall. It's complicated."

"Would it be possible for you to uncomplicate it?" Officer Mead spoke.

"Wait a minute. Is my son in trouble?"

"No Ma'am," Officer Mead said.

"Then we can go?"

"Yes, of course. I think we have what we need for now. Here's my card just in case you lost the last one I gave you. Cullen, in case things get uncomplicated, please let us know. Despite your feelings about Mr. Reid and the incident that happened in class yesterday, we still have a missing person whose family is very concerned about his well-being."

Margaret glanced at Cullen and then back at the officers. "Cullen and I will have a very serious conversation about his actions. I'm sure he had nothing to do with Mr. Reid's disappearance or what happened to that other fellow." As the words left her lips, a fleeting moment of doubt snuck in, catching her off guard. She hated the way it tasted and spit it out as soon as it touched her lips. She stood at the door and waited for Cullen, glaring at him.

Cullen stood up, avoiding eye contact with the officers and Ms. Saunders. His mind reeled with doubt, too. He hadn't forgotten what *Jakob* had shown him. Uncertainty swirled around him regarding the bus incident, but this? This was different. He'd only egged the house, right? Nothing more. Just a stupid prank to get back at a stupid person. He'd have to use *Jakob* for any insight.

As Margaret and Cullen walked down the hallway, Officer Mead called out, "Mrs. Hickey. Can I have just a second? Alone?"

Margaret told Cullen to wait for her in the car. "What do you need?" she asked, exasperated.

The two looked at each other. "I recognize that look in your eyes. Mother to mother?" Margaret nodded. "I know moments like this can be hard."

Margaret's eyes welled with tears. "What would you know?"

"I'm a single mom. I know what it's like to feel like things are unraveling a bit."

"Unraveling?" Tears spilled out of the corner of her eyes and shook her head. "That's a good word for it. My boy has been through so much in life. I'm surprised he's so strong. I would have buckled years ago."

"Hang in there."

"It's hard," Margaret whispered. "I feel like everything is going to fall apart at any second. Those bullies are after him. The police are after him. I'm afraid he'll get cornered, and something is going to give."

"We're not after him, but there are questions that need addressing. We want him safe. Most of all, we recognize he's a boy. Not much different from my own," Officer Mead tried to reassure. "In the meantime, keep your eyes open for anything. Details. Conversations. I hope that if Cullen is involved with anything, he comes to you before anything gets out of hand."

Concern revealed itself in Margaret's eyes. She attempted a smile as a tear escaped her eye.

When Margaret arrived at the car, she wasted little time reprimanding her son, "What the hell is happening, Cullen?"

"Mom, I only egged the guy's house. It wasn't anything horrible."

"Since when is damaging property not considered anything horrible?"

"Like he didn't have it coming?"

"That's besides the point. It's not something we do."

"Don't we? How about when Dad came back for that short time and then left again? It was you that spray painted his car, right?"

"This is different. It was a different time."

"How is it different? I'm young too. It feels like it's exactly the same," Cullen argued without a stutter.

Margaret shot a look at Cullen. "I haven't always made the best of choices, but I'm an adult. What happened between us was much different from someone trying to get under your skin."

"I don't see how it is."

"It just *is* Cullen! When you get older, you'll understand!" she shouted. Silence fell over the two of them as she drove. Finally, she pleaded, "Tell me who these new friends of yours are."

"They're just friends."

"I feel like it may not be best to see them for a while."

"Why?"

"Because maybe they're a bad influence on you."

"They're not."

"They got you to egg Mr. Reid's house."

"It was just something stupid kids do. I went along with it."

"What if they had something to do with Mr. Reid's disappearance? Have you stopped for a second to think about that?"

The truth is, he hadn't, but that was only because it couldn't be true. He thought he knew what happened but couldn't be one hundred percent sure. Then a dark thought covered him. "Mom, do you think I did something to Mr. Reid?"

Her brief hesitation in answering frightened him. "No, honey. I don't think you have that in you."

"You don't *think*?"

"I didn't mean for it to come out that way. I mean, you don't have it in you."

Uncertainty blanketed both of them. "I don't think I do either," Cullen responded.

"You don't think?"

"Yeah." Cullen said with more sureness than expected.

Margaret was silent the rest of the car ride home. Doubt parked itself into her stomach, and it nauseated her.

Chapter 39

CULLEN SAT ON THE floor with *Jakob* in his lap. For the first time, the device scared him. Fear cloaked him in uncertainty and consumed his thoughts. He hesitated in putting it on his head, pushing the button, and seeing what *Jakob* was about to reveal to him. If he were to get any answers, he knew he had to. It was the only way. He lifted *Jakob* and held it to his forehead as if it were staring at him.

He fixed *Jakob* on his head and hoped to find Zeke and Val there to tell him something encouraging. Anything that would reassure him that everything would be okay. Reaching next to him, he put the sketch pad onto his lap and held the pencil. After a deep breath, he lowered *Jakob* onto the bridge of his nose and pushed the button. The machine whirred for a second and the light flashed on, and Cullen tracked it. The familiar message welcomed Cullen and droned through the directions.

"Show me something, *Jakob*," Cullen whispered.

The background image inside the VR goggles slowly came into focus. The sun was still holding onto the last moments of day. In the distance, a faint orange sunset gave the day its last light before the streetlamps kicked on. It didn't surprise Cullen to be in front of Mr. Reid's house. Outside of the session, the pencil in Cullen's hand raced across the sketch pad.

Inside, through his own eyes, he watched from behind a bush as Mr. Reid's car pulled into the driveway. He was on his cell phone. Cullen felt adrenaline coursing through his body. What was he waiting for? What was he going to do? He looked at his hands to confirm they were his own as he flexed them and turned them to see the backs of them. A child's laugh echoed behind him. Cullen spun around to see the boy from his last session. His features were more defined, looking less like a ghostly figure and more like a child. Shadows that danced around like smoke remained around the edges of his body.

"Hello Cullen," his voice echoed.

"Why are we here?"

"I want to show you something."

"Mr. Reid?"

"Of course. I want to help you understand that for you to take your power, you will need to do more."

"This is too much."

"Listen." The words echoed around Cullen.

In the driveway, Mr. Reid opened his car door but remained inside, so Cullen could hear the conversation. "Yes, Shelly. I understand. Look, I didn't think the kid lacked a sense of humor. I was just joking around. Everyone else in the class seemed to get that message except for him." He listened. "Uh-huh. Right. I get it. Yes, I understand he's been through a lot. Yes. Okay, I'll apologize to him tomorrow and make it right. Okay. See you then."

Cullen turned to the boy. "Who is he talking to? The only Shelly I know is Ms. Saunders. He's talking about me, isn't he?"

The boy urged, "Wait for it."

"It seems like they've handled it. He feels bad about it, and he's going to apologize."

"Does he?" The boy tilted his head down and pointed at the car. "I don't think Mr. Reid...gets it."

Cullen felt his body move swiftly through his eyes towards the car as Mr. Reid placed one foot out of the car. "Freak. Gonna get me in trouble? Can't take a joke," he muttered as he shifted his body to exit the car.

"See, I told you. You know what you have to do," the boy suggested.

Through his eyes, Cullen watched what appeared to be his own hand as it gathered a handful of Mr. Reid's hair from the back of his head, and with one motion, the hand rammed Mr. Reid's face into the steering wheel. Then his other arm reached across the front of his neck and secured a choke hold. After a brief struggle, Cullen felt Mr. Reid's body go limp. He watched as his hands tucked under Mr. Reid's armpits and pulled him out of the car. The boy trailed Mr. Reid's body as it dragged him down the driveway and across the lawn.

"You're just a freak to him, Cullen."

"I don't want to do anything like this."

"Don't you? I've been inside your mind, Cullen. So much pain."

Hoping for a voice of reason, Cullen asked, "Where are Zeke and Val?"

"They didn't want to play with me anymore. So, they left." The boy pouted his lips and put his hands up. "It's more fun playing with you, anyway," the boy laughed.

Cullen ripped *Jakob* from his head and tossed it to the floor beside him like it was haunted. He tried to inhale, but his lungs resisted. He stood up and grabbed the plastic water bottle on the nightstand and guzzled it. The last few drops choked his throat, and he bent over to cough. His hand stopped midway through wiping his mouth when he glanced at the image he'd sketched on the pad. He picked it up and held it to the light from the window.

The sketches of the pencil drew out an image of Mr. Reid's face. The bridge of his nose caved in. His terrified eyes struggled for a way out as an arm squeezed across his throat. In the rearview mirror, the shadowy boy watched from the backseat, a devious smile across his face.

Cullen put the pad down, and for the first time, he cried. He didn't know what to think. Doubt and confusion swirled in torrents inside his mind. *Am I the freak they think I am?* Twice now, *Jakob* had shown him something horrible. Both times, Cullen couldn't say for sure if he hadn't committed those atrocities.

The phone in his pocket buzzed. A text from Lori. **Hey. Everything good?**

Ya, Cullen lied as he punched the letters.

What's going on? Y were the police here?

I can't talk about it right now

Wym? Lori texted. **Cullen. Ppl say that it had something to do with Mr. Reid.**

Cullen exhaled sharply. **Don't believe everything u hear.**

Ok... tell me

Nothing. It's a big misunderstanding. U'll see

Okay. If u say so

He thought of a response, but nothing came to mind. Instead, a tap sounded from the glass. Cullen charged to it and found Zeke and Val. Cullen unlocked and opened the window.

"Hey kid, how's it going?" Zeke asked.

"How's it going? How's it going?! I'm in so much trouble."

"Relax," Val said, snapping her gum.

"How do you expect me to relax? The world feels like it's crashing down around me."

"C'mon out. Let's talk about it," Zeke suggested.

"I'm not even supposed to be talking with you guys."

"Well, that's not good," Val pointed out, a bubble bursting from her lips.

"Not good at all."

"Well, where's your mom now?" she asked.

"She had to go back to work."

"Okay. You've got a few hours, right?" Zeke asked.

"Yeah, but Dr. Morris' hours are usually crazy. So, who knows when he'll be here?"

"Cullen, you really need to stop worrying, man. Get out here. Tell us everything."

"Argh. Fine, but things are awful. Terrible." Cullen attempted to climb out of the window, but he slipped and tumbled out instead. Val and Zeke laughed. "It's not that funny. One of you could have caught me."

"Oh really, Cullen? I would have ended up flat as a pancake."

Cullen got to his feet and tried to be angry but snickered instead. "Look, everything that could have possibly gone wrong went wrong."

"How's that?" Val asked as she strutted toward the street, and the boys followed.

"Remember how I told you that Mr. Reid was missing? Well, it turns out that he's missing-missing. No one's heard from him. He's not answering his phone. His family can't find him either."

"How do you know that?" Val asked.

"It's all the buzz at school. And to make matters worse, the police came to school to question me!"

"You?" Val and Zeke asked.

"Why did they do that?" Val continued the questioning.

"Because we were there, guys. I told you it was a bad idea. I had to admit that we egged his house. And apparently, there's a video from a neighbor's doorbell cam. Probably from the lady that chased us away."

"Are you on it?" Zeke asked.

"Dunno, but they know all about what happened at school."

Zeke ran his fingers through his tight, wavy hair. "What did they say?"

"I felt like they think I had something to do with his disappearance. I'm terrified."

"Look," Val tried to offer, "what they have right now is a video. You're probably on it, but you're just throwing eggs. Nothing else, right?"

"Not that I know of."

"So, that's a good thing, man," Zeke insisted.

"How is that a good thing?" Cullen asked, exasperated.

"Once they get that, you'll be fine, right? It wasn't you," Zeke said.

Cullen looked down at his shoes. He knew the timeline of their trip to Mr. Reid's house and there was absolutely no time to do anything like what he saw inside *Jakob*. However, he'd lost track of time after the bus that night. There were hours in which he held no account of.

"What's wrong?" Val asked.

"Here's the thing. I'm almost one hundred percent sure that I had nothing to do with what happened to Mr. Reid," Cullen stuttered.

"Dude, how can you not be sure?" Zeke asked. "We were with you! You didn't do anything."

"But I can't be sure."

"Explain," Val said.

"The last few times I've been in a therapy session with *Jakob*..." Cullen's voice trailed off when he saw Zeke and Val glance at each other. "What? What's that look?"

"It's nothing," Val hesitated.

Cullen shook his head and continued. "Anyway, I've seen things that have made me doubt myself. Remember the night when you guys found me on the bridge? The Winter Formal night? That incident on the bus?"

"With that Daryl guy?"

"Yes, well, it turns out after I got off the bus, somebody beat him up really badly."

"Was it you?" Val asked.

Cullen swallowed hard. "I-I don't know. *Jakob* showed me something that scared me to death. I was watching those guys get off the bus. Like I was watching with my own eyes. I followed Daryl and when he wasn't looking, it appeared that I attacked him."

"Seriously?" Zeke questioned. "I can't say he didn't have it coming."

"There's more. Just before you guys came over, I was using *Jakob* again. Trying to get some clarity. The same thing happened; except this time, I was at Mr. Reid's house. As he was getting out of the car, it appeared that I smashed his face against the steering wheel and then dragged him out of it."

"Can't say he didn't have it coming either," Zeke laughed.

"Guys, you aren't taking this seriously. The police are asking questions about me and the two of you!"

"Us?"

"Yeah, I told them I egged Mr. Reid's house with some friends. I just don't know what to think anymore. I'm not sure what's going on. Lately, *Jakob* has shown me things that are scaring me. And what's worse is I don't have you two in there with me."

Val and Zeke shot glances at each other again. "Okay, what the heck? I feel as if you guys are hiding something. If you have any information at all, you've got to let me know."

Val took a deep breath and stood in front of Cullen. "There's something you need to know about *Jakob*."

Dr. Morris pulled into the driveway of the Hickey house. A few weeks earlier, Margaret had offered him the key. She had said it was a shorter ride home from the hospital to her house than it was from the hospital to his townhome on the other side of town. Given the closeness they'd developed, he'd seen right through the gesture. Over the last two weeks, he had spent more evenings staying there than he had at his own place. The transition was gradual and eventually; he imagined he would live there full time. Eventually. For now, the move would keep him close to Cullen and *Jakob*.

When Cullen wasn't home, he made adjustments to the settings and upgraded *Jakob's* programming. At first, he was doing it for Cullen's therapy. It was true Cullen had become more independent in his everyday life and needed *Jakob* less. That was the plan, wasn't it? Then, the day he saw one of Cullen's sketches, the one with Daryl and his son, Jakob, his priorities changed. He'd taken a picture of it with his phone and gazed at it often.

Jakob was taken from Dr. Morris. No, stolen. Ripped from his arms. And now here he was, years later, showing up in Cullen's drawings. Now he wondered if it was possible to get his boy back. He wasn't sure in what way, shape, or form that would be, but if he was showing up in the VR goggles named after him, then any form, regardless of its capacity, was enough for Dr. Morris.

He knocked gently on Cullen's door. "Cullen? Are you in there?" After receiving no response, he slowly turned the doorknob, opened the door a crack, and called again, "Cullen?" He pushed the door open where the empty room greeted him.

Jakob rested on the night table. Dr. Morris pressed his lips together like someone expecting a cold drink after a long run. The phone in his pocket buzzed. He fished it out of his pocket. It was Margaret. He silenced the notification, so the call went straight to voicemail. Seconds later, the phone chimed. A text message. Dr. Morris slid up the home screen to read. ***Call me. Something else happened with Cullen. I don't know what to do.*** He felt a little guilty for not answering, but he needed to answer another call.

Jakob summoned, and Dr. Morris longed to see him. As he approached, he stared in wonder at Cullen's latest sketch. "How does he do this?" he questioned out loud, tracing his fingers over the pencil marks of Mr. Reid's battered face. "Ah, there you are." His eyes moved up to the drawing of Jakob. Tears edged in his eyes.

He put the pad down and picked up *Jakob*. His thumb massaged the white plastic of the VR goggles across the decal display of his son's name. Before placing *Jakob* on his head, Dr. Morris felt the chill from the open window. He looked out of it expecting to see Cullen but was just met with a cool breeze. He pulled the window down halfway.

His focus shifted to *Jakob*. Even though he wore a suit, he sat like a child in the middle of the floor with his legs crossed in front of him. He pressed his lips against *Jakob's* name before placing it on his head. He clicked the button and watched the light pace back and forth in front of him and allowed his eyes to follow. They searched for Jakob. He knew in his mind that he wasn't real, but his heart hadn't stopped aching since finding him that day. "Where are you, my boy?" Dr. Morris sang quietly.

The background of Jakob materialized, and Dr. Morris found himself in the boy's bedroom. He watched through eyes he believed were his own. In the shadowy corner of the room, Jakob cried. "What's the matter?" Dr. Morris asked.

Jakob faced the wall, but his sniffles echoed in Dr. Morris' ears. "They keep doing it. They won't stop."

Dr. Morris remembered this moment. It was just a few days before Jakob had taken his own life. Dr. Morris searched for something else to say, something different that would change the events, but he only said the same thing. His mind wrestled with the unfolding scene. He wanted to scream, "Jakob, we love you and we'll be with you every step of the way. You are the world to us and when you hurt, we hurt. We can overcome this together."

Instead, what came out bordered on dismissive. Tears spilled from his eyes as he heard himself say, "Buddy, this is just a moment in time that will get better. You don't have to worry about this. We'll talk with your teacher." He knelt and hugged his son and told him it would all work out.

While embracing his son, he caught his reflection in a mirror and wanted to spit at himself. The guilt and contempt he held festered since the day he held his boy's limp body.

From behind him, Dr. Morris sensed another presence. As he held his boy in the memory, wisps of black and gray smoke danced in the corner. "I could never understand why they did that to me, Daddy," Jakob wondered.

"I don't know, son. I knew you were in pain, but I didn't know what to say. I'm a psychiatrist and should have known better," he scoffed at himself.

The shadowy figure moved towards his father and placed his hand on his shoulder. In the reality of Cullen's room, Dr. Morris felt the weight of the boy's hand.

"What would you say differently if you had known?" Jakob asked.

Dr. Morris' chest heaved. "The truth?"

"Yes, Daddy."

"I'd tell you to fight back. I would have encouraged you to stop at nothing to deliver the type of pain you'd received. I would have said, 'Jakob, do whatever it takes—even if you get hurt—to send a message to anyone who dares hurt you.' I'd tell you to keep coming, Jakob. No matter how many times you get knocked down, get up and show them you mean business."

"Even if I get hurt? What if someone makes me bleed?"

"I'd say…" Dr. Morris clenched his jaw as he delivered his advice. "I'd say you make them bleed more, Jakob! Make them hurt more! The only actual way to stop those bullies is to become a bully to them."

Jakob touched his father's face and kissed his forehead. "I wish you would have told me that, Daddy."

"I'm sorry, Jakob. I'm so sorry," Dr. Morris cried out inside *Jakob* and Cullen's room.

"I know you are, Daddy," Jakob's voice echoed. "We have to help Cullen. He needs more. Let him hear the words you always wanted to tell me, Daddy. He's strong, but he needs you."

"I know he does, my son. I'm doing everything I can to help him."

"Do more, Daddy. Let him face all of them."

"Yes. It's the only way he can heal. You're right. My goodness, you would have been an incredible psychiatrist. I love you." Dr. Morris kissed his boy and felt nothing, but the image was enough to satiate him.

He flicked the button to switch off *Jakob* and gently pulled it off his head and returned it to the night table.

"What is it you need to tell me?" Cullen begged Zeke and Val.

Val started walking back to the house. "Are you two coming?" Zeke and Cullen caught up with her. "Something's wrong with *Jakob*."

"What do you mean?"

"Exactly that, man," Zeke said. "Things got weird. Someone else started showing up inside."

"Who?"

"Think," Val probed, rolling her eyes.

Cullen thought of the shadowy boy, how he started appearing inside *Jakob* and in his sketches. "Okay. Yes, there's a boy. He wasn't there when I was in the hospital, right?" Cullen scoured his mind.

"Yes, it wasn't until you were home that he started showing up," Zeke reminded him.

"Who is he?"

"It's Jakob," Val revealed.

"Wait, what the heck are you guys talking about?"

"Jakob lives inside *Jakob*. It's a home made for him," Zeke added.

"That doesn't make any sense."

"Oh my goodness, Cullen. Who made *Jakob*?" Val asked, waiting for Cullen to catch up with their thinking.

"Dr. Morris."

"Okay, who is *Jakob* named after?" Zeke continued leading Cullen.

"He named it after his son." Then as if it hits him all at once. "He *named* it after his son. But why would his son just start showing up?"

"We don't know, man. All we know is once that kid started showing up, we found ourselves gradually pushed out until..." Zeke started.

"...we found you at Watkins Bridge," Val finished.

"I don't understand. This kid's been showing up in my sketches. It's strange," Cullen confessed, as they approached the window of his bedroom. Suddenly, he heard a voice, and the three of them put their backs against the house. "Is that Dr. Morris?"

"Sounds like it," Zeke nodded.

"What the heck is he doing in my room?"

Val shrugged her shoulders and pointed to her ear and then the window.

They heard Dr. Morris say, "I know he does, my son. I'm doing everything I can to help him. Yes. It's the only way he can heal. You're right. My goodness, you would have been an incredible psychiatrist. I love you."

Cullen twisted his mouth. "What was that?" he whispered to Val and Zeke. They put their hands up as an answer eluded them.

Val suggested, "You better get inside. Find out but be careful. Don't let on about what you've heard."

"Why not?"

"I don't know. It just feels like a bad idea," Val said.

"Okay. We'll catch up later."

Cullen snuck around the house and slipped inside. He opened the door to his bedroom and acted surprised to see Dr. Morris there. "Whatcha doing in my room?"

"Oh, hello Cullen. I-I," Dr. Morris started. "My goodness, you gave me quite the scare. I didn't think anyone was home." Cullen noticed drops of sweat form on Dr. Morris' forehead.

"Sorry next time, I'll announce my arrival," he feigned a chuckle. "Imagine how scared I was to see a grown man in my room. Right? So, why are you here?"

"I'm sorry Cullen. I didn't mean to invade your privacy. As you know, I've been updating some of the software in *Jakob,* and I needed access. Wait until you see how clear the graphics are now. I just gave him a whirl."

"Him?"

"Pardon me?"

"You said that you gave *him* a whirl."

"I did?" Cullen nodded. "Him. *Jakob.* You know I named it after my boy, after all. I guess I just feel such a strong connection to him. It. Whatever." The two stared at each other for an uncomfortable moment before Dr. Morris collected himself, took off his glasses to clean them, and asked. "So, you're home early. Is everything okay?"

Cullen naturally moved into therapy mode, which is where Dr. Morris wanted him. "Today? Today couldn't have gone any worse. I'm not sure if you've talked to my mother yet, but Mr. Reid is missing."

"Missing? Who said that?"

"It's all anybody was talking about at school. Then the police pulled me out of class."

Dr. Morris, who just sat down on Cullen's bed, shot up. "Why would the police pull you out of class?"

Cullen felt a wave of embarrassment wash over him. "Because I was at Mr. Reid's house yesterday. Before dinner."

"Why were you there?"

"Me and a couple of friends thought it would be funny to egg his house. You know, after what he did to me in class. We didn't think we'd get in trouble."

"Oh, Cullen," Dr. Morris fretted, not out of disappointment, but something else that Cullen couldn't quite put his finger on. "What friends?"

"You don't know them. It doesn't matter. The police acted like I had something to do with his disappearance."

Dr. Morris gulped hard. "That's preposterous."

"Well, whatever that word means, the cops don't think so. They have a video from a neighbor. I don't know if I'm on it or not, but there was a lady who saw us and chased us away."

"Like from a doorbell camera?"

"Maybe a neighbor across the street caught what I was doing?"

"Did they actually see you do something to Mr. Reid?" Dr. Morris asked.

"If they did, I imagine I'd be in jail right now. The officers said they were going through the footage."

"Were they the same officers from the other night?"

"Yup."

"It feels like the world is collapsing around me again. It all started with that video. I'm sure Evan had something to do with it. I wish he never existed."

Dr. Morris grew silent. The weight of something held him in place.

"Dr. Morris?"

He snapped his head up. "Yes."

"Everything fine?"

"Yes, I was just thinking about my boy. You know, when things started going bad for him, I never really listened. I figured it was something that would work itself out."

"That must have been hard."

"I made a promise at his funeral that I would listen better, especially for those closest to me who are crying for help. That's my promise to you, Cullen."

"Just talking about it always makes me feel better, so thanks." Cullen wanted to mention what he heard inside his room, but it felt as if it were less important at that very moment.

CHAPTER 40

AS EVENING FELL, CULLEN laid on his bed. He hadn't heard from Lori all afternoon and now that he'd had taken the time to recover from his day, he texted her. **Hey**

Three dots showed she was answering back, disappeared, and then showed again. It was a while before the message went through. Finally, a simple message appeared, too short for the time it took to write, **Hey**

Cullen waited before responding. When he couldn't take it any longer, he typed, **Everything all right?**

Again, he waited. Finally, she responded. **Cullen, what the heck is going on? There are all sorts of rumors flying around school.**

Bout what? Mr. Reid?

Of course, Mr. Reid. What else? People are labeling you. Have u seen the things out there?

No. I've had my phone off. Needed a break.

Three dots again. Finally, the message came through and a video popped up. Across the top it read, *Where's Mr. Reid?* The video was of Cullen angrily holding his desk in Mr. Reid's class. To the left of the video, the text read, *Wanna Bet This Guy Knows?*

The lyrics to *Bohemian Rhapsody* played on a loop, "Mama, just killed a man. Mama, just killed a man." Cullen sat up in his bed.

"What the hell is this?" he cried out.

He responded. ***Lori. I had nothing 2 do with Mr. Reid. We just egged his house. That's it.***

No text came through for two minutes. Then finally, she responded, ***Y were the police at school? Were u arrested?***

What?! No. Cause I didn't do anything. I'm home. Sitting on my bed. Not in jail, Cullen punched out in frustration.

I don't. I can't.

What do u mean?

After a long pause, Lori responded, ***My parents won't let me see u anymore.***

I thought u said u'd be there for me.

I know what I said, but... Three dots emerged again. After a moment, she responded, ***I'm sry.***

But... was all Cullen managed.

In frustration, he threw his phone down on his bed. His spirit, filled with hope just days ago, now felt crushed. The feeling of inevitability settled in his mind once again: Helplessness. Hopelessness.

The phone buzzed, and Cullen jolted up. Maybe it was Lori. Instead, it was just a notification. Cullen swiped up and opened Instagram and found Lori's profile and clicked on the first image. As he scrolled through her pictures of them together, both a smile and a tear developed. What he felt about these pictures was something special. Happiness. Yes, he understood the idea was a normal thing, but never for him. It seemed like something reserved for other people. He thumbed to a picture that made Cullen laugh. He, Lori, Chandler, and Tasha enjoying a day at the mall, standing in front of a bunch of mannequins in a storefront window. The four of them posed in goofy, mannequin-like poses with funny faces. The post read, *Happiest days of our lives*. Before he scrolled up to the next photo, something caught his eye.

A shadowy reflection in the store window. At first, Cullen thought it was a reflection of someone walking by or a trick the lighting played with the photo, but when he pinched the photo to get a closer look, he nearly dropped his phone. Buried inside the shadows was a boy's face. The one he'd sketched several times now. Jakob's face. "What in the world?" he whispered to himself.

On the second look, it looked as if Jakob was posing with the group. He rubbed his eyes, thinking it was just his eyes playing tricks on him, but when he opened them again, he was there. *How many other pictures are you in?* he wondered, but unsure he wanted to know, but he had to look. Sure enough, there were other photos on Lori's feed displaying the shadowy image of Jakob. He was there on trips to the park, coffee shops, a basketball game, and Winter Formal. Whenever Cullen was in the picture, Jakob was there. And with each image, his image became bolder. Cullen's mind pulsed with confusion. *How was this possible?* There was only one person who could explain. Jakob.

Cullen grabbed the headset and sat on the floor, his sketch pad on his lap. He took a deep breath, put it on his head, and clicked the button. The familiar welcome announced itself and the light paced back and forth. Cullen allowed himself to follow the light and seconds later, an image appeared. He recognized this place. His mindroom. The four walls breathed. He watched them beat to the sound of a heart. Not Cullen's. Something else. Someone else. Cullen sat on the floor inside the room and waited. After a moment, he called out. "Jakob?" The walls pulsed. "Jakob. Come out."

From the darkness, a shadow emerged, pulling itself forward. From around Jakob, the wall attached itself like smoke that refused to dissipate but was part of the shadow. Cullen could see the boy's face. "Hello, Cullen. Did you come for help today?"

"No. I came for answers."

"Answers? Is there a memory you need access to?"

"No."

"I'm confused. What is it?"

Cullen inhaled deeply and cleared his mind. "Are you always like this? Is there a way you can sit with me as the boy you were?"

"I can." Jakob stepped forward, shedding the cloak of dark shadows. What emerged was a young boy in shorts and t-shirt. Freckles and a missing tooth completed his boyish looks.

"That's better. I knew you were just a boy, but it's nice to see you like this. Jakob, why did you show up in my memories? You weren't there before."

"My father thought it was a good idea that you and I spend time together. We have a lot in common."

"But Jakob, you are dead. Right?"

"Yes," the boy looked down at his feet.

"So, how is this possible?"

"My father put me in here, silly. To help you."

"Help me?"

"Yes. He put me here to help you sort through your frustrations. Cullen, you are becoming very strong."

"It doesn't feel that way."

"Not yet."

"Why are you showing me those things? Those bad things? To Daryl and...and to Mr. Reid?"

"Because Cullen, your mind tells me that these are things you wanted to do." Cullen sat up straight. The walls inside the mindroom reverberated. Jakob looked at the walls. "Is that not true?"

"I don't know," Cullen admitted.

"I can't possibly know things unless you think or feel them. You wanted that to happen to Daryl. It was you who didn't want to stop at breaking his finger. You wanted to rip the entire thing off."

Cullen breathed heavily. He wanted to deny it, but it was true. "I did. I wanted to send him a message."

"There's no denying who you are, even if you aren't that way all the time. But, it's in there."

"What about what happened after Daryl got off the bus that night?"

"What about it? Didn't you want that to happen to him?"

"I don't know. That seemed extreme."

"But you didn't mind that it happened." It wasn't a question.

"If you're asking me if he deserved it, then the answer is yes."

"Don't they all? That's what your mind is telling me." The walls pulsed as a blood red color seeped into it, replacing the black.

"What about Mr. Reid?"

"Yes?"

"Did I feel he deserved that, too?"

"Only you can answer that, but..."

Cullen swallowed hard as the next question rose in his throat, but he was afraid he wouldn't like the answer. "Jakob. Did I do those things to Daryl and Mr. Reid?" A tsunami of red rippled through the walls and screamed as if in pain, waiting for the answer.

"Does it matter if it was you?"

"Yes. More than anything else, it matters."

"Cullen, as much as you agree with their punishments, it wasn't you."

"Oh God," Cullen called out as waves of relief overcame him. The walls of the room relaxed and changed to a sunset orange. "Then who was it?"

"Shh," Jakob put a finger to his lips. "That's a secret, but just know that it was done to protect you."

"Protect me?"

"Yes. There are others too."

"Others?" Panic edged in Cullen's voice.

"You will find out soon enough. When the time is right"

"I never asked for this."

"But isn't it what's needed? Getting back at those people. They are like the monsters that did the same things to me. Made me feel small. Unwanted. Unloved. Made me feel terrible about myself as they tortured me. This is why my dad brought us together. Who better to help you than someone who has been where you are?"

"Jakob. This isn't what I want."

"Zeke and Val said the same things."

"Is that why you got rid of them?"

"They were just holding you back. Interested in playing children's games instead of dealing with the problem. Egging a house?"

"But aren't you just a child?"

"I was, but I had to grow up fast. Just like you."

"I liked having Zeke and Val here. I felt safe."

"What does it matter? You have them on the outside."

Cullen thought about bringing up their concerns, but his mind shifted back to the boy in front of him. Dr. Morris had told him about the bullying. The decision to end everything. "Jakob, what happened to you? I only know what your father told me."

"You know I was bullied."

"I do."

Suddenly, the walls of the mindroom revealed Jakob walking home from his bus stop. Lip bloodied. "During the two weeks when it started, it just got worse and worse. One day, one of them led a group of kids off the bus. It wasn't even their bus stop. They surrounded me and shoved me around the circle." Jakob narrated the scene unfolding on the walls. Cullen watched as each person took turns pushing Jakob. The kids hurled insults at him.

Baby Punch.

You can't get anything right.

Squirrel.

You'll never have any friends.

Jakob tried to exit the circle and run away to the safety of his house.

"When I realized they wouldn't let me go, I fought back. It was my only chance to escape. So, I swung as hard as I could and hit one kid." Cullen watched as Jakob connected with one boy. The boy fell to the ground. Everyone, including Jakob, looked astonished.

Get out of there! Cullen thought.

"I started running, but they were too fast." Jakob pointed to the scene again of him walking with a fat, bloody lip. "It wasn't my first fat lip, but it was my last."

"Is that why you did what you did?"

"What was it that I did?"

"Commit suicide."

"I never wanted to die."

"But I thought that's what happened to you."

"I've always had trouble in school. Out of my seat all the time. Paying attention to everything around me. Calling out. Teachers didn't know what to do with me. The word ADHD was passed around, and my father put me on medication that made me feel like a zombie. So, he experimented with different types for me. He gave this orange tasting pill that tasted good, but it still made me tired. So, my teachers went from complaining that I was too hyper and started saying I wasn't paying attention because I was zoning out. So, I stopped taking the pills. I thought I could just force myself to pay attention, be a better friend, and make my teachers like me. I tried to be normal."

The walls showed Jakob sitting at the table with the bottle of pills in his hand. He opened it up and, one after another, put them into his mouth.

Cullen stood up and called out to the horrific scene, "Jakob, stop! Stop!" Tears formed in his eyes as he ran to the walls. He pleaded with Jakob as he watched him empty the bottle into his mouth. "Why? Why would you do that? You said you didn't take your life!"

"That's true."

"But..." Cullen watched Jakob sit on the couch and turn the television on. Time passed and Jakob dropped to the floor and a seizure took over his body.

"I just wanted to be normal. I figured if people expected me to be normal, the only way I could be was with the pills. That way, I would behave like everyone needed me to. I'm just a kid. I didn't know."

"Oh, Jakob. It was an accident?" Although he witnessed the horror, the realization oddly relieved him—not that Jakob hadn't taken his own life, but that what he'd endured hadn't driven him to the edge that Cullen visited in his own thoughts.

"Jakob, answer me this. Why is it you've shown me these horrible things?"

"Because, Cullen, I want to protect you."

"I appreciate that. Can you answer me another question? How is it you've shown up in pictures outside of the device?"

"*How* isn't really important. I never got to do the things you are doing in your life. Hanging out with friends. Doing things. Freedom." Jakob walked backwards towards the wall as long tongues of black reached out for him and welcomed him back into it.

When Cullen pulled *Jakob* off his head, he looked down at the sketch pad. He sketched a snapshot of Jakob sitting at a table in a kitchen. Pills scattered across the table in front of him. A prescription bottle rested in his hands. Cullen looked closer at the bottle. Adzenys. Cullen reached for his phone and looked it up. The internet revealed it was a drug for Attention Deficit Hyperactive Disorder designed to have a desirable taste for children who struggle to swallow pills. Another search found the effects of an overdose including seizure, coma, and death. Cullen looked up from his phone. His heart broke for Jakob. Cullen stirred inside, yet he felt his energy strangely restored.

Learning that he wasn't responsible for Daryl and Mr. Reid was also a relief. But if it wasn't him, then who?

Outside his room, he heard the front door close. Seconds later, he heard a knock at his door. His mother came in, "Hey, you. Got a minute?"

"Of course," Cullen said, moving his sketch pad to his night table.

"I've got ice cream." Cullen rolled his eyes. "Too big to have a bowl of ice cream with your mother?"

"Never," Cullen smiled. "Where's Dr. Morris?"

"Oh, he got a call and needed to be back at the hospital. I don't know how he does it. Always on call. Always having to listen to people's problems." Cullen shrugged his shoulders. "I'm still angry at you, you know. Egging someone's house?"

"That's the least of it. Have they heard anything about Mr. Reid?" Silence settled between them as Margaret shook her head. "You believe me that I had nothing to do with whatever happened to him, right?"

She scooped in the spoonful of chocolate before answering. "I'm one hundred percent sure. You would never, but I don't think the police will stop questioning you until he's found...hopefully safe."

"It's all just so crazy," Cullen acknowledged.

"It is. How are you doing, you know, with all of this?"

"Considering Lori broke up with me?"

Margaret gasped, "Oh no, Cullen. I'm so sorry."

"Her parents said she's not allowed to see me. It sucks, but I get it. They gotta protect their daughter."

"From whom?" Margaret questioned, already knowing the answer. She put her hand on Cullen's neck, just below the ear, and gently squeezed.

"The freak from Arlington." Cullen smiled as conflicted thoughts consumed him.

"Oh, you stop that talk. After this all gets resolved, we'll get you back on track."

"Is it okay if I take a couple of days off from school? Everything I'll need is online."

"Of course, I don't blame you. But don't fall behind." Cullen nodded as his mother grabbed his bowl and stacked it upon her own. "Get some sleep. I'll see you in the morning."

Cullen crossed his fingers behind his head and stared at the ceiling. Thoughts raced, crisscrossed, and collided through his mind. Part of him still felt unstable, but after talking with Jakob—whether or not he was real—a sense of clarity washed over him.

CHAPTER 41

MARGARET GLANCED AT THE clock in the kitchen. 9:05. Late again for work. She'd spent much of the hours before midnight waiting to hear from Dr. Morris before going to bed. He usually would text an update, but it wasn't unusual for her to wait a while for a response. No response came, and she dozed off on the couch. When she woke suddenly at two in the morning, she reached across to the coffee table for her phone. A lone text waited for her. ***Sorry, my dear. We had a situation with a patient. So as not to wake you, I'm going to head to my place tonight. It's been a few days, anyway. Need to make sure the place hasn't burned to the ground. Ha ha. See you tomorrow evening?***

Margaret threw a makeshift lunch into a bag and collected her keys. The news, which was on every morning, served more as background noise and updates on the weather. A report started that caught Margaret's ear. She dropped everything and listened.

"Thank you, Susan. I'm here outside Arlington High School where beloved teacher, Jonathan Reid, has been missing for several days now. Mr. Reid didn't report to school yesterday. This wouldn't normally be a concern because he hadn't been missing very long, but his car was found in the driveway with the door open and the keys still inside. Police suspect foul play, since there appeared to be signs of a struggle. Police are working on some leads thanks to doorbell camera footage from neighboring homes. Needless to say, nerves are rattled in this usually quiet neighborhood. We spoke to one neighbor, who preferred to not have her face shown."

"I heard a noise like a kid laughing and shouting. I looked outside my window and saw someone. It was getting dark when I ran outside, but I saw someone throwing eggs at Jonathan's house. At the time, I thought it was just a thoughtless prank, but now I'm scared because that could have been the person involved with his disappearance."

"Susan, when I talked with that neighbor off camera, she described Mr. Reid as a quiet neighbor who always had a smile and a wave for all the neighbors. The school's planned a vigil for this evening for this beloved teacher."

Margaret put her hand to her mouth. *Beloved teacher? After what he did to Cullen? Maybe he'll learn a lesson.* She felt slightly guilty about thinking this, but she shifted her thoughts to Cullen. It was best he didn't go to school today. She wondered when, if ever, it would be okay for him to return. She jotted down a note for Cullen. *Get some rest today. Love you!*

Later that afternoon, Margaret sat at her desk. After ignoring phone calls from an unknown number, she finally answered in an exasperated tone, "Yes, Margaret here. How can I help you?"

"Hello, Mrs. Hickey."

"Look, if you are trying to sell me something, I'm not interested. Please remove my name from this calling list."

"Mrs. Hickey. It's Officer Mead from the Arlington Police Department."

"Oh, my goodness, I'm so embarrassed. Please forgive me." Then a realization washed over her. "Is there something wrong with Cullen? Please don't tell me there's something else. I don't think I could handle one more thing."

"Well, that's why I'm calling. I wanted to tell you this in person, but I thought you should know this immediately."

"Okay, Officer Mead. You're scaring me."

"We looked over additional doorbell camera footage and we've concluded that Cullen had nothing to do with Mr. Reid's disappearance."

Tears filled her eyes and relief settled in. "Oh, my goodness, thank you. Thank you. I told you he had nothing to do with it." For the first time, she was one hundred percent sure of it.

"Yes, Ma'am."

"Is that it?"

"No, Ma'am."

"Of course not. What else is there?"

"In looking over that video footage from other neighbors, we could see that evening from different angles."

"Were you able to see who did it?"

"I'm not able to discuss this with you, but I will say it definitely wasn't Cullen."

"So, what else did you find?"

"It's Cullen, Ma'am."

"But you said–"

"Yes, he's in the clear. However, his story doesn't add up."

"Excuse me?"

"Cullen mentioned that he went to Mr. Reid's house with some friends."

"Okay. But–"

"Ma'am, listen," Officer Mead pleaded. "Cullen was there alone."

Margaret furrowed her eyebrows. "What do you mean *alone*? Are you sure?"

"Ma'am, without a shadow of a doubt. In one video, Cullen appears to be talking to someone just off camera, but in reviewing the new footage, it shows there was no one there. He...he wasn't talking to anyone."

"What the hell are you talking about? He was there with friends."

"I know this is shocking news, but as a parent myself, I wanted to call you. He was certainly not there with anyone else. I rarely do this, but I can send you one of the videos. What's your email address?" Margaret was silent. After some moments, Officer Mead asked, "Mrs. Hickey?"

"I'm here," Margaret finally choked out.

"May I have your email address? I can send the video over to you."

"Yes, sorry," Margaret felt her chest tighten.

Seconds later, the email came through, no subject. Nothing was written in the text's body. Just the video with the title *APD Reid Evid. #3*. Margaret closed the door to her office and sat down at her desk. Her hand shook, and she brought the mouse to the icon and clicked. The video popped onto the screen, and Margaret clicked play.

The video showed the back of what was undeniably Cullen. It started off with him throwing three eggs, which found their mark on the front of the house. Then his attention turned to the short bushes where cartons of eggs were sitting upon. It looked like he was listening to someone. Cullen picked up another egg and shouted, "I hate him!" The egg flew through the open door of Mr. Reid's car. "I won't let him do that again to me! Take that!" Cullen frantically grabbed one egg after another until he bent over, seemingly exhausted. He stood up, looking towards the bushes again. "I do. I really do!" he shouted. Cullen high fived...the air.

Then someone off camera yelled something which Margaret couldn't make out, but Cullen looked towards the street and shouted, "Oh crap! Let's get out of here!" Cullen turned and ran down the street. Alone.

Margaret's heart thumped in her chest. *Who were you talking to, Cullen?* Her eyes flicked back and forth as if the answer was somewhere in the office. As the room spun, she scrubbed through the video three times before rushing to the bathroom to throw up. Tumultuous thoughts flooded her mind. Dr. Morris. He'd know what to do. He always knew the right thing to say.

She texted him, ***Joshua. Call me as soon as you get this. It's important.*** No response. She sent four more texts and still he didn't respond.

She called him. Straight to voicemail. She pleaded, "Joshua, call me! Something's up with Cullen. I don't know what to do."

She watched the video several more times, pausing it and pinching the still frame to enlarge it. Hoping. Praying that she would find whoever Cullen was talking to. But after scanning and scrubbing, she was convinced there was no one else. After several attempts to call and text Cullen and Dr. Morris, she fell back into a chair, buried her face in her hands, and cried. "Why isn't anyone answering me?" she whispered between tears.

CHAPTER 42

LATE IN THE AFTERNOON, a clap of thunder shook Cullen from his nap on the couch. The sound of rain pattered against the windowpane. He tossed and turned all night, unable to turn his mind off. The conversation with Jakob had stirred the deeper parts of him. Each time he closed his eyes, the story about how Jakob died jolted him awake. He screamed and begged for the boy to stop taking the pills.

With every evening's stirrings, new questions arose. Had Dr. Morris altered the way *Jakob* worked? And what was he really doing in his room yesterday? Cullen wished he hadn't spoiled his chance to confront him yesterday. What happened to Mr. Reid? And who beat up Daryl? He longed to talk with Zeke and Val. They always knew what to say.

Cullen picked up his phone and saw that he'd missed several calls from his mother. As he was going to listen to the voicemail, his phone chimed. A text message from Dr. Morris. ***Cullen. Can you come out to St. Mary's? I want to share something with you. Upgrades. A new prototype, like Jakob.***

I really can't leave. It's raining like crazy out. Can't u bring it back to the house? Cullen texted back.

Well, I was hoping for you to see it in action. I'm very excited for you to see what I've added. Bus 15 will take you straight to St. Mary's. Please, Cullen.

After moments of thinking, Cullen finally agreed. ***The next bus is at 3:45. I can catch that one.***

Great. I will see you around 4:30. You won't be disappointed, Dr. Morris responded.

Cullen placed the phone next to him and wondered about Dr. Morris' request. His stomach tightened and couldn't quite get the feeling why, but he knew he had to go. The feeling there was something more loomed greater. Something beyond *Jakob*. One thing he knew for sure: he didn't want to go alone.

He dressed quickly and left a note for his mother instead of texting because he didn't want to answer questions. *Beg for forgiveness later*, he decided. He threw his hoodie over his head and struggled to dodge the large, cold raindrops as he bounded to the bus stop a block away.

By the time the bus pulled up precisely at 3:45, the storm unleashed its fury with a blinding rain. Cullen's shoes squished as he stepped on the empty bus and pulled out his phone to scan his ticket. He recognized the bus driver from the night with Daryl and his buddies.

"You aren't going to make trouble, are you?" the bus driver asked.

"No, sir. I'll even sit right up front if you like," Cullen stuttered nervously. To his surprise, the bus driver smiled pleasantly as Cullen sat down in the front seat. He looked down at his phone and scrolled through more images of happier times: images of he and Lori, a fun trip to the park to feed the ducks. *How had things gotten so far out of control?* he thought to himself.

"Here," the bus driver said, tossing Cullen a towel. "Don't worry, it's clean."

"Thanks," Cullen dried his face.

"I gotta tell you, I can't say that I approve of your methods, but those thugs had it coming. Picking on a kid like that," the bus driver said apologetically. Then he chuckled, "Not that you look like a kid. I bet they're gonna think twice the next time they try coming up on a fella again. It's a shame because you looked all fancy that day. Did you come from an event?"

"Winter Formal."

"Well, didn't you have a date or friends that you at least went with?"

"I did. But I...I had to leave early. Something came up. Something bad."

The bus driver's belly rolled with another chuckle. He adjusted his hat, which covered his graying hair. "Looks like bad followed you all the way to the bus."

"You're telling me. It pretty much hasn't stopped since," Cullen paused. "I'm sorry about the other night."

"Well, I'd be lying if I said you didn't give me a scare. I wasn't sure what you were gonna do after that. As I saw it going down, I was going to pull over and give those men an earful, but then you did what you did and..." he laughed again. "I didn't know who to help. You handled yourself just fine."

There was an ease about the bus driver that Cullen liked. There was no accusation in his words and his laughter made Cullen smile inside.

"I'd never won a fight before," Cullen's shoulders sank.

This time, he let out a roar of laughter. "Son, I wouldn't say that was much of a fight."

"I guess there's a first for everything."

"You sure you've never won a fight? I mean, a kid your size? I wouldn't think anyone would dare take you on."

Cullen didn't know why he was divulging this information, but the bus driver was easy to talk to. Probably part of the job. "To be honest, I've spent most of my life running from people like that."

"Is that so? It's a damn shame to hear that." Cullen put his head down. "My name's Al."

"Cullen. Nice to meet you," he stammered.

"Cullen. That's a strong name. Listen. I see something in you. You've got a good heart. Don't ask me how I know, I just have a sense about these things. Can I give you some advice? You can take it or throw it away, but I feel the need to say this." Without waiting for an answer, Al continued. "You gotta pick your head up. I noticed something during our talk. Each time you say something to me that makes you feel uncomfortable, you drop your head. You can't go through life with your head down. How are you gonna see the bright future you have ahead of you if you're looking down at your feet? You strike me as a kid who's weathered a lot of storms in your life." Cullen nodded and was careful to make sure he didn't drop his head. "See this storm brewing its way outside here? This is just a season. If you are feeling alone, just know this. It can't rain every day. It can't rain forever. So, on days it ain't storming, you gotta lift your head and enjoy the sunshine."

Cullen listened intently as emotion overcame him. He felt embarrassed, but Al's words connected with him. "Thanks, Al."

Al laughed gently. "Sounds like that was something you needed to hear. I don't know what told me this, but Cullen, you keep your head up and everything is going to work out for you." Cullen shook his head. "And do me a favor. If there's a next time you get into a scuffle, try to keep the man's finger on his hand," Al laughed from his belly again. "It was a dang mess."

"Well, I can't make any promises," Cullen smiled.

"In that case, make sure it's on someone else's bus," Al smiled back.

As the bus pulled up to the stop, Cullen stood. "Thank you for the ride...and the advice."

Al stopped the bus and put it into park. He turned toward Cullen and extended his hand. Cullen met his grip. He wondered if Al would make a joke about taking it easy, but he didn't. Instead, he offered, "Cullen, it was nice having some company today. You're going to be alright; I promise you. Just give yourself a chance."

"Thank you, sir. Have a good night. I'm sure I'll see you again sometime."

"Looking forward to it." Al looked out of the open door. "See, the rain's already letting up. I told you it can't rain forever. Be safe, Cullen."

A ray of sunshine broke through the clouds as Cullen walked off the bus. He took a moment to let it warm his face and headed towards St. Mary's.

CHAPTER 43

As HE APPROACHED St. Mary's, his phone chimed. A text from Dr. Morris. ***Don't bother heading into the main hospital. Meet me at the old wing.***

Old wing? Cullen punched into his phone.

Yes, you will need to walk around the corner. There's a gate that looks like it's locked. It's not.

Okay, but why r we meeting in the old wing? Cullen texted.

It's easier to show you. Just come through the gate and into the building straight ahead.

As the afternoon gave way to dusk, so did Cullen's courage. Confusion filled his mind as to why Dr. Morris would want to meet there. He trusted Dr. Morris, but he wished he hadn't come here alone. As if an answer to his concern, he looked ahead to the approaching corner and saw Zeke and Val. His mouth dropped in excitement, and he took to a sprint to meet them. "What are you guys doing here?"

"I don't know. Something told us you needed some help today," Val smiled, yet a seriousness loomed under the surface. Zeke nodded.

"I can't tell you how excited I am that you met me here. You guys always have a way of knowing these things."

"What can we say, man? That's what friends are for. We've got you," Zeke said, patting Cullen on the back.

"Dr. Morris was being all sus' about meeting here. He wants to show me something about *Jakob*."

"Why couldn't he just show you at home?" Zeke asked. "I told you, since he's been adding those upgrades, things have gotten weird."

"We tried to tell you," Val snapped her gum.

"Oh, I heard you. I just didn't know what to make of it."

"Well, there's no better way to find out than seeing what the man has to show you," Val said, putting out her hand for Cullen to lead the way.

When they arrived at the gate, they found the padlock opened. Cullen cautiously pushed the chain link fencing open. "So, this is where he wanted to meet you?" Zeke asked. "Doesn't the man have an office?"

The old wing of St. Mary's was an abandoned portion of the hospital, shut down after they built the new one. It was scheduled to be demolished in the spring. As the three approached, the apocalyptic feel of the building made Cullen's stomach turn. The cracks in the steps sprouted with weeds. Cullen tried to peek into the window, but black paint covered them. He found the two doors locked. Finally, the third one opened. He looked back at Zeke and Val with a concerned expression.

Margaret weaved erratically in and out of traffic. In as little as thirty minutes, her world was upended. Her heart sank the moment Officer Mead told her about Cullen. At first, she didn't believe it. How could she? These were things someone only saw in movies. But once she saw the video, the confirmation set her soul into a panic.

She raced down the block leading to home. Dark. Everything is dark. Where's Cullen? She pulled the car into the driveway and charged inside. "Cullen? Cullen?" She pushed open his bedroom door, hoping to find him sitting on the floor with *Jakob* on his head. Instead, darkness erased that hope.

She pulled out her phone and texted him, **Cullen, where are you? We need to talk.** After a few moments, she tried again, **I'm so upset right now. Where are you?**

She took in a deep breath and flopped onto the couch. Her mind ached about where he could be. Then, Cullen's note caught her eye.

Mom, Dr. Morris asked that I meet him at St. Mary's. I took the bus. He'll probably give me a ride home. Love you, Cullen.

"Wait. Why would Joshua text Cullen, but he couldn't text me back?" Margaret wondered aloud in frustration. Things weren't adding up, and the room spun wildly. She tried to get to her feet, but confusion anchored her to the sofa's cushion. *I must get to St. Mary's. I don't know how I know this, but he's in trouble.* Trouble? Officer Mead. She searched her purse and found the card she'd given her. She thumbed the phone number.

"Hello Officer Mead. It's Margaret Hickey."

"Hello, Mrs. Hickey, is everything okay?"

"I wish I could say that it was. You told me I can call you if anything comes up, right?"

"Yes, Ma'am."

Margaret took a deep breath. "Cullen's missing."

"Missing?"

"Well, not missing. I know where he's gone."

"Mrs. Hickey. That makes little sense. Are you in trouble? Can I connect you with someone to talk to?"

"I'm not crazy. Give me a second." Margaret rubbed her head, struggling to organize her thoughts. "Okay. Cullen isn't home right now. He left a note that he was going to St. Mary's to meet Dr. Morris. You remember him, right?"

"Yes, of course. But I don't see how this is an emergency. You know where he is."

"That's the problem. After you gave me the news about Cullen being at Mr. Reid's house and I watched the video, I reached out to Dr. Morris. He was Cullen's doctor when he was in the hospital."

"Yes, I remember that. Please start making sense. I don't have time for this right now."

"Dr. Morris and I have been seeing each other, which I'm sure you gathered. Every day, he would go to work at St. Mary's."

"Okay. So far, I'm not hearing anything suspicious."

"Well, I've been texting both of them all afternoon and neither of them has responded."

"It isn't a crime to not answer text messages. There could be several reasons to explain this."

"I have a sick feeling that something bad is happening. Call it mother's intuition."

"Mrs. Hickey. I'm sorry, but I don't know what you want me to do."

A desperate thought rushed to her lips, "Officer Mead. I'm concerned about Cullen's stability. Can you please, please meet me at St. Mary's?" Her heart thumped in anticipation of her answer. "Mother to mother?" she pleaded.

Officer Mead let out a long sigh. "St. Mary's Psychiatric Hospital? Okay. I'll see you there. Are you leaving now?"

"Yes. Yes. Thank you!"

Margaret rushed out of the house, into her car, and raced through the heavy rain.

Inside the old wing looked as apocalyptic as the outside. A layer of dust covered the sleek tile and discarded papers scattered across the floor as if its last inhabitants left in a hurry. A dim light shone from down the hallway. Cullen, Zeke, and Val followed it and found themselves at a door. From inside, terrified screams echoed. "Who is that?" Cullen asked, panic spilling from his voice.

"Dr. Morris?" Val whispered.

"No, that wasn't him."

"Wait. Listen," Zeke gasped.

"No, no, no. Stay away from me! Please don't..." a female voice screamed from inside begging for help.

"That's not just one person," Val said.

"Oh, God, please make it stop!" another voice shrieked.

"What should we do? Call the cops?" Cullen asked.

"Maybe it's not what we think it is," Zeke wondered, but for the first time, his voice betrayed him.

Cullen's hand trembled as he reached for the door handle. Before turning it, he looked back at Val and Zeke, who both urged him on. The handle turned with ease, and he pushed the door open slowly. At the front of what appeared to be a conference room, three chairs sat on a small stage. Duct taped to the chairs were three people, each with a *Jakob* over their eyes. Lights spotlighted each of them like stars in some twisted horror movie. Their bodies convulsed and jerked in panic. Screams, now clearer, were deafening as if each one was experiencing excruciating pain or panic.

Shocked, Cullen, Val, and Zeke walked down one aisle toward the front. Cullen climbed onto the small stage while Zeke and Val looked on. He stood in front of the three. Deep down, he knew who they were, but denied himself the answer.

From behind, Dr. Morris startled him. "Isn't this fantastic?" he asked in a peppy voice that didn't match the moment.

"Dr. Morris. What's going on? Who are these people?"

"Oh, Cullen, my boy, do you not recognize them?"

"It's a little hard to tell," he lied. "Why don't you tell me?"

"They're your predators. Here in chair number one is the man-child himself who doesn't know how to leave well enough alone. Mr. Reid."

Mr. Reid, who sat in his bloodstained shirt, cried out, "Who's there? C'mon. Get me out of here! Whatever it is, I'm sure we can talk about it! Please. Please, let me go!"

"Pathetic," Dr. Morris called out and then pushed a button on a device he held.

"No, not again! Please!" He pressed his back against the chair as if something were in his face and he desperately didn't want it to touch him.

"This lovely lady right here is Claire. She led you to the darkest of places. Remember how she tormented you and embarrassed you in school? She made you feel so insignificant."

Dr. Morris clicked the button again, and Claire jolted back into her seat. "No! Don't. Don't touch my face! No one is going to think I'm pretty! Please stop!" She screamed and her head thrashed back and as if someone were striking her. "I'm bleeding!"

"And in chair number three is a genuine celebrity," Dr. Morris announced and waved his hand as if he were revealing a secret prize behind a curtain. "I'd venture to say if you're Batman, this here is the Joker. Evan Stephens, who single-handedly made your life a living hell. With every insult, every punch, he reduced you to a mere shell of yourself."

"Who's there? How do you know my name? When I get out of here, I'm gonna–" Dr. Morris pressed the button and Evan's attention pulled somewhere else. "Why are you here? Stop it. Don't touch me. Please. Nooo!"

"But why, Dr. Morris?" Cullen asked.

"Why?" Dr. Morris laughed as if the answer was obvious. "What an odd question. Cullen, these people right here are the bad guys in your world. It's time they learn what it's like to be hunted. Don't you think? This right here is how you get to show your strength. You finally get to show them what actual power is." He balled his hand into a fist and held it up.

As Dr. Morris stepped into the light, Cullen noticed his bloodshot eyes and messy hair as if he'd been up all night. "Dr. Morris. You're not thinking straight." Cullen looked over at Val and Zeke, their faces encouraging him.

"As you will see, Cullen. I'm thinking very straight. This here is the solution."

"Why are they each wearing a *Jakob*?"

"Because this is the ultimate crash course in EMDR Exposure Therapy. I told you I made some upgrades to *Jakob*. I've created the most authentic viewing experience. Real enough to trick the mind. So, I'm not really doing anything to them. They're facing their fears. Looks like they have lots of them. See, they're not that different from you."

"Why are they reacting like that?"

"Because of this." Dr. Morris held up what appeared to be a small remote control with three buttons on it. "Every time I push one of these buttons, I force them to face all their fears at once. Want to give it a whirl?" he asked, smiling deviously.

"I'd rather not."

"Cullen, I'm so disappointed. I've served them up on a golden platter for you. I thought you would be delighted."

"Delighted? Dr. Morris, I don't want to hurt anyone."

"Technically, you aren't hurting anyone. They are just fighting with their own demons."

"But why?"

Then Mr. Reid shouted, "Hey. Whoever's there? Please. Please let me go. I've got a family!"

"You're a liar. You have no one waiting for you at home," Dr. Morris spat. He pressed the button on the remote control.

Mr. Reid flailed his head back and forth. "Not again." He shouted at the images inside *Jakob* while his body convulsed.

Dr. Morris marveled at hearing his screams before releasing the button. "Cullen, how can you ask me why? This is how we get our revenge."

"Our revenge? What do they have to do with you?"

"Everything!" Dr. Morris shouted with a laugh. He took his glasses off, held them up to the light and cleaned them. "These people are the same ones responsible for the death of my son. You know this."

"Dr. Morris, these people did nothing to Jakob."

"The faces change, but their actions are always the same. Always the same, Cullen. This is our chance."

"No. We have to let them go."

"Let them go?" Dr. Morris scoffed. "Cullen, I've seen your drawings. I thought *Jakob* was helping you. He brought you out of that catatonic state and back to your mother. However, as I looked through your drawings, I knew you would never truly get better until you actually got to face off against them. To give them the same torment they delivered to you. Now's your chance. We've got them right here," Dr. Morris passed his hand in front of him as if he were revealing a surprise.

"This isn't what I want."

"Isn't it? Don't deny that it didn't feel good to stand up to those hooligans on the bus ride." Cullen didn't respond, but his mind raced. "I'll take your silence as a yes. How could it not? I felt such satisfaction after I took care of that thug afterwards."

"Daryl?"

"Yes."

"But how did you know where I was?"

"Ah, your mother's phone. She's got that tracking app. She's always forgetting about it. I convinced her a while ago that as your doctor, it may be important to know your whereabouts in case of an emergency, so I downloaded an app to keep track of you. Lori called her to say you had left the dance. So, I looked at your mother's phone and found out where you were. When I saw you getting off that bus, and the condition of that other guy, I knew that he and his friends had harassed you. So, I followed him and when he wasn't looking, I beat him senseless with a trash can lid. I imagined it would be hard, but when I thought about what my boy went through in his brief life, the fat lips and endless tears, it was freeing. Even easy."

"Wait, that was you? And you let me doubt myself?! I mean, the police came and questioned me. Dr. Morris. How could you?"

"Oh, Cullen, you would never get in trouble for that. If it had gotten to that point, I would have handled it."

Upon hearing this information, Evan shouted out. "I don't know what you two are talking about, but you keep saying Cullen. Is that the Cullen that I know?!" Dr. Morris put his finger on his lips to tell Cullen not to speak. "If that's you, freak, you're in big trouble! You are going down for this once I get out of here!"

"See, you will always be nothing in the eyes of these people. They will keep coming and coming and coming. Just push the button. Take it for a spin. It's liberating!"

Cullen wanted to give Evan what he deserved. "Okay." He reached out his hand to Dr. Morris' delight.

Margaret marched up to the front desk of St. Mary's. Officers Mead and Kowalski followed her from a distance. An older lady looked up from her computer. "Well, hello there, Mrs. Hickey. How's Cullen doing? I'll tell you what, he was one of those kids that the entire office staff here was really rooting for. What brings you back here?"

"Hi, Janet. I know that this may sound weird, but have you seen Cullen? He left me a message that he was coming here to see Dr. Morris. I've been texting both of them but haven't gotten a response." As she said the words, more waves of nausea gripped at her stomach.

"Mrs. Hickey, did you say Dr. Morris?"

"Yes. Dr. Morris. Cullen's doctor?"

"Yes, of course, I know that. Sorry."

Margaret drew in a deep breath as she felt her patience waning. "Well, have you seen either of them?"

"Mrs. Hickey. I don't think you understand. Dr. Morris took a leave of absence back in January. Two months ago."

Margaret's face looked as if someone had slapped her. "No." She looked back at the officers and then back to Janet. "That can't be true. Perhaps there's a different Dr. Morris. Joshua Morris?"

"Mrs. Hickey. I assure you we only have one Dr. Morris, and he took a leave of absence in mid-January."

"Are you sure?" Margaret's voice wavered.

"Yes, of course I am," Janet smiled uncomfortably.

Margaret looked around the hospital lobby as if he'd come in at any moment. "That can't be right." She looked at Janet, who pursed her lips. "Then where the hell has he been going every day?!" Margaret slapped the counter with both hands, causing Janet to bolt up from her desk and back away.

"I'm sorry. But he hasn't been here," she whispered and continued to back up as if at any moment Margaret would be upon her.

Officer Mead stepped forward and whispered in Margaret's ear, "Mrs. Hickey. You heard what she said. How about we let Officer Kowalski talk with the nice lady, and we can go outside and make sense of things?"

Margaret broke into tears. "Where's he been going all this time? I feel like such a fool."

Officer Mead looked at her partner and nodded. "It's okay, Mrs. Hickey. I'm sure there's a logical explanation. Let's go outside." She directed Margaret to the exit.

Once outside, Margaret placed her hands on her knees and struggled to catch her breath against the cold air. *He's been lying to me the whole time.* Her mind churned with confusion. The one person who would have answers was a liar. "He's living a double life. No. That's not right. It's an alternate life. Completely different. I'm such an idiot!"

"Like I said, Mrs. Hickey. I'm sure there's an explanation here," Officer Mead attempted to reassure.

"What could that possibly be?" Margaret's mind sprinted. "He didn't have time for anything else. He was always so–" she stopped herself as a storm of thoughts overwhelmed her.

Of course, he had time for other things.

If he wasn't going to work all these days, then what the hell was he doing?

If he wasn't getting called out for emergencies at the hospital, where was he going?

What I should be worrying about is Cullen and not some person who's been lying to me.

After all the pain she'd been through, she was angry at herself for finally letting her guard down. "Stupid. Stupid. What was I thinking?" she questioned while thumping her palm against her forehead.

"I'm sorry, Mrs. Hickey. I truly am," Officer Mead said.

Just then, Officer Kowalski came through the door of the hospital.

"Is it true?" Margaret asked, clinging to the hope that this was all a nightmare.

"I'm afraid so. She showed me the paperwork for his request," Officer Kowalski confirmed.

"I feel sick. Did you see Cullen in there?" Margaret's desperation continued.

"No, Ma'am. Are you sure he came here?" Officer Kowalski asked.

"Well, that's what his note said. Where else could he be?"

"I don't mean this to sound disrespectful, but since we've met Cullen, he's been all over the place. Watkins Bridge. Mr. Reid's house. Places that you never expected," Officer Kowalski pointed out.

"This isn't a part of his usual behavior," Margaret gritted out.

Officer Mead put a hand on Officer Kowalski's shoulder to say ease up. "Mrs. Hickey. Do you happen to have an app that can show Cullen's whereabouts on your phone?"

Margaret's eyes lit up. "Yes! She fumbled for her phone and opened the app. "C'mon. C'mon. Okay, here it is." She looked at the icon for Cullen. "See, it says he's here," Margaret sounded confident. "Right here at St. Mary's."

"May I?" She handed the phone over to Officer Mead.

Officer Kowalski looked over her shoulder. "He's not *here*."

"What?" Margaret asked.

"This area here is the hospital. Cullen's icon is in the old wing, which was shut down after they built the new hospital."

"Where is that?"

"Right around the corner," Officer Mead replied. "It's completely abandoned. The city's got it scheduled for demolition."

"That can't be good. If that's where Cullen is, then we've got to get there right now," Margaret pleaded as her stomach sank.

Officer Mead suggested to her partner, "Let's call for another black and white, just out of caution."

As Officer Kowalski clicked the mic on his shoulder, Margaret asked, "A black and white?"

"We're calling for backup. Let's head over there. Mrs. Hickey, I know you may want to rush in there to make sure he's safe, but please allow us to go in first. Okay?" Margaret agreed. "Let's go."

Cullen stared at the remote control. In his hands rested the power to get back at these people who have teased and tormented him. The point that he could exact revenge on these people scared him and excited him at the same time. It wouldn't be all of them, but it would be a start. When he looked at Zeke and Val, their stares concerned him. He wondered what they were thinking, but they stood silently. Finally, Val shook her head.

"Before I do this, Dr. Morris. I want to let you know something about Jakob."

"The VR set?"

"No. Your son."

Dr. Morris pinched his eyebrows. "What is it you can tell me about my boy?"

"If you've seen my drawings, then you know he started showing up in my sessions. He started as a shadow and, as I continued using *Jakob*, I saw him more and more. I'm guessing that you knew that and that's why you continued to make changes to *Jakob*. Upgrades."

"Yes. They are astounding, aren't they?"

Cullen didn't answer. "I only found out much later that it was your son. Soon, he was the only one that showed up in my sessions. I'm guessing that's when you started using *Jakob*."

"I felt guilty about that, Cullen. I really did. But the upgrades to *Jakob* brought my son back to me. I know it's not real, but I feel as if I got to spend time with him."

"I spent time with him too." Cullen paused. Dr. Morris stared in disbelief. "He dropped hints to me about everything that you did. To Daryl. To Mr. Reid. I bet if I put *Jakob* on right now, he would show me what you did to Evan and Claire." Cullen took a deep breath before asking, "How could you do those things, Dr. Morris?"

"What do you mean? I did that for you. Now you have the opportunity to stand up to them. To take back your power." He clenched a fist.

"But at what cost?" Cullen ran his thick index finger along the remote control. "To have the power to do this was all I ever wanted."

"Me too, Cullen. You can finally get revenge on those people who hurt you. To get back at all those people who hurt my son and others like him," Dr. Morris bit through gritted teeth.

"I want to, but not like this."

"But..."

"If you have seen Jakob in the headset, then you must know the truth about how he died."

Dr. Morris scoffed, "Cullen, I know how my son died. He took his own life. I found him. I don't need to be reminded."

"No, I'm sorry, but that's not what happened. When I used *Jakob* yesterday, he told me what really happened. His death was accidental."

"No. That's not true! I found him! He took his life!" Dr. Morris shouted.

Cullen pressed, "He was on ADHD medication, correct?"

"Yes. How do you–?"

"It was Adzenys, right?"

"Yes." Dr. Morris cocked his head, bewilderment draping over his face.

"After trying several kinds, you put him on that medication. But even though it tasted better, he hated it because it made him feel tired all the time and not like himself. He didn't want to take it anymore because he would get in trouble in class for falling asleep because it made him tired, right? So, he stopped taking it. But it wasn't long before his ADHD bothered those around him."

"But–"

Cullen continued. "The day he died, they picked on him. You're right about that. When he came home, he grabbed the bottle of Adzenys, but not to kill himself."

"Yes. He killed himself because of them!" Dr. Morris shouted and pointed to Evan, Claire, and Mr. Reid.

"No. He was just ready to give in and take the medicine. That way, he wouldn't get picked on and would have some control over his life. Because the pills tasted like candy and he was just a nine-year-old kid, he didn't know that taking all of those pills would hurt him. To a kid, he thought if one or two pills would help him, then more would be better. He so desperately wanted to be normal."

Dr. Morris dropped to his knees, tears swelled in his already bloodshot eyes. "He told you this?" he whispered.

From his pocket, Cullen pulled a folded piece of sketch pad paper and handed it to Dr. Morris. He inhaled sharply as he unfolded it. When he saw what Cullen drew, his hand covered his mouth to stifled a gasp. Tears poured from his eyes. His fingers touched his son's sketched hair.

"Yes, Dr. Morris. It was just an accident. There's no one to blame. Those kids didn't push him to take his life. And I won't take theirs." He ran the remote control between his fingers and looked over at Zeke and Val, who met him with wide grins. Cullen took the remote and smashed it on the wooden floor. Dr. Morris flinched.

Cullen knelt next to him and rested his hand on his shoulder. "I'm so thankful for you. Without your help, I would probably still be in the hospital. But this? This isn't how I want to regain my power. This is not how I show my strength. I feel as if I'm getting stronger. Sure, there will be setbacks, but it's because of them I'm getting better each day. Strength shouldn't come by dishing out revenge."

Teardrops fell on the sketch of Jakob as Dr. Morris whispered as if he were talking to his son. "Oh, Jakob. Was it really just an accident? Why didn't I listen to you? I'm so sorry." Dr. Morris pulled the drawing to his chest.

"Dr. Morris?"

Staring up to Cullen, realizing what he'd done, he responded, "Cullen, my boy. I've spent so many years trying to help kids like you. When I saw how *Jakob* helped you, I knew I was onto something great. Then when I saw my boy, my poor Jakob, I became blind." He looked over at the three captives as if seeing them for the first time and choked out, "Oh, my God. What have I done?"

"We have to make this right," Cullen said, helping Dr. Morris to his feet.

"Yes. Yes, Cullen. I'm so sorry." He pulled Cullen and hugged him tight.

From behind them, a CRASH broke into the moment. Dr. Morris and Cullen spun around to find Evan, who had freed himself and smashed the *Jakob* he was wearing on the ground. "It *is* you, Cullen. You couldn't leave it alone, could you? You are going down for this. But first, I'm going to finally teach you a lesson. You need to know your place." He moved towards Cullen, but Dr. Morris stepped in his way.

"No, no, please. It was all me. I did it all. If you're going to take it out on someone, take it out on me."

"Oh, don't worry, old man. I'm gonna to give it to you first." Before Dr. Morris could react, Evan grabbed Dr. Morris by the shoulders and threw him to the floor like discarded trash. "Finally, Cullen, you and I are going to get to do this."

Cullen felt his nerves react and with that, he stuttered, "E-Evan, w-we don't have to. I g-get it. I-I'm n-not g-going to fight you."

"Oh, really? You're n-not g-going to f-fight me?" Evan mocked. "Then, this is going to be easy."

Cullen felt his confidence wane. From behind him, someone gently squeezed his shoulder. Cullen turned around to see Zeke. He and Val nodded their heads. "We've got your back," Zeke reassured.

"You've got this," Val said, snapping her gum. Cullen smirked and nodded his head.

"What the hell are you looking at, you freak? No one's coming to help you."

Cullen breathed deeply. "I'm not a freak," he insisted without a stutter.

"You're not? I'm not shocked that you know that guy." He pointed to Dr. Morris. "Freaks have a way of finding each other. I'm done talking!" Evan shouted and took two big steps forward and stood chest to chest with Cullen. Evan's eyes showed a fleeting moment of uncertainty when he realized his adversary was nearly a head taller and much broader.

"I'm going to enjoy this!" Evan shouted. He thrusted both hands into Cullen's shoulders, but instead of shoving him backwards, Cullen's body seemed to absorb the effort and didn't budge. Evan tried again to the same result.

"You don't have to do this," Cullen pleaded.

"But I do," Evan smiled and laughed maniacally. He drew back his left fist and delivered a punch to Cullen's right cheekbone. Cullen's head turned hard to his left. The color left Evan's cheeks when Cullen, unfazed, turned his head back to face Evan.

"I won't fight you," Cullen said.

"You have to. Just because you can suddenly take a punch, you think you're better than me?"

"Better than you. Is that what you really think?" Then a thought hit Cullen. "Wait a minute. You *are* no different from me."

"Oh, please," Evan mocked. "I'm much better than you."

"No, Evan. You're not. I get it now. You're just as insecure as I am. That's what this has always been about."

"You shut your mouth."

"Oh, my God, after all these years, you needed me to take the insecurities you feel off yourself."

"I said shut up!" In a fit of rage, Evan uncorked a barrage of fists at Cullen—most connecting with his face and body.

During the beating, Cullen felt himself travel back to his mindroom without the use of *Jakob*. Everything became quiet, and he found himself sitting on the floor. The walls pulsed and changed through a spectrum of color. Out of the walls, Jakob emerged. "Cullen, you see. You don't have to be scared anymore. The power isn't always in the things we do, but the things we don't do."

"How will I know the difference?"

"You'll know. Go and take care of yourself."

Once again, Cullen was aware of the bombardment of blows delivered by Evan. Cullen's left hand stopped Evan's right hand, mid-punch and then his right hand did the same to the left. Evan's eyes grew panicked.

Suddenly, Dr. Morris, who was watching from the floor, lunged towards Evan and tackled him to the ground. "Leave him alone!" Dr. Morris shouted.

Evan got to his feet and turned to Dr. Morris. Before Cullen could stop him, Evan slapped Dr. Morris with the back of his left hand, sending him sprawling across the floor.

"Dr. Morris!" Cullen ran to his side. "Are you hurt?"

"I'm okay, Cullen. Thank you. I'm so sorry I let this get so far. Will you ever forgive me?"

Cullen, whose nose trickled blood and his right eye swelled, smiled at Dr. Morris.

From behind, Evan grabbed the VR headset off Mr. Reid's head and stormed towards Cullen. With both hands, he smashed it on the top of Cullen's head. He collapsed in a heap and held his head with both hands. "Stay down if you know what's good for you," Evan shouted.

Val and Zeke checked on Cullen. "Hey man, you okay?" Zeke asked.

"C'mon Cullen, you gotta get up. Be strong," Val encouraged.

A fire burned inside Cullen and was ready to erupt. His fist flexed in anger, exposing white knuckles. Slowly, he got to his feet and faced Evan. His chest heaved with anger. Blood trickled down his face.

"*We* gave you a chance to walk away," Cullen growled, rage boiling under the surface. Fear cloaked Evan's face.

From the back of the small meeting room, Officers Mead and Kowalski cautiously opened the door. Behind them, Margaret followed. When she saw Cullen, she gasped at his battered and bruised face. She screamed, "Cullen!" Everyone in the room turned their heads towards her shriek. Everyone except for Cullen.

Like a lion fixated on its prey, Cullen slowly stalked towards Evan. Today would be the last day Evan would ever pick on him or anyone else. Flanking Cullen, Val and Zeke moved in unison with him. "Evan!" shouted Cullen. "*We* aren't going to take this any longer! You! You're the one who couldn't leave it alone! *We* were happy in our new life, but you wanted to ruin everything. *We're* done with you!"

"Who are you talking about, you freak?"

In one movement, Cullen grabbed a fistful of Evan's shirt and lifted him off his feet.

Officer Mead yelled, "Put him down, Cullen!"

Dr. Morris called out, "It's okay, Cullen. Don't hurt him. He's learned his lesson."

Cullen looked down at Dr. Morris and shouted without stuttering, "He had his chance! But like you said, he just kept coming and coming! But it ends today!"

"Cullen Hickey. Put him down right now!" Margaret demanded, running to the small stage.

Cullen set Evan down and put an arm across his neck in a chokehold. "I'm done being called a freak, Mom! Done with it. Today is the day *we* do something about it!"

"Cullen. Honey," Margaret pleaded. "What do you mean *we*? Who are you talking about? There is only you."

"Zeke and Val are right behind me."

"No, Cullen," Dr. Morris noted, his eyebrows pinched in confusion. "Your mother is right. It's just you."

"What are you, blind? They're right here," Cullen said with spit dripping from his mouth, looking from one side to the other as Evan gasped for air.

"No, Cullen. No one's there," Margaret slowly moved towards her son.

"What are you guys talking about?" Cullen loosened his grip on Evan and let him drop to the floor. He looked behind him. "No, Zeke and Val are right here..." his voice trailed off. He spun around and called, "Where are you guys?"

"Cullen, my boy, there's been no one here but you," Dr. Morris broke the news, concern edging in his voice.

"No. This can't be. They were right here. You had to see them, right?" He looked down at Evan and he shook his head.

"No?!" Cullen shouted. "Why can't you see?"

"Oh, honey, you're the only one," Margaret's voice softened.

Suddenly, Cullen's mind careened back to his mindroom. He waited for the walls to offer answers. An image appeared from the day he was going to take his own life, and the first time he saw Val and Zeke outside of *Jakob*. *Who talked me off Watkins Bridge?* The walls lit up and revealed the scene. Through his own eyes, he looked down at the rushing water and then heard Val's voice whisper behind him, *"So after all we've been through, you're just going to end it?"*

Val? Is that you? Inside his mindroom, he spun around and thought out loud, See, *she's right here. Wait. Where are you?* He searched, and neither Val nor Zeke were on the bridge.

What about when I stormed out of Mr. Reid's class? Again, the walls revealed the moment. Zeke's voice echoed into the room, *"Look, man. You running away like this ain't gonna help. You playing the victim ain't cutting it, man."*

Tears drizzled like rain as he recalled the day. *"But I am the victim,"* he whispered as he searched for Zeke, but he wasn't there.

You were there when I egged Mr. Reid's house, right? His thoughts cried out loudly in his head, but when his mindroom displayed the evening, only Val's voice resonated, *"Care to do the honors?"*

You handed me the egg, didn't you, Val? Cullen asked. He turned to high-five his friends, but they weren't there.

What about at school that day? You were there in front of everyone, right? Others had to see you guys. The mindroom disclosed the day when Cullen talked with his friends in the alcove.

He heard Zeke's voice whisper, *"You didn't do anything but throw some eggs."*

Why do you guys keep saying I'm going to be fine…You were there too. Don't forget that, Cullen voiced the conversation they had. *Weren't you? It all felt so real. The reason Lori didn't see them at school is because…*

They weren't there.

Then everything came into focus each event played over in his mind. Like a rollercoaster racing downhill, reality snapped back. Cullen's head spun, and the room went with it, nauseating him. Cullen felt that at any moment that he would throw up. He anchored himself to the only thing he could: his mother.

"It was just me? Me all alone? How? Val and Zeke were my best friends." Cullen dropped to the floor and heaved years of torment.

"It's okay. Let it out," Margaret's emotion matched her boy's as she draped herself over him.

The officers arrested Dr. Morris and freed Claire and Mr. Reid. Once paramedics arrived, they treated them, including Evan. A team of police officers came and took statements.

Officer Mead approached Margaret and Cullen. "You're going to be fine," she consoled and gave a tight-lipped smile towards Margaret. "Can I get either of you anything?"

"No. Thank you," Margaret whispered.

Then Officer Kowalski approached. "Mrs. Hickey, Dr. Morris confessed to everything. We just need to get him down to the station for processing."

Cullen stirred and scanned the scene in the room searching for Val and Zeke—hoping to see them to prove they were real, but he knew they weren't. He watched as Evan's parents came to the scene and embraced their boy. It was true. Evan was just like him. Insecure and searching for his way. Perhaps, he and Evan, and people like him, were more alike than he thought. Even though confusion lingered like a fog in his head, this thought offered some comfort.

Evan stood to leave and looked over at Cullen. As their eyes met, Cullen expected Evan's usual disdained glare. Instead, Evan's bloodshot eyes softened, and he nodded his head slightly before leaving the room.

CHAPTER 44

Two Months Later

An emptiness weighed over Cullen like a heavy blanket. He'd mostly come to terms with the fact that his friends didn't exist, but their absence left a void in his heart. Often, he pulled *Jakob* out from under his bed, which he kept hidden from his mother, and placed it on his head. Not because he needed the therapy, but because he hoped to see his friends again. They left so abruptly, and he never had a chance to say thank you.

In the weeks that passed, Margaret found a therapist, ironically referred by Dr. Morris. Although he likely would need much more therapy, Cullen learned to deal with the past. His therapist suggested that to truly heal and move on to the next phase in his life, he should do something symbolic to get there.

Cullen peered over Watkins Bridge and watched the white foam from small rapids cascade over the rocks. It reminded him of the way the walls moved inside his mindroom. He pulled his hoodie over his head to brace against the chilly mist. Like Charlie Watkins, he closed his eyes and listened.

"You aren't thinking about jumping again, are you?" Zeke's voice sounded out over the roar of the water.

"Yeah, last time we had to save your butt," Val laughed and blew a pink bubble.

Cullen turned and smiled from ear to ear. There they were. Zeke, in his familiar stance, arms folded across his broad chest. Val's blue streak sparkled as bright as day.

"I hoped you would meet me here!"

"Well, you know we would," Zeke laughed.

Cullen rolled his eyes. "I've been looking for you!? I never thought we'd be together again."

"Here we are," Val laughed. "How have you been holding up?"

"Better. Much better. I've been taking some medicine that, you know, has been helping."

"That's good, man. We're happy for you."

"I couldn't have done it without you. You guys gave me strength when I needed it."

"Really, Cullen? You're the one who made us," Val smiled.

"What's that mean?"

"That means your strength has always been there...inside of you. You don't need us anymore." Zeke winked.

"I know, but I really don't know where I would be without your help. I can't thank you enough. In a lot of ways, you saved me. You helped bring me back to my mother, and you gave me the confidence to face things. Zeke. Val. You were the best friends I ever had," Cullen teared. "So, where will you go?"

"We're going to take the Watkins plunge. That way, if you ever need us, you can come to this spot and talk with us just like that Watkins guy did," Val smirked.

"That didn't turn out too well for him. He went in after his family."

Zeke smirked. "We said come and talk to us, not join us."

Val wondered, "You've moved past thinking like that, right?"

"Yeah, I'm good." Warm tears cut tracks down his cheeks. "I'm going to miss you guys."

Val and Zeke smiled.

"It's time for us to go," Val said.

"Do you have to?" Cullen asked, knowing the answer already. He took one last look at his friends and lunged in to hug them.

When they finished, Zeke hopped onto the steel girder of the bridge and reached out his hand for Val. The two of them looked down at Cullen. "There's no reason to cry, man. We'll always be here to listen if you need us," Zeke reassured.

"You're going to be fine. No. Better than fine. You're gonna be great." Val said, as Zeke, with his arm across Val's back, nodded with that confident smile.

"We gotta go," Zeke insisted. Then he and Val leaned back and fell back off the bridge.

Cullen rushed to the girder and looked over in time to watch them disappear into the mist of the river. He took a deep breath and sighed, fighting back tears.

By his feet rested a small duffle bag. Out of it, he pulled out *Jakob*. For one last time, he held *Jakob* up to his head as if he was staring eye to eye with the VR set. "Thank you, Jakob," he whispered. He held the headset over the rushing water. A smile pulled at the corners of his lips as he let it fall from his hands and watched it splash into the river.

"You aren't thinking about pulling a Charlie Watkins, are you?" a familiar voice called out.

"Turns out that living is much better. How are you, Lori?" Cullen turned and heart leaped.

"I'm glad you remembered me."

"Why would you say that?"

"After our last conversation, I wasn't sure if you wanted to."

"I can't lie. My heart shattered into like a million pieces." He examined the floor. "Oh, look. There's another piece right there."

Lori looked down for a second before realizing his joke. "Hilarious. There was nothing I could do."

"I know. It doesn't make the hurt any less, but truth be told, I completely understand. I definitely wasn't in a good place."

"Are you still upset with me?"

He looked over the bridge and felt the cold mist on his face and inhaled. "No. I was never upset with you."

"I'm so relieved to hear that."

"So, are you here by chance?" he asked her.

"Well, I was looking for you."

"You were?" Cullen smiled. "How'd you know I'd be here?"

"You know the story. Charlie Watkins came to this spot because he missed his wife so much."

"Are you saying that you came here because you missed me?" Cullen nudged her shoulder.

"Don't you miss me, too?" She nudged him back.

"Every day. I'm not sure I could lose another person I care about."

Lori moved next to Cullen and looked over the edge of Watkins Bridge, inching closer to him. Lori touched his arm and stretched to kiss him on the cheek.

Cullen felt the realness of her kiss and felt at peace. He looked over his shoulder, expecting to see Zeke and Val, and smiled slightly when they weren't there.

"Everything okay?" Lori interrupted his thoughts.

As the clouds gave way to a single beam of late-spring sunlight, Cullen remembered Al's words from the bus drive to St. Mary's. *It can't rain every day. It can't rain forever. So, on those days, you gotta lift your head and enjoy the sunshine.*

Cullen lifted his head and absorbed the sun's warmth. He enveloped Lori's hand as it waited for his. He smiled.

"For the first time in a long time, I'm in the best of places."

Acknowledgments

Although I'm an Indie-Author, my journey is one that isn't taken alone. I have a terrific support crew of friends, family, and the online community that makes a project like this possible.

The first person I'd like to thank is Avery Poznanski. Partnering with you over these last four books has been a pleasure.

Next, I can boast this fact and be comfortable in saying this—my Beta and ARC Teams are the best!! To Lynn and Alisha, I truly appreciate your thoughts, edits, and fun little notes. I never expect the time you put into editing my work, yet you continue to go above and beyond. To my childhood friend, Mike, thank you for taking the time to read Cullen. I love our chats about what works and what doesn't. Finally, to my fabulous nephew, Scott, I know how well read you are (just like your dad was) and your thoughts and insight are incredibly valued and brutally honest.

Finally, none of this is possible without the love of my life! Veronica, I don't know how you put up with my endless conversations about writer's block, plot questions, and my insecurities. Cullen is a better book because of your ideas and critiques.

CALL TO ACTION

FOR READERS:

You can sign up for Solomon Petchers' newsletter, with give-aways and blog information, at

<u>A REQUEST FROM THE AUTHOR:</u>

If you loved this book and have a moment to spare, I would really appreciate a short review on the site where you bought this book. Your help in spreading the word is more appreciated than I can say, and the reviews make an enormous difference in helping new readers find my books. This is true for all authors.

–Solomon

NOVELS BY SOLOMON PETCHERS

A GHOST IN THE ATTIC

FEASTERS: AN APOCALYPTIC TALE

FEASTERS: THE CIRCLE

ABOUT THE AUTHOR

 Born in New York City and raised on Long Island, Solomon Petchers has always had an affinity for scary stories where friends come together to defeat whatever bad guy or entity they face. It's no wonder that Stephen King is his favorite author. Shortly after getting his teaching degree, he moved to Southern California, where he spent all of his 25 years in education. Currently, Solomon lives in Murrieta, California with his wife, Veronica, and three amazing children. When he's not writing or teaching, Solomon spends time with family or going on dates with his wife. His favorite choice of movie? Anything suspenseful or outright scary! In 2019, he fulfilled a lifelong dream and released his debut novel, A Ghost in the Attic. In 2020, he unleashed Feasters: An Apocalyptic Tale. This award-winning novel blended vampire and zombie genres in an exciting, believable way. In 2021, the exciting sequel, Feasters: The Circle was released.

FOLLOW SOLOMON PETCHERS

Website:

Facebook: @authorsolomonpetchers

Twitter: @solomonpetchers

Instagram: solomon_petchers